KU-349-964

MURDER IN THE HAMPTONS

9030 0000 242832

Dear Reader:

Danita Carter has a history of weaving together fabulous storylines with intricate characters and messages to ponder long after the last page has been turned. In her latest offering, *Murder in the Hamptons*, Carter continues to impress as she intersects the worlds of music, money, and murder.

When old money meets new money, after a rapper moved into the famed and glamorous Hamptons, his neighbors are forced to accept both him and his crew. But even if they can learn to live peacefully together, once a horrific crime takes place, all bets are off.

Celebrities are America's royalty. Rappers transcend all races, classes, and gender and many of them have fans not just in the United States but around the world. Everyone wants a piece of their world, a piece of their lifestyle. Danita Carter does a fabulous job of depicting this and much, much more. Filled with drama, erotic sequences, and surprises, *Murder in the Hamptons* is sure to please.

Thanks for giving this novel a chance and it is my hope that you will also pick up a copy of Danita Carter's young adult novel, *Peer Pleasure*.

Thanks for supporting all of the Strebor Books authors. To find me on the web, please go to www.eroticanoir.com or join my online social network, www.planetzane.org.

Blessings,

Zane

Zane
Publisher
Strebor Books International
www.simonandschuster.com

ALSO BY DANITA CARTER
Peer Pleasure

ZANE PRESENTS

MURDER IN THE HAMPTONS

DANITA CARTER

SBI

STREBOR BOOKS

NEW YORK LONDON TORONTO SYDNEY

Strebor Books
P.O. Box 6505
Largo, MD 20792
http://www.streborbooks.com

ISBN 978-1-59309-253-5
ISBN 978-1-4165-9705-6 (e-book)
LCCN 2010925099

First Strebor Books trade paperback edition June 2010

Cover design: www.mariondesigns.com
Cover photograph: © Keith Saunders/Marion Designs

10 9 8 7 6 5 4 3 2 1

Manufactured in the United States of America

For information regarding special discounts for bulk purchases, please contact Simon & Schuster Special Sales at 1-866-506-1949 or business@simonandschuster.com

The Simon & Schuster Speakers Bureau can bring authors to your live event. For more information or to book an event, contact the Simon & Schuster Speakers Bureau at 1-866-248-3049 or visit our website at www.simonspeakers.com.

I'd like to dedicate this book to my mom, Alline;
my brothers, Ronald and Dane; and my sister, Denise.
You guys knew me before I knew myself,
and my life would NOT be the same without
your love and continuous support!!!
Our family means the World to me!
Danita

ACKNOWLEDGMENTS

This being my first romantic who-dunit, I had a great team to help me pull it off, and they are…

My agent, Sara Camilli, we work so well together, and I appreciate all of your help and hard work!

Charmaine Parker, Publishing Director, Strebor Books, thank you for keeping my project on track.

Zane, I appreciate all of your input.

Yona Deshommes, you are the bomb publicist! Thanks for including me amongst your A-Listers!

Keith Saunders of Marion Designs, I want to thank you for taking my ideas on the cover and executing them to perfection! You are the MAN!

To my family, including our newest member, Loghan Iman Cowans, my little Loggie Bear! I love you guys dearly, more than words can express. And to my friends who are like family! I can call, text, Twitter, email, FB, each and every one of you day or night and you're there for a sistah with words of encouragement, and/or an ice-cold martini…LOL! All jokes aside, I love and appreciate you all!!

And lastly, my readers and media outlets, especially Radiah and Charles Hubbert of Urban Reviews, and Carol Hill-Mackey of Black Expressions, who have supported my work over the years, thank you with all my heart!

Much Love, and I hope you enjoy *Murder in the Hamptons*!

Danita

[1]

"Why are all these people still outside? We need to clear out the entire area," Detective Pratt instructed.

"We've been telling everybody to go back inside the boat so that they can be questioned, but they won't go," the police officer said, sounding frustrated.

Detective Pratt stood on the gangplank and looked up at the three-story, multi-million-dollar yacht. There were people peering over the railings from all three decks, staring down into the coal-black water. Detective Pratt knew exactly what was capturing their attention; she had seen it too, the minute she came upon the scene. She looked over at the water again, where police divers were marking off the crime scene with yellow plastic caution strips. She exhaled hard. "Come with me," she told the officer.

The two of them went aboard. "Okay, people, back inside. Nobody goes home until everyone is questioned," Detective Pratt announced to the ogling partygoers.

"Back inside, people. Let's move it," the officer echoed, waving his flashlight like a wand.

Detective Pratt could hear the buzz of whispers as guests eased toward the entrance.

"Oh my God, I can't believe this!"

"It's like something out of a movie."

"Yeah, a horror movie."

They were right. There hadn't been a murder in the Hamptons in quite a while, and when the news broke in the morning, residents would be horrified.

"Who owns this boat?" Detective Pratt asked another officer.

"Liza Lord," he said promptly. Everyone on the island knew that the Lords had the most opulent yacht at the marina. Detective Pratt was new to the island, and wasn't familiar with the Lords.

"Go get her," Detective Pratt said with urgency in her voice.

"Right away," the officer responded, then disappeared into the crowd. A few minutes later, he came back with the owner in tow.

Before speaking, the detective checked out the woman with a discerning eye. Liza Lord was dressed to the hilt in a stark white, silk halter gown, with a thin silver belt wrapped around her slim waist. The belt had tiny rhinestones—or were they diamonds?—encrusted around a square buckle. Large teardrop diamonds were dangling from her earlobes, and her neck and wrists were also dripping in diamonds. Her copper-colored skin was flawless; no wrinkles or any other signs of a stressful life.

One look at her, and anyone could see that Ms. Lord came from money; not only a couple of million, but old money that had lasted for generations.

"I understand this is your boat," the detective said.

"Yes, *Lady Lord* is my *yacht*," she said, making the correction obvious.

"Is this an annual party that you give on your boat?" Detective Pratt asked, deliberately using the incorrect term. She hated the upper-crusty tone that rich people used to talk down to common folk, and whenever she could get in a dig, she did.

Liza rolled her eyes and said with a discerning air, "This is not my affair. I merely provided the venue." Liza had been thrilled to help Donovan plan the party, but this nosey detective was pissing her off. That and a dead body had completely soured her mood.

"Then whose party is it?" Detective Pratt snapped.

"Donovan Smart's."

"The rapper?"

"Yes. It's his White and Platinum party, given to introduce himself to the community."

That explains why everyone is dressed in white and silver, the detective thought. "Where is he?"

Liza shrugged her shoulders and then answered, "I don't know."

"Excuse me, Detective, but they're ready to take the body out of the water now," the officer told her.

"Okay, I'll be right there." The detective then turned

back to Liza. "Can you hang around for a few minutes? I'd like to ask you some more questions."

"Do I need to call my attorney?"

"That's up to you. My questions are standard and will be quick. We can either do it here, or you *and* your attorney can come down to the station. The choice is yours."

Liza exhaled and thought about the situation for a moment. She wasn't about to be carted down to some godforsaken police station. Besides, she didn't have anything to hide. "Okay, I'll be below deck, in my stateroom," she said, and sauntered away.

Detective Pratt made her way out to the dock. She stood there and watched the divers pull a woman's lifeless body from the water. The woman was also dressed in white and silver; obviously she had been on the guest list. The burning questions now were who was she, and how did she end up floating facedown in the bay? Was it an accidental death, or murder?

[2]

The morning after the drowning, Detective Theodora Pratt—Theo for short—pored over her notes. To her amazement, Liza Lord had been extremely cooperative and had filled her in on the major players at the party. There was the host, rapper Donovan Smart, aka TuSmArt; his sister, Reece; and her best friend, Chyna. Also in attendance were Dr. Lars Braxton and his wife, Remi, new money residents of Coco Beach. Troy Hamilton, the chef and owner of Café Coco, was there, as well as a smattering of the old money residents who had summered in that part of the Hamptons for generations.

According to Liza, Donovan had given the party to ingratiate himself into the community. Most of the people who lived in Coco Beach were snobs, and didn't want a rapper disrupting their tranquility. Donovan had wanted to prove to them that he and his crew were housetrained and that there was nothing to be intimidated about. The party had been a success, until someone wound up dead.

"How's it going?" the chief of police asked, coming into her office.

Theo thumped the notes on her desk. "This is going to be an interesting case, to say the least. We have an eclectic cast of characters here. I'm interviewing the rapper, Donovan Smart"—she looked at her watch— "in about ten minutes. After I finish with him, I'm going down the list. I'll probably be here all night." Although she had talked briefly with the guests last night, she wanted more in-depth interviews with some of the key people at the party.

"Okay; let me know how it's shaping up. We're going to need to wrap this case up as soon as possible. The residents will want to know if the woman jumped, accidentally fell overboard, or was pushed. If she was pushed, then it's murder, and Coco Beach hasn't seen a murder in God knows when."

"I'm on it, Chief."

Ten minutes later, right on time, in walked Donovan Smart, looking more like an executive for a Fortune 500 company than a rapper. He was dressed in a navy blue suit, white shirt, and baby- blue tie. The suit fit his brawny frame perfectly, and the white shirt seemed to glow against his chocolate skin.

Donovan Smart's name fit him to a tee. He wasn't merely smart; he was brilliant, a borderline genius. His IQ was right up there with Einstein's. He'd skipped two grades in elementary school and graduated high school when he was only sixteen. His GPA was an astonishing 4.0, and he'd received scholarship offers from Yale, Northwestern, Harvard, and NYU. But to the disappointment of his guidance counselor, he turned down the chance to attend an Ivy League institution, preferring instead to dive deep into his music.

Donovan had been writing rap lyrics since his first taste of the music released by The Notorious B.I.G. The second he heard Christopher Wallace's raspy voice deliver those dope rhythmic lyrics, Donovan was hooked, and knew that he had to be in the rap game.

Unlike the other boys in the neighborhood who hung out playing b-ball all day and night, Donovan would sequester himself in his bedroom, writing songs. He saved enough cash from a part-time job dropping fries at Mickey-D's to buy a keyboard and a secondhand sound system, complete with CD burner and microphone. He set up a makeshift studio in his room and would work on tunes for hours on end, until he had the right track to accompany his words. His songs were profound. He wrote of growing up in a crack-infested neighborhood, where the habit-forming synthetic drug had grandmothers selling their bodies to get a ten-dollar hit. He wrote of teenage mothers struggling to work *and* finish school so they could move out of the 'hood to provide a better life for their children. He wrote of witnessing shootouts and seeing the bullet-riddled bodies of his peers; their young lives snuffed out like insignificant, flickering flames right before his eyes. By the time Donovan had graduated from high school, he had a vast catalogue of work, and was ready to make some noise in the world of music.

Initially, he wanted to be a writer/producer, but he couldn't find anyone with a unique-enough vibe to record his demo. Everybody he auditioned tried to sound like Tupac, Biggie, or Ice Cube. Though each was great in his own right, he wanted originality, not a remix of the classics. Tired of wasting time with wannabes, he went into the studio and laid the tracks himself. To his astonishment, he realized that he possessed within himself the unique sound that he craved.

With the demo complete, Donovan was ready to shop for that elusive record deal. However, he knew from reading trade magazines and watching celebrity profiles on television that it often took years to sign with a major label. He couldn't fathom the idea of wasting his energy running down an A&R exec to get a contract that only paid pennies on the dollar.

Instead of taking the traditional route, he opted to go underground and shave years off the conventional process. He made mass copies—since he owned the music there were no copyright issues—and sold his CDs on the street, keeping one hundred percent of the profit. Donovan couldn't produce the music fast enough. The neighborhood was hooked. His dope rap was the new crack! The message in his lyrics transcended age, touching young and old alike. People would line up outside his apartment door to buy the homemade discs.

It didn't take long for the big boys to come a-callin' once they heard the *ka-ching* of a proven money-making machine. In the music industry (as with all industries), the name of the game was profit with a capital "P." After selling more than fifty thousand CDs in less than a year, Donovan had proven without a doubt that his music was indeed profitable.

The marketing team at Lysten UP Records reasoned that if he could generate a loyal following without the benefit of corporate dollars behind him, then he would surely go platinum with their worldwide distribution propelling him into the stratosphere and beyond. Lysten UP wooed Donovan with SUVs on d.u.b.s., bling, phat gear, and a fat advance check when he signed on the dotted line. Since he'd brought a proven track record to the table, his attorney was able to negotiate top-notch terms in his contract, including creative control for the artist, which was rare for a neophyte.

Six platinum albums and a Brink's truck of cash later, Donovan was the new prince of hip-hop. Though music would always be his first love, he decided to branch out and diversify his dollars in several different arenas. Following the lead of Sean Combs—whom Donovan admired and had studied in the press long before Donovan made his millions—Donovan started his own clothing line—SmArtGeAr. He followed that with a restaurant, simply called Donovan's. And he partnered with real estate mogul Donald Trump to open a trendy boutique hotel in Harlem. Professionally, his life couldn't get much better. He was amassing a vast empire, had three singles on *Billboard*'s Top 20 simultaneously, and was co-producer on another two top singles.

On the flip side, his personal life—or more to the point, his love life—was stagnant. He wrote ballads of unrequited love, but had never experienced the blood-rushing, adrenaline-pumping thrill of giving his heart to a woman.

One of New York's most eligible bachelors, Donovan had a smorgasbord of women at his disposal, from video dancers, to models, to Grammy Award–winning singers. As alluring as they all were, he wanted something more. He didn't only want a woman with killer looks. He wanted brains as part of the package. However, the three "B"s— beauty, body, and brains—was a tough combination to find among the women in his circle.

To save face and to keep his fans satiated with the juicy details of his so-called escapades, his publicist arranged, on occasion, dates with some of Broadway's leading actresses. This media tactic was used to solidify his image as the consummate ladies' man, but in reality, Donovan was as lonely as a castaway on a deserted island.

[3]

"So, Mr. Smart, I understand both your sister and her best friend were at the party," Theo said, looking directly across the desk at Donovan. His eyes were red-rimmed and puffy, as if he had been crying all night. Theo assumed that he was distraught about a death taking place at his party.

He looked down in his lap, took a deep breath, looked up and then said, "Yes, they were. Part of the reason why I threw the party was to introduce my family to the community." Donovan didn't admit that he'd also hoped to find his sister a suitable guy to date. Reece was a bit on the wild side, and he wanted a well-bred man to help calm her down.

"Who else in your family was there?"

"By 'family,' I mean Chyna, my sister's best friend. We all grew up together in the projects. When I signed my first recording contract, I moved my family, as well as Chyna and her mother, out of the 'jects," he explained.

"So you guys go way back?" Theo put her elbows on the desk. "Tell me about your sister and her friend."

A smile spread across his handsome face. "Those two are something else. They're more like sisters than friends. Growing up in the projects, it helped to have someone you trust have your back, and Chyna and Reece definitely had each other's best interest at heart." As he was talking, tears welled up in his eyes, and were soon rolling down his cheeks. Donovan took a handkerchief out of his back pocket, and wiped his face.

"Are you okay, Mr. Smart?"

"No, I'm not. This has been an ordeal. I don't know what else I can tell you. I didn't see what happened," he stood up, "so if you don't mind I'd like to go home."

Theo didn't have any reason to keep Donovan, so she let him go. "Okay, Mr. Smart, if I need anything else, I'll give you a call."

"Sure, no problem." Donovan took a pair of shades out of his breast pocket, put them on, and left.

Theo watched him walk out, and wondered if he was leaving so soon because he was distraught over what had happened at the party or if he was trying to hide something. If it were the latter, she would find out the truth, sooner rather than later.

[4]

Donovan's interview at the police station wasn't as painful as he had thought it would be. The detective was nice enough; she didn't badger him with a barrage of useless questions. He appreciated her directness. Donovan was in a somber mood and really didn't feel like going through something akin to the Spanish Inquisition. She simply wanted to know more about him, his sister, and Chyna.

On his way home, Donovan thought about the previous night's events. He couldn't believe that his party had turned into the scene of a tragic accident, and it got him thinking about his lunch with Chyna a few weeks ago.

THEY WERE MEETING AT A SWANK, NEO–SOUL FOOD restaurant on Thirty-Eighth Street, close to Donovan's midtown office. Chyna was there sitting in the waiting area when Donovan arrived. He was wrapping up a conversation when he walked into the restaurant.

"Yeah, man, I just got out of the meeting," he said into the phone as he approached Chyna. He planted his body close to hers on the sofa and continued his conversation. "Looks like we're going to get the endorsement deal with Mercedes." He smiled, exposing perfectly straight, bright white teeth.

Chyna began to fidget. She hadn't rehearsed a script in advance, and didn't know how to tell Donovan about Reece's addiction. She didn't want to blurt out the information. She knew he'd be shocked, but knowing Donovan's impatience, she didn't want to beat around the bush either.

"Sorry about that," he apologized, after ending his call and pecking her on the cheek.

"No problem." She checked out his high-powered business look. He was dressed in a tailored khaki suit that hugged his broad shoulders ever so slightly, with a light-blue pinpoint cotton shirt and multi-colored, brown and baby-blue Michael Newell tie. "Don't you look like the consummate businessman." She smiled.

"Thanks," Donovan said, slightly blushing. "Come on, let's eat. I'm starving." He got up and headed toward the hostess's podium.

"Hey, Donovan, man. How ya doing?" It was Keith, the general manager, standing next to the hostess.

"Man, I'm good." He slapped Keith on the back. "What about you?"

"Things couldn't be better; business is booming. We hosted a party for Common last night, and it was off the chain." Keith gave Chyna an appraising look, and quickly changed the subject. "Who's your lady friend?"

Since they had grown up together, Donovan was immune to Chyna's dazzling beauty. She was tall with long black silky hair that she inherited from her father, who was half Asian. She had delicate features on a honey-wheat complexion, and a round, sister-girl butt, compliments of her African-American mother. She was slim like Reece, and people would often mistake them for sisters.

Donovan looked over at Chyna, who was dressed in a girly pink floral dress with a generous neckline that show-cased her ripe bosom. Her sexiness made him blush. "Oh, uh, this is my girl, Chyna."

"Damn. You're a lucky man," Keith said, with disappointment.

Donovan laughed. "Naw, man, not my *girl*. She's my homegirl, my homie. We grew up together," he explained.

"That's right," Chyna chimed in. "We're like family."

"That's good, because I'd love to take you out sometime," Keith said without skipping a beat. He quickly whipped out a business card from his breast pocket. "My home number's on the back. Please give me a call."

Chyna reluctantly took the card. He was handsome enough, but she wasn't interested in getting involved in a relationship. She had her sights set on opening a boutique, and didn't need or want any distractions. Men were the worst distraction of all, especially when the sex was good. She hadn't been in a committed relationship in two years, not since her last boyfriend. He was an up-and-coming rapper on Donovan's label, and their attraction was animalistic. They fell into bed the night they met. Chyna didn't smoke, drink, or do drugs; her only vice was sex. Their union had no solid foundation; it was all about fucking. Once the sheets cooled off, so did the relationship. He dropped her like a nuclear bomb. She was devastated when he left her for a dancer. It felt as if a vital appendage had been surgically removed, and in a sense, it had. Once she recovered from the missing dick, Chyna vowed never to become whipped again. She swore that she would get to know her next boyfriend long before they made love. "Okay, talk to you soon," she said half-heartedly and put the card in her purse.

"Let me show you to your table," Keith said, walking them into the dining room. He sat them at a choice corner table near the back of the restaurant. "I'll send the waitress right over," he said, and disappeared into the kitchen.

"So…" Donovan said, peering directly into Chyna's coal black eyes.

She knew exactly what he was asking, even though he hadn't actually asked a question. Since she never invited him out to lunch, brunch, or dinner for that matter, she assumed that he wanted to know why she scheduled this meeting.

"Yes…" she said, stalling.

He let out a slight chuckle. "You know what I mean, Chyna. What's up? Why'd you want to have lunch? I'm sure it's not to sit around and chit-chat." Donovan was one for getting right down to business. He didn't like wasting time on unnecessary conversation. Cutting through the usual trivial preliminary topics, like the weather and sports updates, was one of his many attributes. Donovan could get right to the meat of a situation within seconds, and resolve any ensuing conflict before it escalated. He learned that from dealing with young hotheads in the music industry, when it was better to give it to them straight with no chaser.

Chyna exhaled, and then said, "It's Reece."

"What about her?"

"I don't know how to tell you this…" She hesitated.

He leaned in closer to her. "Tell me whatever the problem is."

"How do you know it's a problem?" she asked, continuing to stall in an attempt to find the right words.

"Knowing my sister, I'm sure it's some kind of problem. Otherwise, you wouldn't be here."

"You're right." Chyna swallowed hard, and lowered her eyes. "She's on drugs."

"What?" Donovan shouted, causing the other patrons to turn around and look in their direction.

"Calm down, Donnie," Chyna said in a hushed tone.

"How can you expect me to calm down when you're

telling me my baby sister is on drugs? What is she on?" he asked, lowering his voice.

"She's hooked on Oxy."

"What?" Donovan couldn't believe his ears.

"OxyContin. It's a painkiller that's highly addictive."

"Yeah, I know what it is."

"Remember the night of your release party?" she asked, but didn't wait for him to answer. "Anyway, Reece was high then." She went on to tell him what had transpired that evening.

"GIRL, I KNOW YOU AIN'T WEARING THAT!" REECE exclaimed, turning up her diamond-studded nose at Chyna's hideous getup.

Standing in Reece's bedroom and glancing in the full-length mirror behind the door, Chyna pivoted slightly so she could get a rear view. "What's wrong? You don't like my outfit?"

Reece looked at the black-and-white polka-dot, baby-doll dress worn over a pair of red satin cargo pants with silver platforms, and snickered under her breath. She and Chyna had been friends since childhood when they both lived in the Red Hook project complex in Brooklyn. Back then, both of their families were so poor that the girls had to shop for back-to-school clothes on the sale rack at Goodwill, and even that was a treat. Those were the lean years and a lifetime away. Now they were living high on the hog, compliments of Reece's brother,

Donovan, aka TuSmArt, the triple-platinum Grammy-winning rapper. "Girl, you look like you been back at Goodwill bobbing for bargains." She laughed.

Chyna took offense. "Ain't shit funny, Reece. Just 'cause yo' brother is raking in the Benjamins don't mean you gotta diss me like that."

"Puleeezze." Reece smirked and rolled her eyes. She couldn't believe Chyna was going down that "Your brother, the star" road. Not only did Donovan take his family out of the ghetto; he had reached back and plucked Chyna and her mother from a life of rats, roaches, and government cheese. He felt a certain loyalty to his next-door neighbor, who was like a second mother to him. The two families would often pool their meager resources, sharing their monthly rations, and making life in the jets bearable. Donovan vowed that once he "made it," money, or the lack thereof, would be the least of their problems, and he had made good on his promise, giving the ladies in his life—his mother, Reece, Chyna, and her mother, Joyce—a hefty monthly stipend.

"Puleeezze, what?" Chyna responded, mirroring Reece's tone.

"Why you didn't go over to Prada and buy something hot?" Reece asked, admiring her new black pleated miniskirt with matching halter. "You know we gots to look fly tonight." They were going to TuSmArt's album release party at NV, one of New York's hot spots.

"I do look hot." Chyna turned again in the mirror.

"Plus, ain't tryin' to drop a few grand unnecessarily when I can shop in my closet. Anyway, I'm tryin' to sack my cash." She smoothed out the hem of her dress.

Reece looked bewildered. "What you saving for?"

"I wanna open one of them trendy boutiques, and have folks drop a few grand in *my* store. There's a ton of money being spent on clothes, and I want a piece of the action."

Again Reece looked shocked; this was the first time that she had ever heard Chyna talk about starting a business. "Girl, I didn't know you were interested in opening a boutique."

"Remember when we were both at F.I.T.? You were studying jewelry design, and I took fashion merchandising classes?" Chyna asked, walking over to the vanity and applying a thin layer of gloss to her bottom lip.

"Yeah, I remember." Reece plopped down on the bed. "But I took those classes as a hobby, for something to do. And I thought fashion merchandising was another one of your phases, like the time when you wanted to direct music videos, or the time when you swore you was gonna write a book about growing up in Red Hook, or the time—"

Chyna rolled her eyes and cut Reece off. "Okay, okay, I get your point." She had to admit that she'd been scattered in the past, hardly ever completing a goal, but now she was serious about getting her life in order and becoming financially independent. "Merchandising wasn't no phase. I got plans." She put the gloss in her purse. "I can't live off of your brother for the rest of my life."

"Why not? He got it like that, and then some," Reece responded cavalierly.

"Tru dat, tru dat, but I still wanna make my own money and be my own woman." She turned to face Reece, who was sitting on the edge of the king-sized bed digging frantically around in a large duffel bag. "You should think about making plans for the future, too. I know you don't wanna be on Donnie's payroll forever. Maybe you could do something with your jewelry designs. I know!" She perked up, as if having an epiphany. "You could sell your ice in my store."

"Thanks, but no thanks. Unlike you, I ain't got no problem being on his payroll." Reece looked up for a second. "Hell, it's better than slaving away at some stupid-ass nine-to-five, and getting a lousy two-bit check at the end of the week." She went back to digging in the bag. "And as far as plans, the only thing I'm planning on is getting more of these," she said, taking a tiny white pill out of a bottle she'd found in the duffel bag.

"You still taking those?" Chyna wrinkled her nose. "Didn't the prescription run out?"

Reece had ruptured her Achilles on the dance floor while trying to execute a complicated move she saw performed on *Soul Train*, but instead of landing on her feet, she landed in the hospital with a severed tendon. To tame the excruciating pain after surgery, the doctor prescribed OxyContin, an extremely potent drug. But that was six months ago, and the pain should've been long gone.

Reece popped the pill in her mouth and chased it with a shot of Belvedere. "I got a couple more left; then I'ma have to shop around, 'cause my doctor won't give me another scrip."

"What do you mean, 'shop around'?" Chyna knew exactly what Reece meant, but she wanted an explanation just the same so she could throw in her two cents. She knew how addictive OxyContin could be, even deadly when misused.

Reece sucked her teeth as if irritated. "Shop around, as in find another doctor who'll write a prescription for my pain."

"Pain? What pain? Your surgery was months ago, and the way you strutting around on them Manolos, I know you ain't hardly in no pain. Girl, Oxy ain't nothing to play with. I read this article in the *Times* where this boy O.D.'d using it as a recreational drug," Chyna cautioned.

"Damn, you sound like somebody's momma. If I needed a lecture, I'd call my *own* momma," Reece hissed.

"Sorry. I didn't mean to step on your toes. I don't wanna see you caught up; that's all," she said, concerned.

"I ain't caught up. I'm just trying to get my party on," Reece responded, snapping her fingers and downing another shot of vodka.

Chyna hated to admit the truth, but they had grown apart. She didn't exactly know when the divide had first occurred, but it was glaringly obvious that their interests were now different. Reece's vision was blurred by the OxyContin flowing through her veins. She didn't talk about anything constructive anymore, no short-term or long-range plans. Her sole focus seemed to be scoring more prescription drugs, drinking, and partying until the wee hours. Chyna, in comparison, had never done drugs in her life, either prescription or the street variety. She didn't even take Tylenol for headaches or cramps. Her father had drunk himself to death, so she drank sparingly. She didn't touch the hard stuff. When she did drink it was mostly wine coolers, and sometimes champagne. She was afraid that she had inherited her father's addiction gene, and didn't want to tempt fate by overindulging.

"Be careful; that's all I'm saying."

"Consider me warned. Now let's go, 'cause I wanna get there before they roll up the red carpet."

Fourteenth Street from Sixth Avenue to Ninth Avenue was one elongated parking lot. Actually, it was more like a luxury car dealership with a barrage of G-Wagons, Range Rovers, Escalades, and Navigators lined up bumper-to-bumper, all pimped out with customized spinning rims, tinted windows, and psychedelic paint jobs. The metallic midnight-blue stretch Hummer carrying Reece and Chyna sluggishly inched toward NV along with the rest of the traffic.

The speakers inside the vehicle trembled with the heavy

bass line of TuSmArt's new CD. Bouncing her head to the jazzy beat, Chyna sang along to the rhythmic lyrics:

I'm from the Hook, but I ain't no crook,
the Streets raised me, but my momma saved me,
from a life of crime, now I spend my time, writing rhymes
and making cheddar, and spending cheese...

"Girl, this joint is off the hezzie!" Chyna yelled over the music, but Reece didn't respond. The back of the car was dark, so she could barely see her friend's face. "Girl, did you hear what I said?" Still no response. Chyna scooted to the edge of the leather seat and nudged her on the knee. "Reece!" she shouted.

Reece's eyes popped open and she sprang back to life. "What? What's the matter?"

"Damn! Are you 'sleep?"

"Uh, I guess I dozed off," she said groggily, blinking hard, trying to adjust her eyes to the darkness.

Chyna shook her head in disappointment. She knew it was the Oxy coupled with the vodka that was making Reece drowsy. OxyContin was an opium derivative and had a heroin-type effect on the body, causing the user to lose consciousness at any given time.

"You'd better get yourself together before Donnie sees you." Donovan was overprotective of his younger sister, always trying to shield her from the trappings of the entertainment world.

Reece sat up, stretched her arms above her head, and

opened her mouth wide, letting out a thunderous yawn. She shrugged her shoulders up and down, trying to ward off the lethargic effect of the drug. "Now I need a toot to wake the hell up, so I can stomp with the big dawgs tonight."

"Girl, I know you ain't gonna mix cocaine with Oxy?" she asked, alarmed.

"If I can find a hit, I'm definitely going to do a line or two or four," she said without a second thought.

"Have you lost your fucking mind?" Chyna shouted over the music.

"What's your fucking problem?" Reece screamed back. "I ain't asking you to partake. Anyway, it's my damn body and I can do what I fucking please."

"I know it's your 'damn body,' but you're talking about mixing a lethal combination." She looked down in despair and softened her tone, trying to convey the seriousness of the matter. "Reece, you could die."

"Cool out. Ain't nobody gonna die up in dis piece." She took out a compact of pressed powder. "I wanna have some fun, that's all," she stated calmly, dabbing her forehead and the tip of her nose with the soft makeup sponge.

From the way Reece was gobbling up the tablets like Tic Tacs, she was, without a doubt, hooked. At a loss for words, Chyna sat back and stared out the window. They rode the rest of the way in silence, with only the music blaring between them.

Another twenty minutes passed before they finally

pulled up to the curb in front of NV. Reece instantly
perked up when she peered through the tinted windows
of the Hummer and saw the throng of paparazzi litter-
ing the fringes of the crimson runner outside of the
club. She loved being recognized as TuSmArt's sister,
and being photographed for the various celebrity sightings
sections of the urban glossy magazines. Though she
wasn't a bona fide celebrity, she was packaged like one.
Reece's complexion was as rich as a chocolate Thin Mint.
She had delicate features and long, wavy, jet-black tresses
that most people assumed were woven onto her scalp.
She was tall and lean with a pair of knockout gams that
rivaled Naomi Campbell's killer legs. Her tight waist
and ample boobage made the skimpy outfits that she
wore look like pieces from Frederick's of Hollywood's
private collection.

Reece retrieved a pair of oversized Aviator shades from
her purse, adjusted them on the bridge of her keen nose,
tossed her hair back dramatically, and got out of the car,
with Chyna follow- ing in her shadow.

"Hey, isn't that TuSmArt's sister?" she heard a photographer ask, as she strolled down the red carpet.

"Yeah, that's Reece Smart. Ms. Smart, this way,"
another photog responded, snapping her picture.

Reece stopped mid-stride and struck a pose like a
model gracing the catwalk, as the bright bulbs flashed
repeatedly in her face. Preferring to remain anonymous,
Chyna hung back, shying away from the glare of the
spotlight.

A short time later, Reece was satisfied that she had gotten a significant amount of exposure. She picked up her pace and strutted toward the beefy bouncer.

"Yo name?" asked the keeper-of-the-gate, holding three different clipboards.

Reece rolled her eyes, obviously annoyed that Mr. Beefcake didn't immediately recognize her face. "Reece Smart. TuSmArt's sister. I'm on the platinum VIP list," she announced with much attitude.

At these industry functions there were several tiers to the "list," the first being the commoner list, which included those who knew somebody who worked on the album. But that didn't necessarily guarantee admittance into the party, especially if the guest was tardy, since this list had a capacity limit. The second tier was the VIP list, reserved for executives and their friends, and guaranteed entry no matter what time they arrived. Finally the list to grace was the VVIP list, also known as the platinum list, reserved for the artist and his entourage. The platinum list not only guaranteed admittance, but also granted total access once beyond the velvet ropes.

The bouncer stacked the clipboards in his massive hands, with the silver colored one on top. He ran his meaty index finger down the list until he spotted Reece's name, with "plus guest" noted in parentheses. He put a checkmark beside her name and unhooked the thick crimson cord. "Go right on in, Ms. Smart."

Reece and Chyna parted a plush shield of heavy drapes

that protected the inner sanctum of the club from the outside world and sauntered inside. As usual, they expected to see a horde of scantily clad hoochies gyrating to a hip-hop beat. Instead, an elegantly dressed hostess in a long, black evening gown greeted them. "Right this way, ladies," she instructed, showing them to a cozy booth along the wall.

Looking around at the dimly lit room, which was set up like a 1920s speakeasy, with indigo votive candles on round tables covered with black linen cloths, Reece couldn't believe her eyes. A smartly dressed quartet was softly playing jazz on an intimate stage. The entire scene seemed surreal. "Are we in the wrong party or what?" Scanning the room for the second time, she wrinkled her nose. "Is this TuSmArt's album release party, or a tribute to some dead jazz dude?"

Before Chyna could answer, in walked Donovan. Dressed in a tailored, black pinstriped suit with pearl-white tone-on-tone shirt and tie, his appearance defied the typical baggy, falling-off-your-butt pants rapper look. "'Z'up, ladies?" he asked, kissing them each on the cheek.

Skipping the hellos and getting straight to the point, Reece asked, "Yo, D, what's up with this so-called party and why you dressed like that?"

"You like my suit?" He held out his arms for appraisal. "I'm changing my image. Whatcha think?"

"I think you look like a damn undertaker," replied Reece.

Chyna chimed in, "I, for one, think you look nice. It's about time somebody stepped up to the plate and showed them young bulls how to dress."

"Thanks," he said to Chyna, ignoring his sister's lack of taste. "Now don't get me wrong, I'm still gonna rock my Timbs and SmArtGeAr, but a little change is good every now and then. That's why I decided to do something different for this release party. Since I sample a couple of songs from *Kind of Blue*, one of the great albums from the master, Miles Davis, I wanted to offset the hip-hop with a little jazz, and give my peeps some cultural exposure for once."

"The only thing I need exposing to is a bottle of Moët and a funky beat," Reece huffed.

He held up his hands in mock defense. "Don't get your feathers all ruffled. They playing my new joint downstairs, so you can get your party on."

"What about the champagne? I need to get my drink on, too."

"Can you have them bring over a bottle of Vitaminwater?" Chyna asked Donovan, hoping Reece would get the hint and lay off the alcohol.

"Sure, no problem. I'll talk to you guys later. I gotta go do an interview with *Uptown* magazine."

Before Donovan had walked far, Reece shouted, "Yo, D, don't forget about my 'pagne!"

"All right, calm down, little sis. I'ma send a bottle over."

Once Donovan was out of earshot, Chyna sounded

off. "Girl, you need to slow your roll and drink some Vitaminwater to flush that shit outta your system."

Annoyed, Reece sucked her teeth hard. "Here you go. Get off my back, Chyna, and let me live my life."

"REECE WAS PRESCRIBED OXYCONTIN WHEN SHE WAS in the hospital for her Achilles operation, and—"

He cut her off. "That was six months ago. Why is she still on that shit?" He looked pleadingly at Chyna, as if she had the answer.

"Evidently she's hooked."

"Are you sure about this, Chyna? I know Reece is on the wild side, and loves champagne, but I've never seen her take drugs."

"Yes, I've seen her take it with my own eyes." She hesitated, debating whether or not to also tell him about Reece's cocaine habit. Since she had cracked the lid on Pandora's box, she might as well blow the entire top off and spill *all* the beans. "She's also using coke with the Oxy."

Donovan slumped back into his seat. He had seen the kids in the old neighborhood strung out on crack, and doing whatever they had to in order to get a fix. Now his little sister was an addict. Even though it wasn't crack, she was addicted nonetheless, and the thought sent a chill up his spine. "What should we do?"

"She needs to go into rehab. I think that's the only way to get her off that stuff. But she won't listen to me. Every time I mention it, she tells me to back off.

That's why I had to tell you. Maybe she'll listen to you. Donnie, you gotta get her in a program before she…" The words stuck in her throat.

"Before she ODs," he said, finishing her sentence. Donovan hung his head. He put out fires on a daily basis in his business, but never thought he'd have to deal with a strung-out sibling. "I'll talk to her as soon as possible. Do you know where she is?"

"No, I haven't talked to her today."

He reached across the table and touched her hand. "Thanks, Chyna. Good looking out. You're a true friend."

"You're welcome, Donnie. I hope you can talk some sense into Reece."

"I'm going to try," he said, with a sad, faraway look in his eyes.

[5]

"Stop, Troy, I gotta go."

"Stop what?" he said, planting another wet, juicy kiss on her neck and pulling her body closer to his.

Pam had managed to get out of his bed after spending the last three hours making passionate love to her boss. She was a hostess at Café Coco, the trendy restaurant that chef Troy Hamilton owned, and though she had been employed less than a week, she was already caught in his seductive web.

She was freshly showered, dressed, and ready to walk out the door. Her mouth was saying "Stop," but her body was saying something totally different. She instinctively jutted her pelvis forward against his heated mound of flesh. His hot mouth sucked her neck until her skin turned a deep crimson. "Troy…" she moaned.

"Yes," he answered between kisses.

"Why don't you save some for later?"

"I want it all now. Besides, you can't leave me like this." He stepped back a half a step so she could get a look at his full-monty.

Pam swallowed with desire as she stared at his massive, rock hard penis that was pointed straight toward her clit. She couldn't believe that he was erect so soon after they had made love. Most of the men she had been with took at least a few hours to recover. Not Troy. He was primed and ready for more. She wanted him badly, but didn't want to be so easy and predictable. Determined to leave, she turned away from him and faced the door in an attempt to escape his advances.

Before she could put her hand on the doorknob, Troy was rubbing his hardness against her backside. He then reached under her skirt and panties, and found her engorged clit. He fingered her until she came.

Her body was reeling with lust for him, and in that moment, she no longer cared about being easy and predictable. All she cared about was getting fucked. She stepped out of her panties, ripped off her skirt, and bent her naked ass over so that Troy could have easy access.

He eased his hard cock into her slippery wetness, grabbed her hips, and rammed every inch of his nine inches deep within her. The sex between them was hedonistic and they howled like wild animals as he grinned and pumped them both into an erotic climax.

"Maybe I'll skip work today, and stay here with you," she said, after recovering.

"Ugh." Troy turned away from her and walked toward the bathroom. "That's not a good idea."

She picked up her underwear and skirt from the floor. "Why not?"

He yelled from the bathroom, "Because there's no one to cover the podium, and tonight's going to be busy."

"Oh." In the heat of the moment, Pam had forgotten all about work. Since she was servicing the boss, she had assumed that she'd be entitled to a few fringe benefits.

Troy came bouncing back into the living room with a terrycloth towel wrapped around his waist. "You'd better get a move on, babe, so you can go home and rest up for this evening's rush."

Pam couldn't believe how drastically his tone had changed. Ten minutes ago, he was begging for her pussy. Now he was kicking her out of his apartment. Pam knew that she was being easy, but she couldn't resist him.

Troy pecked her on the forehead, then patted her naked ass. "Come on, sweet cheeks, the restaurant needs you."

"I thought you needed me," she said, sounding dejected.

Not another needy broad, he thought. He didn't know what it was about women. One or two good fucks and they thought that translated into a committed relationship, when it was nothing more than horny sex. Troy looked into her sad face and knew that he had to pull a quick lie out of his bag of deception. The last thing he wanted was a disgruntled employee. He knew that he should have never dipped his stick into her well, but he couldn't resist, especially after seeing her night after night in that black hostess dress. He had designed the hostess uniforms personally, and purposely chose a thin, flimsy fabric that was practically see-through. Pam's 36Cs filled out the dress perfectly, and with her large nipples pressing against the delicate material, he couldn't restrain himself.

"Come on, babe, you know I need you," he cooed, as he slipped his finger back into her hot box. She was still wet and it turned him on all over again. His dick began to harden as he finger-fucked her into another orgasm.

"Oh, Troy, Troy," she moaned. "I—I love you."

He instantly went limp at the mention of the "L" word, and promptly withdrew his finger. This was more serious than he'd thought. He knew there was nothing more dangerous than a woman scorned, and now he'd have to handle her with kid gloves. "Babe, I'll probably have to go to the police station and answer some more questions about last night." One of the junior detectives had briefly questioned Troy, but informed him that the lead detective would probably have more questions.

Pam hadn't gone to the party and didn't know about the accident. "What happened last night?"

"Someone drowned at the yacht party," he said matter-of-factly, as if it didn't faze him.

"*OhmyGod!*" Pam threw her hand to her mouth. "How did they drown?"

"I don't know." Troy didn't have an appointment scheduled. He'd told Pam the white lie to get her off of his back.

"Why didn't you tell me this last night?" she asked urgently.

"I didn't feel like talking about it, and needed a

distraction from all the drama." Troy needed a distraction, all right! Last night had been total pandemonium. "Anyway, I've gotta get going, and you'd better scoot, too," he said, tapping her on the butt.

"Oh, all right," she said reluctantly.

Once Pam had left, Troy sat on the sofa and thought about the floating body he had seen in the bay last night. He couldn't believe that there had been a tragedy in his quaint little town.

TROY HAD SPENT SUMMERS ON COCO BEACH EVER SINCE he was five. His father's sister, Vivian Hamilton, was a diva in every sense of the word. Light enough to pass for white, she was a mezzo-soprano with the Metropolitan Opera back in the day, and was the grand dame of the island. Twice married and twice widowed, she was childless and spoiled her one and only nephew as if he were her son. Troy was treated like a precious prince by his aunt and her doting friends. The women would fret over the cute, curly-headed child like he was some type of mini-deity. Little did they know that their adoring admiration would turn the innocent little boy into a lying ladies' man.

The attention that he received from the opposite sex was addictive, like a powerful drug he couldn't live without. He realized that he was at the age where he should settle down, find "the one," and start a family. However, the idea of being faithful to one woman was a foreign concept to him. Troy had never in his life been committed to a monogamous relationship, and he doubted that he could honor the strict vows of marriage.

He finished dressing, hopped into his black Porsche, and drove to his restaurant. Café Coco was located on the wharf. The million-dollar yachts that docked at the pier were the perfect accessories for the trendy restaurant, with most of the wealthy boat owners opting to dine on the café's patio. Troy had bought the building—a former shipping warehouse—a few years ago, and had it completely gutted and transformed into a modern, yet charming space. Bathed in a soothing cerulean blue with pure white accents, the nautical color scheme was befitting the environment.

Troy unlocked the heavy, hand-carved wooden door, and walked inside. The cavernous room was still, void of any activity. He loved the quiet, private time with his "baby" before the restaurant became a bustling throng of activity. Most of the diners wanted a good meal, but then there were others who wanted what wasn't printed on the menu—Troy. Naturally, he loved the attention from the ladies, but lately the men had also started giving him the eye, which was unnerving to the full-blooded heterosexual.

He walked past the bar area and ran his hand across the antique ebony bar, admiring its beauty. The piece was a fantastic find. It had been slated for demolition and was sitting inside a salvage yard when Troy rescued the hundred-year-old bar.

"Damn," he mumbled as he traced his finger around a white water stain. He made a mental note to have the manager order a waterproof runner to protect the relic from the martini-sipping, miniskirt-wearing femme fatales who sat perched on the stools weekend after weekend looking either to get a husband or to get rid of one. Troy chuckled at the thought of the desperate women, who unabashedly threw themselves at anything in trousers. Those types were a serious turn-off for him. He was often on the receiving end of their blatant passes, but was clever enough to dismiss their advances with a lingering smile and a drink on the house. By the time he ducked back into the kitchen, the women were so taken aback by his generosity that they were clueless to his sly maneuver.

But there was one woman in particular that he wanted to maneuver right into his bed. Every time she came into the restaurant, her head was buried in a book. She never even looked in his direction, and her aloofness intrigued him. Troy had his finger in several pies around town, but this was one dish he had yet to sample.

[6]

D r. Lars Braxton had come to the island for some fun and relaxation, to escape the pressures of work. However, the yacht party had been anything but fun. His wife had caught him in a compromising position with another woman. He'd tried to talk his way out of the mess, but the other woman kept interjecting, making the situation worse. He persuaded the other woman to leave him and his wife alone so that they could talk privately. Lars did his best back-pedaling act, trying to convince his wife it was the liquor that had made him behave inappropriately.

When the conversation was over, he left the party, went home, and first thing in the morning, he jumped into his car and made a beeline back to the city. He left his wife a note saying that he had an early morning surgery. Lars had had enough excitement and didn't want to stick around in case tempers flared again. He needed some distance to sort out what had become of his life.

Dr. Braxton's multi-million-dollar practice on ritzy Fifth Avenue was a lifetime away from his meager beginnings. Born Larry Brown thirty-six years ago in Memphis, Tennessee, Dr. Braxton was the only child of blue-collar assembly-line workers. His parents came from a long line of sharecroppers, so their work as wage slaves was a step up. Neither graduated high school, but that didn't stop them from instilling in Larry the importance of a higher education. In their opinion, each generation's accomplishments should exceed those of the one that came before, as they had done by moving from the fields into the factory.

Fueled by a desire to succeed and make his parents proud, Larry excelled in school and earned an academic scholarship to the University of Tennessee at Knoxville. Since childhood, Larry had had an interest in medicine, often diagnosing his mother's ailments. More times than not, he was right on the money with his layman's verdict. So it came as no surprise when he chose pre-med as his major. Larry leaned his concentration toward internal medicine, but with one look at his lean, nimble fingers, his professor suggested that he specialize in vascular surgery. During med school, Larry's interest shifted briefly from academics to romance when he met a charming undergraduate.

Remi Boulet, a third-year art history major, was an exotic beauty with hypnotic, hazelnut-colored eyes and a glowing complexion to match. She was hard to miss when she graced the quad with her presence. Larry learned through the grapevine that she hailed from New Orleans, which explained her French surname.

Assuming that Remi would have no interest in a dark-skinned country boy from Tennessee, Larry kept his distance, admiring her from afar. He soon started dating Dena, another med student. Although she was homely, she was interesting and smart. However, fate intervened one Saturday night, changing the course of his life.

Celebrating graduation from med school, Larry and a group of his classmates packed the local watering hole to toast their hard-won accomplishment. To his surprise, Remi was among the crowd of beer-drinking co-eds. She was a friend of a friend, and after a few bottles of suds, Larry got up the courage to ask for an introduction. Though he was easy on the eyes, with a tall, slightly muscular runner's body and a smooth baby face, he was nervous and feared rejection. However, Remi proved extremely pleasant, and they effortlessly chatted the evening away, trading life stories.

After that night, Remi began pursuing Lars. He told her that he had a girlfriend. He was attracted to Remi, but didn't want to hurt Dena. However, Remi was relentless, calling him and showing up at his dorm room unexpectedly. Just when Lars thought he'd have to make a choice between the two women, Dena left school out of the blue. He later learned that she had become ill, and passed away. Lars grieved his girlfriend, but with the help of Remi, got over his grief. He and Remi quickly became an item, with Remi clinging to the aspiring young surgeon.

After his residency at Knoxville General was over,

Larry was inundated with offers from some of the leading hospitals in the country. Vacillating between Northwestern in Chicago and Columbia Presbyterian in New York, he was unable to make up his mind and solicited the opinion of his girlfriend. In true diva fashion, she didn't bat an eyelash when she told him New York would be the better choice. She had always wanted to escape the South and live on the East Coast. Naturally, she assumed that she'd be going along for the ride; after all, they were inseparable—she had made sure of that.

Remi was in the catbird seat; with Larry crazy in love with her, she had the power to call the shots. And call them she did. Remi didn't mince words when she told him in no uncertain terms that she *would not* move *anywhere* as a mere *girlfriend*. Larry got the hint and proposed to her the very next day with a plain gold band. She didn't balk at the non-traditional engagement ring because she knew it was only a matter of time before Larry would be raking in the big bucks as a surgeon, and then she would have her pick of the best and biggest rocks that Tiffany had to offer.

During the lean years, life in New York was anything but glamorous. Larry was working long hours, honing his skills as a vascular surgeon. Though he made a decent salary, he spent the majority of it on rent. Remi insisted that they live on the snobbish Upper East Side. She knew the value of appearances and location was a key element in presenting an affluent front. The first question a New Yorker asked after your name was "Where do you live?" and a prestigious ZIP code could open the right doors. It didn't matter to Remi that they were house poor; what mattered was that they were accepted into the upper echelon circles.

This line of thinking also led her to suggest, no, *insist* that Larry change his name. In Remi's opinion, Dr. Larry Brown had no cachet. She hated his last name so much that she still used her maiden name. After scouring her Bible—the society pages of *Town and Country*—and digesting the aristocratic family names of some of the country's finest Blue Bloods, she concocted the perfect combination: Lars Braxton. Now that was a name that easily rolled off the tongue and said, "I have arrived." Besides, the initials were the same and she wouldn't have to change their monogrammed towels. It took a lot of pouting and several nights of withholding sex to sway him to her side, but Larry finally caved, as she knew he would. Larry was a sexaholic, a closet freak who needed the booty on the regular, and Remi knew exactly how to please him to get what she wanted. And what she wanted was a life straight from the pages of those glossy society magazines—a life of privilege and status with lavish homes in the city and in the Hamptons. Thanks to Larry's hard work, her dreams were only a breath away.

Remi had visions far beyond Larry's narrow scope.

All he wanted was to practice medicine and save lives, but unclogging arteries wasn't glamorous enough and would never bring her the type of recognition she craved. The answer to her prayers came one evening when she was home alone channel surfing and came across a documentary on plastic surgery. Traditionally performed on patients to correct deformities, it had now become elective surgery. The documentary went on to show how people altered their appearance regularly, and how socially acceptable it had become to have body parts reduced or enhanced. Thanks to Hollywood, plastic surgery had become the latest craze and was no longer stigmatized, but was embraced by society. Because the surgery was elective, insurance companies didn't cover the cost, which meant that it was a cash business. When Remi heard this, she danced a jig in celebration of their impending wealth. She ordered a copy of the documentary and viewed it with Lars, who promptly got on board with the plan. He was sick and tired of being house poor, and agreed to take the necessary courses in cosmetic surgery.

Remi assumed a new role, becoming a one-woman marketing team, taking out ads in all the society magazines, and dropping his name with the "ladies who lunch" crowd. With vanity running rampant among this bunch of pretentious buppies, it didn't take long for Lars's new career to take off. Fueled by a high-octane need to surpass the rest, these women jockeyed for position to be the first in their group to get a little nip from Manhattan's latest celebrity surgeon.

The Braxtons had finally arrived. Their net worth rose quickly, easily affording them a lavish penthouse on Fifth Avenue with commanding views of the city and a beachfront home in the bourgeois Hamptons. However, Lars was learning that money wasn't everything.

LARS MADE A PIT-STOP AT HOME, CHANGED, AND THEN headed to the office. The sidewalks on the Upper East Side of Manhattan seemed to be encrusted with diamond dust, which would explain why they sparkled in the moonlight and glimmered under the glare of the noonday sun. Limestone buildings adorned with starched canvas awnings stood shoulder to shoulder like majestic ivory towers, each one more grandiose than the next. Fifth Avenue above Sixtieth Street was a world unto itself. Primarily residential, the area was only a mile or so away from the renowned retail district that boasted the crown jewels—Tiffany, Harry Winston, and Cartier—of the avenue. Daily activities flowed at a civilized pace in this part of the city. Uniformed nannies could be seen leisurely strolling babies in white-walled prams along the Central Park side of the street. The frenzied fight for yellow taxis was unheard of here, since private drivers in luxury sedans chauffeured the over-indulged to their destinations. Even the air seemed rarified amongst this privileged group.

Dr. Lars Braxton moseyed the two short blocks from his penthouse to his office. A highly sought-after plastic surgeon, his practice was thriving with a triple-A list of clients, most of them repeat offenders who were addicted to the scalpel. The roster ran the gamut from wealthy trophy wives who were determined to remain competitive with the young beauties who sought to dethrone them, to television personalities—male and female—who were forced to retain a fresh look if they expected the networks to renew their hefty seven-figure contracts. There were also those who wanted to alter their appearances simply in the name of vanity.

"Good morning, Dr. Braxton," said the white-gloved doorman as he held the door open for Lars.

"Good morning, Porter."

The gray-haired, African-American attendant smiled broadly every time he saw Lars; it did him proud to see a young black man among the sea of white faces he greeted on a daily basis. Lars was the only doctor of color in the suite of medical offices that occupied the ground floor of the luxury high-rise. "Have a good day, Dr. Braxton."

"You, too, Porter."

Lars walked into the building and made a sharp left. He was one of two doctors who had a pricey street view. He unlocked the door to the office, which was actually three large adjoining apartments which had been redesigned. The result was a state-of-the-art medical office with a richly appointed waiting area bathed in tones of taupe with hints of cream. There were a series of examination rooms, and a secret rear entrance for high-profile patients who didn't want to be seen.

Lars flicked on the overhead lights as he entered his office, his home away from home. He spent so much time at work that he had decked out the space with the latest high-tech electronics—a flat-screen plasma television complete with DVD player, and a Bang & Olufsen sound system.

He took off his tailored suit jacket, replaced it with a starched white doctor's coat with his name monogrammed on the left pocket, and settled in behind his desk. Lars had a meeting with a pharmaceutical rep. He'd scheduled this appointment to take place early in the morning, before the office became a swarming hive of activity.

As he was checking the day's calendar, the buzzer rang. He looked at his watch. It was seven-thirty and the sales rep was right on time. Lars walked back to the outer office and buzzed the intercom.

"Dr. Braxton?" asked the attractive woman before him. She was about five foot three, with a short-cropped haircut that accented her round eyes and full lips perfectly. Looking at her small, compact body, he thought she resembled Lil' Kim, sans the long weave and hoochie-momma getup.

He extended his hand. "Yes. Please come in." Lars

was pleasantly surprised. He had only spoken on the phone with her, and had no idea that she was a babe. He grinned a sly smile as he watched her strut into his office. Her form-fitting skirt hugged her round rear end ever so tightly. He could tell from the absence of panty lines that she wore a thong. The thought of a thin strip of material flossing her naked ass gave him a rise. He could feel an erection coming on and tried to stop it, but the moment she turned to face him, his blood rushed straight to his head, and not the one on his shoulders. His penis hardened the second his eyes greeted her breasts, and he was grateful for the long doctor's coat that hid his protruding bulge. He tried to concentrate on her eyes as she spoke, but her 38Ds were pushing against her ill-fitting bra, which he could see through the thin nylon sweater she wore. With one discerning look, he noted that she wasn't saline enhanced. Her breasts hung low enough and her nipples were tilted down ever so slightly. In his professional opinion, her breasts were perfect! They didn't have the fake, balloon-type appearance that some patients preferred.

"It's so nice to finally meet you," she said, bringing him out of his trance.

"The pleasure is mine, Ms....?" His mind was flooded with lewd thoughts, causing him to forget her name.

"Sandra Jackson," she said quickly, ending the awkward moment.

"Come into my office, Ms. Jackson," he said, trying to refocus and get his mind back on business. He had gotten himself into enough trouble last night, and didn't need to further complicate things.

Once they were seated, she went into her spiel, removing packets of samples from her oversized brief-case as she spoke. "This medication is similar to Vioxx." She held up an orange and blue box. "But it's manu-factured by a company in Sweden and is easier on the stomach lining. I also have varying strengths of OxyContin. The white tablet is the lowest dosage, for moderate pain; the pink tablet..."

He knew all about the drug and tuned her out, focusing instead on her full lips as she spoke. He could imagine them wrapped around his dick. It had been months since his wife had given him the pleasure of oral sex, or any sex at all for that matter. He wanted to ask the rep if she had an anti-Viagra pill to deflate his perpetual erection.

Over the years, as their wealth grew, the Braxtons' sex life withered. Remi was no longer concerned with pleasing her husband in or out of the bedroom. The only thing that seemed to make her happy these days was amassing more material possessions. Her latest project was redecorating their beach house, where she spent the majority of her time.

Lars was tired of going home to an empty bed, and of taking matters into his own hands. He'd been the dutiful husband long enough. After all, a man could only take so much jacking-off to late-night porn before desiring the feel of soft female flesh. The need to indulge his desires had led him to his current predicament. Now Lars had two women to contend with. He knew eventually he'd have to make a choice—stay with his wife and leave the other woman or vice-versa—especially after last night. Time was closing in on him, and Lars had some tough decisions to make. But he was a smart man and was confident that one way or the other, he'd make the right choice.

[7]

Theo sat at her desk going over the interview notes. She had spoken to Donovan Smart yesterday, and got a little insight on his sister and her best friend. Donovan left before she really had a chance to dig deep. Theo sensed there might be something he was hiding. Her nearly ten years as a detective had sharpened her intuition, and she knew when a person was holding back. Theo didn't press him; that wasn't her tactic. Every detective had their own way of extracting information, and Theo's was the no-pressure approach. She would let an alleged suspect know that she had enough information on the crime to incriminate them. She then would talk about the sentencing factor, and would point out that a confession usually boded well for lenient sentencing. More times than not, Theo came away with that confession. Donovan wasn't a suspect at this point in the investigation, so she hadn't objected to him leaving her office so soon.

"Hey, Boss Lady, how's it going?"

"Stop calling me that, Rogers," Theo told her co-worker.

Theodora was the new lieutenant of the detective unit at CBPD. Tired of the big city, and wanting a slower pace of life, she had moved to Coco Beach from Manhattan after a bad break-up with her ex-husband. When the opportunity to relocate arose, she jumped at the chance to change scenery. She had been married for eight years and thought that her marriage was secure, but she couldn't have been more wrong. While she was busy solving crimes, her husband was busy sleeping around. Although Theo was a detective, she'd had no clue what he had been up to. He would've gotten away with the adultery if it wasn't for his mistress showing up at their front door—pregnant! When Theo confronted her husband about the affair, he broke down and begged for her forgiveness. She wasn't about to be a part of a threesome that included baby mama drama, so she filed for divorce, packed up, and moved out. That was a year ago, and she still wasn't quite ready to date. Her husband's deception had totally shattered her trust in the opposite sex, and for now, her faith in men was sketchy at best.

"But you are the boss and a lady," Rodgers said, ribbing her.

"How can I forget, when you keep reminding me every chance you get? Rodgers, I would really prefer it if you'd call me by my name," she said in no uncertain terms. Theo was a no-nonsense type of person, and didn't bite her tongue when it came to expressing herself.

"Lighten up, Theo. I was only kidding. You're wound too tight. What you need is some fun in your life. When was the last time you went out on a date?"

Theo looked up from her paperwork and stared at him like he had lost his mind. "What did you say?" she said with attitude, as if to say, "It's none of your business."

"Don't get your knickers in a knot. All I'm saying is you're always here at the station, and that can't be fun day in and day out. Coco Beach is a great little town. You need to get out and experience what the area has to offer socially," Rodgers said, trying to clarify his comment.

He had a point. Theo hadn't even entertained the idea of dating since her divorce. Work was the one constant in her life that she could depend on, so she focused on her job instead of getting into another relationship and possibly getting her heart broken again.

"Tell you what, Rodgers." She got up from her desk. "While I'm *experiencing* a nice lunch, you finish up these case files," she said, handing him a stack of file folders.

"Ha, ha, very funny," he said, with a sour expression on his face.

Theo took her tote bag out of her desk drawer and headed out of the station. Café Coco was down the street, so she walked the few short blocks instead of getting into her unmarked sedan.

When she got to the restaurant, the lunch crowd was thinning out. Theo purposely ate a late lunch in order to avoid the masses. She assumed her normal seat at the bar, ordered a glass of lemonade, and looked over the menu. The food at Café Coco was delicious, with the menu changing on a regular basis to accommodate the fresh produce and seafood that the island had to offer.

"Have you decided yet?" the bartender asked.

"Yeah, I'll have the lobster club and a side of sweet potato fries."

"Excellent choice! The lobster was caught early this morning, and it's extremely succulent," the bartender explained.

"Hmm, can't wait to taste it."

As the bartender put in her order, Theo took a mystery novel out of her tote bag. Not only did she enjoy solving crimes, she loved reading about them as well, and James Patterson was one of her favorite authors. She was thirsty from the walk and quickly polished off her lemonade.

Theo was so immersed in her novel that she didn't notice a pair of eyes following her every move.

[8]

The restaurant was thinning out from the lunch crowd. Troy made his entrance and was eagerly greeted by a group of women who were leaving.

"There you are," said Penelope Black, one of the senior inhabitants of Coco Beach.

Troy leaned down and kissed her on the cheek. "Hey there, Mrs. Black. Don't you look lovely this afternoon," he said, commenting on her lemon-colored linen suit and matching hat.

Mrs. Black blushed at the compliment. Although she was old enough to be Troy's grandmother, she still loved the attention that he showered on her. "Thanks. Aren't you the sweet one."

"Yes, he sure is a sweetie," Wanda Richards said, chiming in. She, too, was smitten with Troy.

Rounding out the trio was Elizabeth Lord, Liza's grandmother. Elizabeth looped her arm through Troy's and smiled up into his handsome face. "So, Troy, when are you going to settle down and get married? I think you and Liza would make the perfect couple."

"Mrs. Lord, Liza and I grew up together like brother and sister. As pretty as she is, I'll always think of her as a sibling."

"Nonsense! I'm well aware of how you two grew up. The fact of the matter is that you are *not* related. And I don't want to hear any more talk about being brother and sister. Is that clear?" she said in a demanding tone. Mrs. Lord was accustomed to ruling over her family, and didn't think twice about brandishing her authority where it didn't belong.

"Yes," Troy answered, sounding like a little boy who had been chastised.

Mrs. Lord then switched gears. "Troy, I assume you were on my yacht the night of that horrible incident," she said.

"Yes, I was there."

"Did you know the young lady who drowned?" Mrs. Black asked.

"They haven't released her identity yet," Troy answered.

"What a shame." Mrs. Richards shook her head. "We haven't had something this awful happen in Coco Beach in years. The newspaper said it hadn't yet been determined whether she jumped or was pushed."

"I knew something like this would happen the minute that rapper and his ilk moved to town," Mrs. Lord said, turning up her nose.

"Those new money types have no couth," Mrs. Black chimed in.

"Especially the entertainers," Mrs. Richards added.

Troy stood back as the matrons bashed the Donovan Smarts of the world. He had met Donovan at the party, and the brother seemed cool, but of course, Troy was too smart to admit that to these ladies. They were snobs in every sense of the word, and would never accept the new money residents who moved to Coco Beach. As far as they were concerned, the town belonged to the long lineage of old money and their heirs.

"Come on, ladies, before we're late for bridge," Mrs. Black said.

"Thanks for coming by. Next time, dessert is on me," Troy told them as they walked out.

As Troy was making his way back to the kitchen, he spotted the one customer who never paid him any attention. She was sitting at the bar, with her head in another novel. Troy didn't know her name, but he knew that she was fine. Her complexion was the color of a ripe pecan. Her reddish-brown hair dusted her shoulders. She had petite features, except for her full lips. Since she was sitting, Troy couldn't determine how tall she was. However, he could see that she was slim.

Troy slowed his gait, stopping at her side. "Hello. How are you this afternoon?"

She looked up from her book. "I'm fine, and you?"

"Couldn't be better." He smiled and extended his hand. "I'm Troy Hamilton, the chef and owner of Café Coco."

"Theodora Pratt," she said, shaking his hand firmly.

Troy looked at her glass sitting on the bar and noticed that it was nearly empty. "Can I buy you another drink?"

"No, thanks."

Troy had hoped announcing that he was the owner of the restaurant would give him some leverage, but it hadn't. Theodora went back to reading, totally unfazed by his charisma and good looks.

Although the owner of Café Coco was fine as hell, Theo was unimpressed. In her line of work, Theo had to quickly assess people, and one look at Troy told her that he was a lady killer. He was tall, handsome, and charming—a lethal trifecta.

"Are you sure I can't get you another lemonade? It's made from an old family recipe. As a matter of fact, I use a lot of my grandmother's recipes, but I put my own twist to them, of course. Take for instance the lemonade, I added Celestial Seasonings Lemon Zinger to give it an extra zing."

Theo smiled half-heartedly. She wasn't interested in idle chit-chat. She wanted to continue reading her book while she waited for her food, but this guy seemed intent on taking up her time. "Of course."

Troy stared at her full lips as she spoke. He could imagine himself kissing her until she melted in his arms, like most women did. Then again, something was telling him that she wasn't like most of the women on the island. For starters she wasn't overly glammed-up. She wore a khaki suit, with a pale blue shirt, and a pair of loafers. Her casual attire set her apart from the other ladies who came to the restaurant decked out in the latest designer labels. Even her tote was regular, not some obscenely priced designer purse. Although she was dressed plainly, she was pretty enough to give the over-aged debutantes some competition. Troy was curious as to where she had come from. Whoever she was, she didn't appear to be concerned with fitting into the snobby Coco Beach mold. "Sooo," he said, taking a seat next to her. "Where are you from?"

Oh here it comes…the twenty questions, she thought. "The city," she answered dryly.

"Which city?"

"Manhattan."

He wrinkled his brow. "Really?"

Theo noticed his expression and tone. "Why did you say it like that?"

"Like what?"

"Like, I don't belong in the city."

"No. I didn't mean it like that. I meant that I also live in the city, and I'm surprised that I've never seen you before."

"Oh, like you know every woman in New York," she said with a slight attitude in her voice. She had met Troy's type so many times before—the handsome stud who ran through women like they were disposable—and it irritated her that he was sizing her up like she was a fine cut of sirloin.

Troy could see that she was getting upset for some reason. He put his hand on her forearm and said, "Sorry if I offended you."

"I'm not offended," she said, removing her arm from underneath his hand.

"Here's your lunch," the bartender said, interrupting their tense conversation.

"Can you wrap it up? I need to get back to work."

"Sure, no problem."

Theo stood up, indicating that she was ready to end this "getting to know you" session. She had come to Coco Beach to escape the Troys of the world. Now here she was in the crosshairs of a serial ladies' man. Suddenly, Theo had an idea that would hopefully get him off her scent. "Can you tell the bartender to have my lunch delivered to the police station?"

"Police station?" Troy asked, looking puzzled.

"Yeah." Theo dug into her bag, took out her badge, and flashed him. "I'm the new lieutenant," she said with a macho edge to her voice. She had been too busy questioning the other guests the night of the drowning to interview Troy, but had his name on her list of interviewees. She purposely hadn't let on that she was the lead detective in the drowning case. Theo had wanted to observe Troy without him knowing who she was. She wanted to see if he betrayed any signs of suspicion. He didn't. The only signs he betrayed were of lust.

Troy was shocked. He now understood why she dressed

the way she did. Theo wasn't in town for vacation; she was the *man*! "Oh, okay, Lieutenant, I'll have it sent over right away." He smiled, and then saluted her.

Theo felt that he was mocking her, but she wasn't about to get into another useless conversation. Now that he knew she was the law, hopefully he would stop drooling over her. Theo took one last look at him before she left, and he still had that lustful gleam in his eye. Obviously, learning she was an officer of the law didn't have an effect on Troy, at least not yet.

[9]

Remi Braxton lifted her dimpled chin slightly and slowly inhaled the fresh country air. She could smell freshly cut grass, lilacs, and wildflowers the moment she turned off Sag Harbor Turnpike. With the rejuvenating breeze in her face, the grime and stench of the city seemed worlds away. The canvas top on her creamy vanilla, vintage T-Bird was neatly folded down. Her hair would've been blowing wildly in the wind, but it had been recently cropped. Remi's yearly ritual was cutting her locks prior to Memorial Day. She couldn't stand the "wool" (as she called it) scratching the back of her neck all summer. She ran her fingers through the short 'do, adjusted her shades, and cruised toward home.

She had taken a drive to clear her head. Remi was still recovering from the ordeal at the party. She had caught her husband, Lars, red-handed with a hoochie. Remi had gone into one of the staterooms to freshen her makeup. She opened the door and saw Lars rolling around in the bed with another woman. She was shocked! Lars quickly disentangled himself and scrambled to his feet, straightening his clothes as he spoke. He was talking fast, telling Remi all of this was a big misunderstanding, and that the woman meant nothing to him. As he was talking, the other chick kept putting in her two cents, saying that she was Lars's lady, and that Remi could take a hike. The woman also spouted off other allegations, rendering Remi speechless. Eventually Lars persuaded the woman to leave so that he could talk to Remi in private. As he spoke, Remi knew the words coming out of his mouth were straight-up lies. She went along with him because she didn't want to exacerbate an already embarrassing scene. Lars made a swift exit after his speech, leaving Remi alone at the party. She didn't mind. Remi had business of her own to take care of.

The Braxtons' summer home was in Coco Beach, one of five private, primarily black enclaves tucked neatly away on the sandy shores of Sag Harbor, where the well-to-do spent the majority of their summer. The area had a rich African-American heritage as a stop along the Underground Railroad, where slaves would hide in secret compartments at St. David AME Zion Church, which had since been classified as a landmark.

The quaint village of a few thousand during the winter months easily swelled to over ten thousand in the summer. Remi loved the serenity of the off-season, but deplored the hordes of people who invaded the area from Memorial Day to Labor Day, most of whom were renters paying through the nose for a temporary piece of paradise. Shying away from the fray, Remi spent most of the time at her beach house, except of course for the occasional meal at Café Coco, the island's hot spot.

Remi could hear the phone ringing inside the house the moment she pulled into the graveled circular driveway. She didn't rush to answer the call, thinking whoever it was would either call her on the cell or leave a message, and sure enough, before she could put the car in park, her cellular phone rang.

"Hey, girl, where are you? I've been calling the house all morning." It was Remi's best friend, Liza Lord.

The Lords were one of the founding families of Coco Beach, and were old money personified. Eli Lord, the family patriarch, had made his fortune from a variety of sources—real estate, banking, import/export—but most notable were his early years as a bootlegger. Rumor had it that he ran booze from Europe directly to the shores of Sag Harbor during prohibition and made millions, then laundered the ill-gotten cash over the years until it became as pure as the driven snow. Some time ago Liza and her family were featured in an article in *Country Classics*—one of the many society magazines that Remi devoured on a regular basis—and after reading the rather lengthy piece, Remi was determined to befriend the rich girl.

"I've been out driving."

"I'm on my way over. I got some news for you!" she squealed into the phone.

Liza was the Liz Smith of Coco Beach. She knew the comings and goings of everyone—who was sleeping with whom, whose house was being foreclosed on due to squandered fortunes, and almost anything else someone was trying to hide. Talking to her was better than reading "Page Six," the infamous gossip column.

Years ago, Liza had gotten the four-one-one from the local realtor the moment Remi and Lars closed on their house. She promptly paid them a friendly visit to satisfy her curiosity. Though straight, she was immediately drawn to Remi's beauty and classy style. Liza had decided on the spot that the doctor's wife was going to be her new BFF, especially since Remi's skin tone fit the color code of the island—lighter than a brown paper bag. Little did she know that Remi had purposely chosen the property based on its close proximity to the Lords' beachfront estate.

"Okay, come on over." Remi grabbed her Marc Jacobs tote bag and headed toward the house.

Their home was over ten thousand square feet of pure luxury and was the third largest home on the beach. The Wellington estate was second, and of course the Lord mansion on sprawling grounds was numero uno. The Braxton property took up three entire acres, which was rare for beachfront property. Remi had the original, century-old, wooden beach house demolished and replaced with a modern, three-story glass and granite structure reminiscent of the Guggenheim Museum. She was a fan of the great architect Frank Lloyd Wright and wanted their house to convey a sense of awe, much like his circular masterpiece on Fifth Avenue.

She unlocked the door and left it ajar for Liza, then headed upstairs to change into her swimsuit.

No sooner had she slipped on her tankini than she heard Liza's heels tap across the terrazzo floor downstairs. As the click-clacking sound of Liza's shoes faded, Remi guessed that her friend had gone into the kitchen. Sure enough, sixty seconds later, she heard a cocktail shaker full of ice being shaken back and forth with a vengeance. Remi tied a sarong around her waist and bounced downstairs, anxious to hear the latest gossip.

"Pardon the mess." Remi waved her hand at the stacks of fabric swatches and paint samples strewn across the kitchen table. "I'm redecorating."

"Again? Didn't you redecorate last summer?"

"I did, but I've grown tried of this black and white color scheme. I'm thinking about keeping the white, taking out all the dark accents, and replacing them with celery or something in the green family for a more tropical feel."

"This mess isn't in my way, as long as I can get to the refrigerator. Thought I'd shake us up a cold one," Liza said, taking two martini glasses out of the freezer and pouring them each a cocktail.

Remi parked herself on one of the white leather stools next to the counter island. "Good. I could use a drink after that long drive."

"Why were you out driving anyway?"

"I needed to clear my mind. The drowning has me freaked out," Remi said, taking a sip.

"Tell me about it. I still can't believe that someone died on my yacht," Liza said, shaking her head.

"Technically the death occurred in the water."

"I hear what you're saying, but I still feel sort of responsible. Anyway, I came over to tell you that I heard the coroner's report will be available soon, and we'll find out exactly what she died from," Liza said, always full of breaking news.

"Is that right? Liza, it's amazing how you find out information before it's public," Remi said in amazement.

"I told you, I have sources all over this island."

"Well, your sources should have told you not to get involved with that rapper and his crew. I tried to warn you, but you wouldn't listen." Remi couldn't help herself. She had tried to warn Liza, but Liza was bullheaded. Remi could still remember the day that Liza found out Donovan had bought a house in Coco Beach. It was the beginning of the summer season, and that afternoon they had also been sitting in Remi's kitchen enjoying cocktails and conversation.

"SO...GIVE IT UP. YOU RUSHED OVER HERE WITH SOME big news; now tell me all the juicy details, Ms. *Entertainment Tonight*," Remi said, scooting to the edge of the stool.

Liza took a seat opposite Remi. "You know I love that

show, but I'll bet they don't have this scoop yet, since the deal was closed only this morning."

"What deal?" Remi put her glass on the counter.

"You'll never guess who bought the Wellington estate," Liza said with a raised eyebrow.

Remi looked surprised. "I didn't even know it was for sale."

The Wellingtons were also one of the founding families of the island, but over the years their entire clan had begun to scatter across the world, except for the eldest son who stayed in the States caring for his elderly mother.

"J.R. told me that he never liked the Hamptons, preferring instead to spend his summers in Capri, and that he only kept the place for his mother. But the minute Mrs. Wellington passed away, he put the estate on the auction block. J.R. also told me, in confidence, that his mother's prolonged bout with Alzheimer's had taken a toll on the family fortune, and that he needed to sell the estate in order to rejuvenate his bank account."

"I'm sure the property wasn't on the market long." Remi admired the stately Wellington place, which resembled a medieval castle complete with reflecting pond; manicured, maze-like hedges; and a prize-winning rose garden full of American Beauties.

Liza drained her glass. "You're right about that." She got up to make another shakerful of martinis. "Like I said before, you'll never guess who bought the estate."

Remi did a quick mental scan of some of the country's wealthiest black families, and then spoke her first choice. "The Cosbys?"

The left corner of Liza's top lip rose into a smirk. "Nope."

"Don't tell me Oprah bought it?" Remi said with glee at the thought of having *the* media queen as a neighbor.

Liza shook her head. "I wish. Try again," she said, enjoying this little guessing game.

Most of Remi's top picks already had houses on the island or at Martha's Vineyard, so she was at a loss. She hunched her shoulders. "I don't have a clue."

"You're not going to believe this," Liza said, prolonging the answer.

Remi leaned in. "Well?"

"Donovan Smart!" Liza grinned, revealing the big mystery.

Remi wrinkled her nose. "Who?"

"Donovan Smart, the rapper." She refilled their glasses. "Actually, his showbiz name is TuSmArt. I'm sure you've heard his music. His latest CD, *Straight from the Hook*, recently went double platinum," she said knowingly.

"I have no idea who you're talking about." Remi wasn't interested in rap music or street culture. She had spent too many years trying to infiltrate the world of high society, and now that she had arrived, she was intent on staying there and only associated herself with those born into this privileged sect.

"Girl, I'm here to tell you"—Liza fanned herself—"he is one *hot* number, and single to boot."

Remi rolled her eyes. "As if you'd ever take a rapper home to meet your family. Your parents would have simultaneous heart attacks, and your grandmother would promptly disinherit you."

"You got a point there, but that doesn't mean I can't have a little summer fling with a cute roughneck." She laughed.

It amazed Remi how casually rich folks regarded their station in life, as if nothing or no one could ever shake their foundation. While she, on the other hand, prayed every night that she would never misstep and lose her footing while trying to keep up with the Lords. "With all the eligible bachelors in Coco Beach, why would you ever even consider dating down?"

Liza exhaled loudly. "I'm sick of these tired, stuck-up Negroes, with their pedigrees and pompous posturing, always trying to trump each other with their outrageous toys. Besides, it's not like this Donovan person isn't rolling in the dough. He must be loaded. He paid cash for the Wellington estate."

"How do you know he paid cash?" Remi asked, before realizing that Liza was privy to the most proprietary information through her various connections.

"Come on, Remi, there's very little I *don't* know around these parts. He closed on the estate this morning and is moving in next week. I've decided to be a one-woman welcoming committee. I'm dying to see how the other side lives. I wonder if he has that new Bentley?"

"You already have a Bentley. Remember?"

"Not the new one," Liza whined, like a spoiled child in need of another unnecessary trinket.

Remi grunted. "Like you couldn't afford to buy one for yourself."

"Sure I could, but it's sweeter coming from a man."

"What strings do you think will be attached to a car that cost more than most homes?"

"Oh, don't be such a wet blanket. What's a few hundred grand to someone like that? He probably has a fleet of cars and trucks. You know how rappers like to flaunt their wealth."

"Be careful. Those people are notorious for shootouts and drive-bys."

Liza laughed. "You sound like one of the old biddies who play bridge with my grandmother."

"Okay, you're laughing now, but you won't be laughing once those 'old biddies' find out that you're dating a rapper, and the word spreads like wildfire across the island," Remi said, point blank.

"Trust me, I won't get caught. I'm not trying to marry the guy. I only want to have some fun." Liza laughed.

THAT WAS BEFORE SOMEONE HAD DIED. Now nobody was laughing, least of all Liza.

[10]

On Liza's way home, Remi's words reverberated in her head. She hated to be told "I told you so," but Remi did have a point. Of course, Liza couldn't see it in the beginning. She was too hell-bent on meeting Donovan. As she cruised along the country roads of Coco Beach, the day she set off for Donovan's house played again in her mind.

LIZA HAD QUIETLY CRUISED ALONG DONOVAN SMART'S tree-lined flagstone driveway in her drop-top Bentley. Though the car was five years old, it was impressive nonetheless, with its rich indigo exterior and creamy ivory leather interior piped in the same rich blue as the body of the car. In the distance, she could see a swarm of activity. She couldn't make out faces, but she could clearly see bodies milling about in front of his house.

"Maybe they're shooting a video. Is this my lucky day, or what?" She grinned from ear to ear. "My first visit and I'm going to be in a music video. I'ma be in a video. I'ma be in a video," she chanted, with urban verve.

Thinking that rap music would make her appear hip and help her blend in, Liza reached over to the stereo, slid in TuSmArt's latest CD, and pumped up the volume as she got closer to the mansion. Luckily, she had memorized the lyrics that were printed on the jacket, and knew every word. She sang along like a true rap-nista. "I'm from the Hook, but I ain't no crook…"

Liza pulled in behind a row of pimped-out SUVs and parked in the driveway. All eyes turned to her. Suddenly, she felt like a guppy swimming in shark-infested waters. Liza thought about hitting the gas pedal and getting the hell out of Dodge. What was she thinking? She was completely out of her comfort zone. She knew nothing about this culture except for what she read in magazines and saw on television. But she had made her grand entrance, rolling up in a Bentley, so now was not the time to turn tail. Besides, she was a Lord, and Lords could conquer anything. She adjusted her oversized Gucci shades and turned off the ignition.

"'Z'up, ma?" asked one of the gangsta-looking guys sitting on the bumper of his truck smoking a blunt, wearing jeans, a white wifebeater, and Timbs.

Liza mimicked his slang, and nodded back. "'Z'up?" She glanced in the rearview mirror and spotted two women walking in her direction.

"Yo. Who are you?"

Liza didn't know what to say. She wasn't expecting the ghetto Gestapo. Liza looked at the first young woman and recognized her from the social scene section of *Uptown* magazine. It was Donovan's sister, Reece Smart. Liza plastered a phony, toothy smile on her face and extended her hand through the driver's side window. "Hi. I'm Liza Lord."

Reece looked down at her hand with no intention of making contact, and then twisted her face into a grimace. "Who?"

"Liza Lord. I live a few houses down, and thought I'd welcome Donovan to the neighborhood."

"Donovan? You know my brother?" Reece asked in an over-protective tone.

"Uh…"

"Yeah, I thought so." Reece rolled her eyes to the sky. "You ain't nothin' but another wannabe groupie."

"Excuse me?" This was not going according to plan.

"You heard me."

"I beg your pardon, but I am not a grou—," she could hardly get the word out of her mouth, "groupie." Liza's blood began to boil at the implication. Her family fortune could buy and sell the likes of TuSmArt and his entire clan. She was two seconds from telling Reece where she could put her "groupie" label, but backed down and regained her composure. She had come here for one reason, and that was to meet Donovan, not spar with his sister.

"Whatever you are"—Reece smacked her lips—"he ain't here."

Liza doubted that she was telling the truth, but had no grounds to challenge the claim. "Tell him 'L' stopped by," she said, giving herself a hip nickname. She put the car in drive and sped off, leaving Reece in her dust.

"Don't worry, I'll be back," Liza mouthed into the rearview mirror as she watched Reece and her friend retreat into the house.

As LIZA DROVE ALONG, SHE WONDERED what would have happened had she never pursued Donovan. Maybe the life of the woman who was found in the water would never have come to a tragic end. Liza knew that was a stretch, since she had nothing to do with the woman's death. Nevertheless, she was still wracked with guilt.

[11]

Theo couldn't believe the gall of Troy. Even after he knew that she was on the police force, he still undressed her with his eyes. He obviously regarded women as nothing more than sex objects. Theo hated to be viewed as a piece of meat. She had worked hard over the years to prove that she was more than just a pretty face. Working in a predominately male environment, she had learned how to deal with male chauvinists, and that was to give as good as she got. If they teased her or made sexist jokes, her comeback was equally as harsh, if not harsher. Although she was as pretty as any super-model, she didn't play up her looks with makeup or fancy hairdos. She wore simple clothes so as not to draw attention to her toned body, preferring instead to focus on her brains.

"Rodgers, call Café Coco and get Troy Hamilton on the phone. Tell him I need to talk to him ASAP!" Theo yelled from her office. She planned to show him that she wasn't one of his groupies, but a woman who demanded and deserved respect.

"Sure thing, Boss Lady!" he yelled back.

Theo slammed her fist on the desk. "I told you not to call me that!" she hissed.

Rodgers heard the angry tone in Theo's voice and knew that she was dead serious. "Okay, okay," he said, holding up his hands in defense. He picked up the phone and made the call. "He'll be here in an hour," Rodgers said after he hung up.

Theo didn't look up or answer him. She simply nodded. She wanted to make sure that Rodgers knew not to tease with her anymore. Theo picked up the phone and called the coroner's office.

"Hi, this is Detective Pratt. I'm calling to find out if the coroner's report is back for the Lord yacht accident?"

"It's back. Do you want to pick it up?" asked the technician.

"Yes. I'll be right over," she said and hung up. Theo grabbed her tote bag and walked out of her office, closing the door behind her. "I'll be right back. If Mr. Hamilton comes in before I get back, have him take a seat," she told Rodgers.

"Sure thing, Lieutenant," he said, using her correct title this time.

It was a warm, sunny day with a slight breeze coming in from the water. Theo dug a pair of shades out of her tote, put them on, and made her way to the black unmarked Crown Victoria that she drove for work. She got in and rolled down the windows, instead of using the air conditioner. She loved the feel of the balmy air on her skin. Summer was her favorite season and she wanted to soak up as much warmth as possible before the chill of autumn set in.

Theo cruised down Main Street. With its quaint storefronts and centuries-old buildings, it was reminiscent of yesteryear. The idyllic town was picture-perfect and from the looks of the neatly arranged flower boxes and manicured lawns, no one would suspect that a tragic death had taken place nearby less than forty-eight hours ago. People were strolling along and shopping like any other ordinary day, and to them it was. But for Theo, it was day two of having a dead body and no answers. She hoped that the coroner's report would be the key to unlocking the mystery.

Theo pulled into the parking lot of the medical examiner's office, parked, and got out.

"Detective Pratt, here to pick up the report for the Lord yacht case," she told the receptionist and flashed her ID.

"Here you go," the receptionist said, handing her a manila envelope.

"Is the coroner available?" Theo thought that since she was here, she might as well talk with the medical examiner personally.

"I'm sorry. He's gone out for lunch. Do you want to leave a message?"

"No message. If I have any questions, I'll call him later," she said and walked out.

Once inside the car, Theo tore open the envelope.

She couldn't wait until she got back to the office. She was too anxious to see what the report said, and had to read it now. Her eyes scanned the length of the page and back again.

"Cause of death, drowning," Theo said aloud. She then read the toxicology findings. There were lethal amounts of OxyContin found in the victim's bloodstream.

"Hmm." She scratched the side of her head. "Oxy-Contin? Did she accidentally OD, or did someone slip her the pills?" Theo wondered aloud. "Maybe she was so wasted that she fell over the side?"

Theo read over the report again, and this time noticed that the coroner had noted that the victim had bruises on her back, as if she had been attacked. Theo's earlier assumption was now shot down. Obviously the victim didn't accidentally tumble overboard. Theo thought for a minute. "Looks like someone pushed her from behind," she said, coming up with a logical conclusion. This was definitely murder.

Theo put the car in drive and headed back to the station. When she walked inside, Troy Hamilton was sitting at Rodgers's desk, waiting for her.

"Hello, Detective," Troy said. He smiled broadly, showing a pair of sexy dimples.

"Come into my office, Mr. Hamilton," she said, walking swiftly past him, ignoring his killer smile.

Troy got up and followed her. "Twice in one day," he said, sitting down.

"Excuse me?"

"It's a joy to see you again so soon," he said, clarifying his statement.

Theo sat behind her desk and put the coroner's report down. "Mr. Hamilton, do you do drugs?" she asked point blank, not wasting any time.

He looked shocked. "Excuse me?"

"I said, do you do drugs?" she reiterated, looking directly into his eyes.

"Oh, yeah. I'm a bona fide crackhead; can't you tell?" he answered with a grin on his face.

"This isn't a laughing matter. A woman is dead. Do you understand that?" she asked sternly. "So answer the question."

"No, I don't indulge in drugs. I don't take anything stronger than Tylenol," he said, this time without the smile.

"Uh-hmm." She nodded her head. She told him the victim's name. "Did you know her?"

"No, I didn't."

"Really? I'm sure you know a ton of women," she said suggestively.

"In my business, I meet a lot of people, men and women, but I didn't know the deceased."

Theo gave him a scrutinizing look, trying to decide if he was telling the truth. She didn't detect any hints of lying. Either he was a good actor, or was indeed being honest. "Okay, Mr. Hamilton, that'll be all," she said, dismissing him.

Troy rose slowly, keeping his eyes on Theo. "You're

finished with me already?" he said, his smile returning.

This guy is relentless! she thought. "Fortunately for you, I don't have any more questions," she said, and then picked up the phone. "If you'll excuse me, I have an important call to make."

"Sure. No problem. I'll see you at the restaurant, and next time, the lemonade is on me," he said, still flirting.

When he left, Theo put the phone down. Theo refused to get caught up in Troy's web of seduction. Although she was lonely as hell, she for sure wasn't about to become another notch on his belt.

[12]

Donovan was in his study, writing lyrics to a new song. *When I first saw you, girl, I knew you had to be in my world.* "No, that's not it," he mumbled and crossed out the last verse. His creativity wasn't flowing like it normally did. He was naturally gifted and wrote hit songs effortlessly. Today, however, was a different story. He had a mental block and couldn't concentrate on work. His mind was too preoccupied with the tragic drowning. Now Donovan wished that he had never bought the estate or had the party. He sat back in his oversized leather chair and remembered the day that he had the idea to throw the bash of the season.

HE'D HAD A RECORDING SESSION THAT LASTED MOST OF the night, and had been calling his sister throughout the evening. When he still hadn't heard from Reece by morning, he began calling around, trying to find her. He had recently found out that she was using drugs, and wanted to keep close tabs on her to make sure that she stayed out of trouble.

"Chyna, have you seen Reece?" he asked frantically the moment she picked up the phone.

"Hey, Donovan. What time is it?" Chyna asked in a groggy voice.

"A quarter to seven. I just got out of the studio. I've been calling Reece since yesterday. Her phone was ringing; now it's going straight to voice mail. I've left a ton of messages, but she hasn't called me back," he said quickly, almost running his sentences together.

"Calm down, Donnie. I talked to her yesterday, and she's at the house in Coco Beach."

"Then why in the hell isn't she answering my calls?! Did you tell Reece that I know about her abusing Oxy? Is that why she's avoiding me?"

"No, Donnie, I didn't tell her anything. Knowing Reece, she probably forgot to bring her charger, and her phone is dead. Did you call the house line?" Chyna asked, trying to ease his mind.

He exhaled loudly into the phone, breathing a sigh of relief. "Reece threw such a fit when she found out the house was in Coco Beach that I didn't expect her to be there. She thinks Coco Beach is too snotty."

"Isn't it?"

"It's old money. And if that's snotty, then so be it. I'm tried of being viewed as some lowlife rapper. I got the cash; now I want the status, and being a homeowner in Coco Beach is a start. I told Reece that maybe she'd find a nice guy up there to settle down with, instead of those hoodlums she's been running around with."

"Come on, Donnie, you know as well as I do that Reece ain't hardly into quote, unquote 'nice guys.'"

"Yeah, I know. She hasn't met the right guy yet. Hey, I got an idea! Why don't I throw a cocktail party and invite some of the locals? There's bound to be a *nice* doctor, attorney, or businessman in the group."

"That sounds like a good idea."

"Maybe if Reece had a good man in her life, she wouldn't feel the need to do drugs," Donovan said optimistically.

"Maybe." Chyna wasn't so sure a man was the answer to Reece's problem. The girl needed rehab. But she didn't want to rain on Donnie's parade, so she kept her mouth shut.

"I'm finished in the studio for a couple of days, so I'ma head home, pack up a few things, and head out to Coco Beach. If I'ma have the bomb party, I need to start planning it ASAP," Donovan said, his voice now much happier than before.

"Sounds like a plan."

"You wanna ride out with me?"

"Sure. Why not?" Chyna didn't have anything going on in the city. She wasn't into bar hopping anymore, and the thought of going to dinner alone once again was depressing.

"Okay. I'll pick you up in an hour."

"Cool. See you then."

Donovan got into his sleek black Lamborghini and sped off. Twenty minutes later, he was pulling into the parking garage of his building. Being a born and bred Brooklyn boy, Donovan couldn't (nor did he want to) get out of the borough that he loved. When the record money starting pouring in, he bought a small warehouse building in DUMBO. At the time, the area in south Brooklyn, known as Down Under the Manhattan Bridge Overpass, was a seedy part of town, with abandoned warehouses, artists' studios, and little else. Donovan had the foresight to be one of the area's pioneers, and bought the building when it was a steal. Now DUMBO was trendy, with one-of-a-kind boutiques, cute restaurants, and pricy lofts going for over a million dollars. Donovan rented out the ground floor of his building to a curator, who turned the space into one of the community's hottest galleries. The second and third floors of the building had been renovated and transformed into a two-level loft. Donovan had hired a talented interior designer who brought Donovan's visions of urban living to life. His loft was a combination of modern, art-deco, and African motifs. The top floor was the party floor where he hosted private affairs. The area was complete with two fully stocked bars, a lounge area, dance floor, and a terrace that spanned half the length of the building.

He entered the loft, went into the kitchen, and made a smoothie. Donovan was a health nut, and blended a combination of spinach, ginger, celery, wheat grass, and orange juice. He drank the green concoction on a daily basis, to the chagrin of most of his friends.

Donovan polished off his breakfast and went upstairs to his massive bedroom. The room took up nearly half the second floor. He had a custom-made, extra-wide, extra-long king-sized bed, which was the room's focal point. There was a sixty-inch plasma television mounted to the wall, with surround sound speakers concealed in the walls. The room was painted in a rich mocha, and original African artwork hung on three walls. Donovan went into his boutique-sized closet and began throwing clothes into a Tumi duffle. He then took a quick shower and changed into a black warm-up suit, sneakers, and his trademark shades.

Forty minutes after arriving in the loft, he was out and back in the car. Donovan called Chyna and told her that he was on the way. Chyna also lived in Brooklyn, but had moved from the projects of Red Hook to Brooklyn Heights, near the Promenade. Her condo faced the East River and had a spectacular view of Manhattan. She was standing on her stoop when he pulled up.

"You're looking quite Hampton-ey," Donovan said, as he got out of the car to help Chyna with her luggage.

"Thanks. Thought I'd blend in with the crowd." She wore white jeans, a white linen shirt, and a pair of aqua Tory Burch ballerina slippers.

"Always the fashion plate." He chuckled.

"Donnie, you know I love clothes. As a matter of fact, I'm planning on opening my own boutique," she told him once they were settled in the car.

"Really?" This was the first time that he had heard of

her plan. "I didn't know you wanted to go into business."

"Yeah, I do. I mean, I can't expect to be on your payroll forever."

"Why not? My sister certainly has no problems spending my money."

"Don't get me wrong. I truly appreciate everything you've done for me and my mother, but it's time that I stand on my own two feet. I want to feel a sense of accomplishment, and not be a moocher for the rest of my life."

"That's admirable. Chyna, you know that I don't mind taking care of you guys. You're like family to me. I'll never forget how our families used to take care of one another back in the day. When we ran low on food, your moms would come over with a bag of groceries."

"And your moms did the same thing when we didn't have anything to eat," she said, remembering the lean times.

"Back to your store; have you found a location yet?"

"Yes and no. The places that I like are a little too expensive, so I'ma have to wait and save more cash before I can sign a lease."

"Chyna, why didn't you tell me this before? I'll be more than happy to give you the startup capital."

"Thanks, Donnie, I know you would, but you're already giving me a monthly allowance, and I don't want to impose any more than I already have." Chyna didn't tell him that at one point she'd thought she had found an investor. Kalvin was a friend of a friend who wanted to invest in her boutique, but after several meetings, he began coming on to her, and it wasn't hard to guess that he only wanted to fuck her. She cut off communication with him, but the guy kept calling. He was relentless. He even showed up at her apartment unannounced. Chyna had cursed him out, and after that she hadn't heard any more from him. She thought about telling Donovan this, but she didn't want to worry him.

"Damn, Chyna, when did you grow up and become such a responsible adult? I can remember, not too long ago, when you and Reece were hanging out 'til the break of dawn," he said, seemingly shocked at her maturity.

Chyna blushed slightly. "I guess you can say I got tired of partying without a purpose. I'm tired of being a fixture at the industry functions." Chyna had enough memories of hanging out with hip-hop's crème de la crème at parties, on video shoots, and at award shows to last two lifetimes. Besides, memories were non-negotiable intangibles that didn't trade on the open market. And she wanted to secure her future, so that she and her mother wouldn't find themselves back at Red Hook relying on the government for a measly handout. "I wanna make a future for myself, like you did with your music."

"And I have no doubt that you will. Now if we can knock some sense into Reece, then I'll be a happy man."

"Are you planning on having a talk with her?"

"Yep. As soon as we get to Coco Beach, my first order of business is to have a heart-to-heart with my baby sis."

For the rest of the ride, Donovan and Chyna were quiet, each in their own world. Chyna was mentally going over her business plan. And, as Donovan raced along the Long Island Expressway, zipping in and out of traffic, his mind was on the right words to say to Reece to get across to her that doing drugs was anything but cool.

Donovan pulled into the circular driveway of his estate, and was appalled at what he saw. Lounging all over the front lawn were a few of his homeboys from the old neighborhood, Reece, and some other chicks whom he had never seen before. They were barbequing, pitching pennies, and dancing to blaring music coming from inside the house. Donovan released the door handles on the car, and they slid up. He and Chyna stepped out of the butterfly doors. They both stood still and looked around. This was not the vision that Donovan had when he bought the esteemed estate. He had dreamt of cocktail parties with people dressed elegantly, not of front-lawn cookouts with scantily clad women and roughnecks running around drinking forties.

"Turn off the music!" he yelled at the top of his lungs.

"What you say, D?" Reece asked, turning a miniature bottle of Moët up to her lips.

"I said, turn off that damned music!" he yelled again, getting more furious by the minute.

Reece turned around to the guy who was pitching pennies near the front door and screamed, "Yo, Hasan, go in the house and turn off the stereo."

A few minutes later, the song stopped playing, putting an abrupt end to their party. Everyone turned and looked at Donovan like he was the one wiling out.

"I don't understand why you all have to hang out on the front lawn when there are acres of beautiful grass in the back. This is not Red Hook, where we have to be bunched together in front of the building. In case you haven't noticed, there's a pool, and tennis *and* basketball courts in the back," he said, reading them the riot act.

"Yo, D, why you trippin'?" Reece asked, with her hands on her slim hips.

"I'm 'trippin'"—he put his fingers up to mimic quotation marks—"because you're acting exactly like the locals thought we would act. I'm trying to clean up our image, and you all are playing right into the stereotype of how they think rappers and their entourage behave."

"Fuck what they think!" Reece huffed.

"Damn, Reece, can't you see that Donnie is only trying to make a better life for us?" Chyna said, irritated at the way Reece was acting.

Reece rolled her neck and eyes at the same time. "Whatever!"

"Naw, it ain't whatever. This is my house, and if y'all going to hang out here, it's going to be by my rules. And rule number one is absolutely no hanging out in the front! Rule number two, no blaring music. There are speakers out back, so there's no need to pump the stereo up from inside the house. It was so loud, I'm sure the neighbors could hear every word. And rule—"

"Okay, okay, we get it!" Reece said, cutting him off.

"And one more thing. I'm planning to host a party and invite some of the locals, so I want everyone to be on their best behavior. Is that understood?" he said, looking around at the motley bunch.

Nobody said anything; they all nodded their heads.

"Now, if you don't mind, will you please take that grill and these blankets out back?" Donovan added.

As the group was gathering their belongings, Donovan went over to Reece and took her by the arm. "Come inside. I want to talk to you."

"Didn't you do enough talking out here?" she said flippantly.

"You got some mouth on you, girl. Now come on. I'm not playing," he said, tightening his grip on her arm.

Though they had been raised by the same woman and had grown up in the same household, Donovan and Reece were like day and night, oil and water, and the rest of those tired old clichés. Donovan was driven and worked hard for his success, while his sister was as lazy as an old English bulldog. All she wanted to do was sleep, shop, and party, exactly in that order. At times he thought about taking away her monthly allowance, forcing her to work for a living, but he knew that would only be a lesson in frustration. Reece was beyond stubborn and hated for anyone to tell her what to do. If Donovan demanded that she get off her butt for a change, she would only dig her heels in deeper. Besides, he could never deprive his little sister of anything. Growing up poor, and with a father who had run off with another woman, abandoning his old family for a new one, had been rough on Reece, and Donovan felt a certain obligation to take care of her.

In the process of ensuring her welfare, Donovan had created an ungrateful little beast by spoiling her with excess cash and indulging her every whim. Now he wanted to tame the monster, but it was too late. The most he could hope for at this point was that she meet a nice guy and settle down.

Once inside, Donovan led her to his office, which was to the right of the foyer. He shut the door behind them and went over to the oversized black leather sofa, sat down, and then patted the cushion next to him. "Have a seat."

Reece begrudgingly did as told. She plopped down and folded her arms in front of her chest.

Now that he had her in the room, Donovan didn't quite know what to say. He didn't want to betray Chyna's confidence and cause a rift between the two best friends. He didn't want to straight-out accuse Reece of using drugs either. He knew that if he made an unfounded accusation, she would lie her way out of it. Donovan decided a more loving approach might work better, so he exhaled, and began talking. "So, Reece, what's been going on?" he asked, his tone much softer than it had been outside.

"Nothing much," she answered, tight-lipped.

"You haven't been in the studio lately so I was wondering whatcha been up to."

She bristled. "I ain't been up to nothing."

He put his hand on top of hers. "Calm down. I didn't mean anything by it; it's just that you used to love coming down to the studio to watch me lay down tracks."

"Yeah, that was when you first started, and being in the studio seemed exciting. Now it's boring. I got better thangs to do."

"Like what?" he asked.

"Like, shopping, partying with my friends, and hanging out."

"Who you been hanging with?"

"Keisha, and 'em."

"Was that Keisha outside?"

"Yeah, Keisha and her sister Tanisha."

"Where do you know them from?"

"From the club. Hey, what's this? Twenty Questions?"

"No. I only want to know who your new friends are, that's all."

Reece sucked her lip. She was getting tired of this inquisition.

"What do they do for a living?"

"Keisha work at Starbucks, and Tanisha ain't got no job."

"If she doesn't work, how can she afford to hang out and party?"

"I dunno." Reece hunched her shoulders. "I guess she be getting money from her boyfriend."

"Is he a drug dealer?" Donovan asked, sensing this was the perfect segue into talking about drugs.

"How the hell do I know?"

"Calm down," he said, again. "I'm concerned, that's all." He looked into her eyes and continued. "Reece, there are a lot of bad drugs out there on the street, and I don't want you to get mixed up with anybody who uses or sells drugs."

"Whatcha talkin' about? Why you trippin'? Ain't nobody said nothing about drugs!"

Now that the lid on Pandora's box was open, it was time for Donovan to ask Reece what he had been trying to get at since they sat down. "I'ma ask you this, and I want you to tell me the truth. Are you using drugs?"

Reece jumped up and waved her arms in the air. "Where the hell did that come from? Did Chyna tell you I'm using drugs?"

Donovan also stood up. "No, Chyna didn't tell me anything. So, are you using?"

"Hell no!"

Donovan had known that Reece was going to deny being on OxyContin. "Okay, I'll have to take your word

for it, but, lil' sis"—he put his arm around her shoulders—
"if someone ever offers you coke, or any prescription
drugs, please say no! I don't want to see you get mixed
up in that scene. Promise me you won't get caught up,"
he said, gripping her shoulder tight.

"Don't worry; I won't get caught up."

"Promise?"

"Yeah."

"Good. 'Cause it would kill me if something happened
to you."

Reece wiggled out of his embrace. "Damn, D, lighten
up. Ain't nothing gonna happen to me. Now, if you're
done with your speech, I'ma go for a swim."

"Go 'head. I'll be out there in a few."

Once she was gone, Donovan sat back down on the
sofa and put his head in his hands. His sister had lied to
his face. He hadn't personally seen her do drugs, so he
couldn't call her a liar. The only thing that he could do
was keep a close eye on her, and that's exactly what he
planned on doing for the rest of the summer.

DONOVAN HADN'T KEPT HIS EYE ON REECE, and he sadly
regretted it. Now there was a death, and he felt the
weight of the world on his shoulders. Maybe if he had
been more attentive to Reece and her drug problem,
none of this would have happened. However, that was
beside the point now. The deed was done, and all the
money in the world couldn't undo the damage.

[13]

S and sifted through Remi's perfectly manicured toes as she strolled along the shore. She dug her heels deep into the finely ground, abrasive particles, using the sand as a natural exfoliant—not that the bottom of her feet needed sloughing, but it felt good anyway. The sun had yet to reach its peak. The surface of the sand was cool to the touch, unlike late in the afternoon when the temperature soared into the high nineties and beaming rays ignited the tiny granules, making them feel like burning hot coals.

Remi loved roaming the beach this time of the morning when the air was still. There was little activity. The children who splashed about in the calm waters of the bay during the afternoon were still in bed. Remi didn't have a maternal bone in her body, so she avoided the local rugrats like a contagious virus without an antidote. She was far too selfish to share her life with an all-consuming baby. Lars was busy with his practice, and to her delight, didn't press the family issue.

The sea quietly lapped at the damp sand, creating a

hypnotic, melodic rhythm, while turning the tiny granules into soft mush. Remi bent down, stuck her hand in the water, and retrieved a tiny seashell. She looked at the intricate details of the minute specimen, turning it over for further inspection, ensuring that it was suitable for her collection. She rubbed the shell on the leg of her jeans, knocking off the excess sand, and then tossed it in the wicker basket that hung from her wrist. She continued her trek along the shallow shore, stopping every few steps to examine another floating crustacean. Remi spotted what appeared to be a large conch shell lodged in the sand. She reached down and tugged on the pointed tip, unearthing the perfectly formed mollusk. Instinctively, she put the shell to her ear and closed her eyes to listen to the ocean. Instantly the sound of crashing waves reverberated loudly in her ear. Remi knew it was an old wives' tale and the noise she heard was really blood rushing through her ears, but she smiled anyway.

Remi opened her eyes and could see the gray, weather-beaten wharf adjacent to Café Coco. She put the treasure in her basket and turned back toward the house. She had ventured farther than expected and was too close to town. She kicked up her pace. She didn't want to be seen by anyone, at least not yet. Not until she had shed her sandy, waterlogged jeans and T-shirt. She had appearances to keep up, and wanted to look perfect for her lunch guest.

She slid open the glass door to the kitchen, dusted the sand from the bottom of her feet, placed the basket of seashells on the floor, and padded inside. She washed her hands in the sink and dried them on a paper towel. Remi filled the coffee carafe with water and poured it into the machine. She put a heaping spoonful of hazelnut coffee into the filter and turned on the coffeepot. Once it was finished brewing, she poured herself a cup of coffee, then went upstairs to find the right outfit for her lunch date.

She flicked on the lights in her private boutique and moseyed inside. She stood in the middle of the enormous closet, glancing around at the colorful garments that hung on padded hangers. She walked over to a row of suits and fingered the arm of a beautiful, peach linen jacket.

No, that's too dressy, she thought. Most of the two-piece ensembles were reserved for the "ladies who lunch" crowd.

She did a slight pivot toward her many swimsuits with matching covers and sarongs. Thinking that a bathing suit might be more appropriate for the occasion, she pulled out a chartreuse one-piece with a deep, plunging neckline. The suit was sexy yet classy, exactly the look she was going for. The sleeveless duster in the same, greenish-yellow color was the perfect complement.

Now that Remi had selected the perfect outfit, she went back downstairs and went into the kitchen. The smell of coffee was permeating the air, and she inhaled the delicious aroma. Remi poured herself a cup, and sat at the kitchen table. She positioned the chair so that she could see clearly out of the glass doors. The beach was gorgeous, and she lingered in the kitchen enjoying her coffee and the view. Before long morning was approaching afternoon. She polished off the last of the coffee, and headed back upstairs to make her transformation.

Remi showered, shampooed her hair, and then gelled her short locks back behind her ears. She polished her skin with a rich La Mer body cream, squeezed into the swimsuit, and adjusted her breasts so that her cleavage was displayed correctly. Born an unimpressive 32A, she was now a va-va-voom 36D, compliments of her husband. She slowly applied her makeup. Satisfied with her au natural look, she went back into the closet and grabbed a dramatic Patricia Underwood straw hat with an oversized brim. She adjusted it on her head and left the house en route to her clandestine meeting.

The drive into town was brief, but long enough for her to make one important call to the marina. A short time later the dock attendant greeted her as she pulled into the marina's private parking lot. "Good afternoon, Mrs. Braxton."

She didn't remember the guy's name, so she offered a polite "Hello."

"We just got your call to clear away the tarp and have the boat wiped down, but Herman isn't finished yet. You wanna wait, or come back in about thirty minutes?"

"Thirty minutes!" she hissed.

"Yes, ma'am. Herman went to work the second your

call came in, but it takes longer than a few minutes to do a good job," he tried to explain, sensing her impatience.

Remi exhaled louder than necessary. She hated being called "ma'am"; it made her seem like an old woman. But more than that, she hated being kept waiting. She didn't care if it was her fault. She dramatically looked at her watch, then said, "Can't he possibly speed it up? I don't have all day."

"Let me see if I can pull Rod off another detail." He unclipped the two-way radio from his waistband and spoke quickly into the mouthpiece. "Rod, pick up. Rod, pick up."

"Yeah, boss?" Remi could hear the man on the opposite end.

"I need for ya to drop everything and hightail it over to *Nipit/Tuckit*, and help Herman with the clean-up."

"But I'm in the middle of detailing *Blue Seas*."

"Yeah, I know."

"Tell ya what. I'll get to *Nipit* once I finish."

"No, I need for ya to do it right now." He looked at Remi. "I got Mrs. Braxton here, and she's anxious to come aboard."

"Okay, boss. I'm on it." *Click.*

"Shouldn't be too much longer, Mrs. Braxton. You wanna come into the office and have an ice-cold Coke while you wait?"

"No. I'll wait in my car," she said. Remi thought about calling Liza to pass the time, but didn't want to explain what she was doing for the afternoon.

I guess I should call home. She hadn't spoken to Lars since he had left the party. Remi took out her phone and hit the speed dial to his cell. She knew that she'd get his voice mail during office hours, and that's exactly what she wanted.

"Hey, it's me. I was calling to tell you that after you left the party there was an accident. Somebody fell overboard and drowned," she said, filling him in on what she knew. That night she had started to wake him and tell him what had happened, but she was still too upset at catching him with another woman. Instead she slept in the guest room with intentions on telling him in the morning, but he had left before she awoke.

"Call me back when you get a chance. We still need to talk about what happened at the party. And by the way, don't have too much fun in the big bad city all by your lonesome." Remi used one of the oldest tricks in the book—reverse psychology—to put Lars on the defensive. Now he would be the one trying to explain his whereabouts, and not delving into her business.

She made a second call and ordered a take-out picnic basket from Café Coco. The restaurant was known for their gourmet lunch on the go. Rather than the ordinary picnic fare of sandwiches and chips, this basket included French brie on toasted baguettes; lobster and lump crab cakes; guava, mango, and star-fruit salad; and a chilled bottle of Pommery.

As she put the phone back into her tote, the attendant appeared at the driver's side of her car.

"Mrs. Braxton, you're all set to board." He smiled a nervous smile. "Sorry for the inconvenience," he apologized, even though it wasn't his fault. He knew that one derogatory word to his supervisor from a trophy wife could cost him his job.

Remi didn't respond, other than to return his smile with a weak one of her own. After he'd walked back into the office, she flipped down the visor, adjusted her hat brim down over one eye, grabbed her tote, and got out.

The lightweight, sheer cotton duster flowed freely in the midday breeze as she strutted down the gangplank to *Nipit/Tuckit*, appropriately named after the costly cosmetic procedures that enabled them to afford the luxurious craft. The exquisitely built Marquis was seventy feet of floating elegance, from the customized, bright-white pearlized hull, to the blond wood, wraparound deck, to the richly appointed staterooms.

Remi boarded and disappeared below. She whisked past the highly polished mahogany paneled living area and headed straight toward the master stateroom. She tossed her hat on the chaise lounge adjacent to the bed and went into the adjoining bathroom to check her makeup. Today was a scorcher, and the heat from the noonday sun had caused a sheen of perspiration to form over her entire face.

As she was removing the unattractive glow with a dusting of translucent powder, she heard someone walk across the deck above. Remi quickly returned the makeup to the vanity drawer and rushed back into the bedroom.

She scooted to the center of the bed and propped herself up on one elbow. Spreading her legs suggestively, she waited with hedonistic anticipation.

Her doorway darkened less than two seconds later. "Delivery, ma'am?"

"It's about time. I'm ravenous. I need you to feed me that big dick of yours!"

"Your appetite is insatiable." He crooked his finger at her. "Get over here and give me some of that ass."

Remi stood up, slipped out of her swimsuit, sauntered over, and backed her rear up against his groin. "Is this how you want it?" she asked, looking over her right shoulder.

He grabbed her hips and pulled her to him. "You know I like fucking you from behind." He slapped her naked butt. "Damn, girl, you got a pretty ass." He slapped her again.

"Ouch!"

He then rubbed the same spot, trying to take the sting out. "Sorry, baby. Here, let me make it better," he said, leaning down and kissing her ass.

"Ooo, that feels so good," she purred, as he circled his tongue around her left cheek.

"Not as good as my dick is going to feel." He took a condom out of his pocket, held it in his mouth and then unzipped his pants, kicked them off and stepped out of his boxers. Standing there naked from the waist down with a stiff erection, he was ready for action. He tore open the package, took out the condom and rolled it on.

He parted her butt cheeks and eased his long, stiff rod into her waiting pussy. He then grabbed her legs and held them up against his waist, plunging in and out of her wetness.

Remi held on to the chair in front of her for support. This man was rocking her body exactly the way she liked it—hard and rough—and it felt beyond good. She closed her eyes and enjoyed the ride. Sex with her husband was never this explosive, not even in the beginning. After so many years of mediocre lovemaking, Remi had decided to take charge of her needs and find pleasure outside her marriage. Divorcing Lars wasn't an option. He was her financial rock. Since she had a hand in building his practice, Remi felt entitled not only to his money, but also the clout that came along with being married to a prestigious surgeon. Instead of ending her marriage, Remi committed adultery. She wasn't worried about Lars discovering her dirty little secret. He rarely came out to Coco Beach, and what she did on the island, stayed on the island.

"Oooo, that's it!!" Remi yelled as he hit her G-spot.

He opened her legs wider, wedging himself further inside her canal. He loved to hear a woman scream in ecstasy. Giving pleasure made him even harder, and he worked his pelvis like a porn star. "Come for me, baby," he said, giving her another hard thrust.

Remi bit the side of the chair as he punished her pussy. She was in a zone now, and unable to speak. Drool escaped the side of her mouth as he brought her to climax. Once she came, her body relaxed. Remi eased over and collapsed into the chair. "That was awesome," she said, finally catching her breath.

He walked around and sat on the edge of the bed. "Better than your husband?"

"Now, now, let's not compare notes." Although Lars wasn't the best lover, Remi didn't want to disclose that much of her personal life. What went on between her and her husband was nobody's business.

He smiled broadly. "I'll take that as a yes."

She shook her head. "You are one cocky man."

"I thought that's what you liked." He pulled on his dick. "My cockiness."

"Ha, ha. Aren't you the comedian?"

"Comedian and chef." He laughed.

Remi had called Troy earlier that morning and told him that Lars was back in the city, and that they could resume their regular lunch dates. He was more than willing to oblige her.

"I hate to fuck and run, but I need to get back to the restaurant. We're totally booked tonight and I want to make sure the kitchen is running according to schedule."

Remi stood up, went over to him, stood between his legs, and ran her hands through his curly hair. "Troy, it's been a pleasure as usual. I don't know what I'd do all summer if I didn't have you to play with."

He kissed her stomach and patted her on the butt. "I

love our play dates, too. Now, I've got to run." He stood up, retrieved his pants and underwear, and quickly dressed.

"Am I going to see you tomorrow?" Remi asked before Troy left the yacht.

"I can't tomorrow. I have to go back into the city for a business meeting."

Remi poked out her bottom lip. "Oh, poo. What am I supposed to do all day?"

"I'm sure you'll think of something." Troy bent down and kissed her on the lips. "See you when I get back." He picked up the wicker picnic basket that he had brought in with him, and left.

"Okay. I'll look forward to it."

When Troy got above deck, he stuck his head through the doorway to make sure that no one was lurking about. He didn't see any people on the neighboring boats, so he made his escape. In the event that he was spotted leaving Remi's yacht, he would simply say that he was delivering lunch, as evidenced by the basket that hung from his arm. Troy walked swiftly down the gangplank and made his way back to Café Coco without being spotted by any of the town's gossipmongers. The last thing he needed was to get linked to a married woman. *I gotta stop fucking around with Remi, and stick to the single ladies*, he thought, his mind suddenly drifting to the hot Detective Pratt. Now she was a challenge worth pursuing. If Troy could get with Theo, he would give up all the booty in Coco Beach *and* Manhattan.

[14]

Lars was bubbling over with excitement. He had purposely scheduled his last appointment at three o'clock in the afternoon, which was rare. Normally his work day didn't end until after eight p.m. He had abnormally late office hours to cater to his wealthy patients, but not today. With Remi safely secluded on Coco Beach, he was free to roam the city and go buck wild.

His last consultation sat across from his desk, blabbing on and on about her desire to roll back the hands of time with an extreme makeover.

"Dr. Braxton, I want a brow lift, cheek implants, and this"—she gently pulled on the loose skin hanging from underneath her chin—"pulled and tucked for a more youthful appearance."

Lars nodded in agreement, though he actually thought that she only needed the brow lift and a few injections of Botox around her eyes to smooth out the tiny crows' feet. But he wasn't going to argue with a paying customer. He had learned over the years that when these pampered

Upper East Side mavens came into the office with a laundry list of wishes, it was to his benefit to grant each and every desire within reason. If he didn't accommodate them, another surgeon would be more than happy to take their American Express Centurion card.

"I've also been thinking about getting a tummy tuck." She stood up and pinched a marginal amount of fat on her lower abdomen. "What do you think?"

"You don't need a tuck." On this assessment he had to disagree. There really wasn't anything to cut away. He would look like a quack going into the operating room with barely an inch of skin to remove. "Actually, liposuction is a better alternative," he suggested, finding a resolution that would suit them both.

"Yes, I thought about lipo, but doesn't the fat return if you gain weight?" she asked, returning to her seat.

"Not exactly. Once the fat cells are removed from your midsection, they will not reproduce. However, if you don't control your weight, then fat will be stored in other areas of the body where fat cells are prominent," he explained.

"I'm not an overeater. Therefore, weight gain is the least of my problems," she said, as if offended at his suggestion that she couldn't control her caloric intake.

Lars wanted to shake his head. This woman sounded like a schizophrenic. One minute she's asking about weight gain, and the next saying that she didn't overeat. "Then why in the hell are you wasting my time talking about tummy tucks and liposuction?" he wanted to say, but naturally held his tongue. "Of course, Mrs. Billingsly, I didn't mean to suggest that you're an overeater," he said politely, nodding his head in agreement. Lars despised being at the mercy of his super-rich, super-spoiled patients. Oftentimes, he felt like a puppet, being controlled by the strings of commerce.

His childhood visions of practicing medicine and helping people with serious illnesses seemed like a life-time ago. Now the only help he offered was to those who didn't need it—patients who abused cosmetic surgery, going under the knife for mere vanity. Being a slave to the mighty dollar was beginning to weigh heavily on Lars, but he couldn't give up his practice. The monthly expenses on both homes and rent on his office space, coupled with Remi's excessive spending, were nearly six figures. It seemed the more money he made, the more she spent. Lars felt a tension headache coming on, and needed a shot of vodka and an Oxy-Contin tablet for a little release.

"Okay, Mrs. Billingsly." He rose from his chair. "Schedule your next appointment with my receptionist so we can do your pre-op work-ups."

"Will do. I'm anxious for my new look." She smiled, showing the tiny crows' feet around her eyes.

"It'll be hard to improve on perfection, but I'll try." He chuckled and walked her to the door.

"Oh, Dr. Braxton, you're such a kidder," she gushed, before leaving.

Lars locked the door for added privacy once his patient

left, and made a beeline straight to the gray metal filing cabinet that was adjacent to his desk. Digging into his pants pocket, he retrieved a small yellow envelope. He opened the flap and dumped a mini key into the palm of his hand. Lars stuck the key into the cabinet's lock, turned it to the left, and released the catch that secured the drawers and his secret. He quickly thumbed through the various manila folders until he reached four medicine bottles deep in the back of the drawer. He took out one of the amber-colored bottles, carefully lined up the red arrows on the white cap, and popped open the top. He then removed a tiny Ziploc bag from his breast pocket and emptied a couple of pink pills from the bottle into the waiting pouch. Returning the drugs back to their hiding place, he locked the cabinet and slipped the pills into his pocket.

"Tonight's going to be fun." He smirked and patted the outside of his pants.

Lars tidied up his desk, putting the various consultation notes and drawings in their proper place. He hurried over to the coat rack, removed his doctor's smock, and replaced it with a navy linen blazer. Before he could hightail it out of the office, the phone rang. Lars stepped to his desk and picked up the receiver.

"Yes, Martha?"

"A Detective Pratt from the Coco Beach Police Department is on the line," his assistant informed him.

"Tell the detective I'm not available," he said. Lars

was ready to leave and didn't want to talk. Remi had left a message telling him about a drowning, and he assumed that's why the cop was calling. He had left before the party was over, and didn't have any information to share with the police.

"Okay," his assistant said, and released the line.

Five seconds later, she was buzzing his office again.

"Yes, Martha, what is it now?" he asked with an edge to his voice.

"The detective said that it's important, and won't take long."

Lars sighed into the phone, and then said, "Okay, put him through."

"Hello, Dr. Braxton; thanks for taking my call," Theo said pleasantly.

"What can I do for you, Detective?" Lars was surprised to hear a woman's voice on the phone. He had automatically assumed that the detective was a man.

"I understand that you were a guest at Donovan Smart's party, held on the Lords' yacht," she said, changing her tone, sounding more businesslike.

"Yes, I was there, but I left before the accident happened," he said, assuming that's why the detective was calling. He then added, "My wife filled me in on what happened."

"This was no accident, Doctor." Theo told him the name of the victim. "Did you know her?"

"No," Lars said quickly.

"Since you're a doctor, I'm sure you have occasion to prescribe OxyContin," she said, going into a different line of questioning.

"Of course I prescribe the painkiller. Why do you ask?" Lars asked calmly, even though his underarms had begun to sweat. *Why the hell is she asking me about Oxy?*

"The victim had OxyContin in her bloodstream, and I was wondering if she was a patient of yours?" Theo asked, omitting the fact that the deceased had an unusually high amount of the drug in her system.

"I told you, I didn't know her, not as a patient or personally," he said sternly. "Now if you don't have any more questions, I'm late for an appointment," he added, attempting to end the inquisition.

"When are you coming back to Coco Beach?" she asked, ignoring his comment.

"I don't know. Look, Detective, I've got to run."

"Of course, sorry to keep you, but when you come back to town, I'd love to sit down with you and go over a few more questions," Theo said, her pleasant voice returning. She was trying to schmooze him. She didn't have any evidence to link him to the murder, and couldn't order him to come into the station.

"Sure thing," he said, hanging up. He had no intention of going into the police station to be interrogated. It was unfortunate that the woman had died, but this wasn't his problem. He wasn't a suspect, and planned on steering clear of the cops. He had his own issues to deal with and murder wasn't one of them.

Lars turned off the lights in his office and headed out.

"Good night, Martha," he said to his office manager.

"Good night?" Martha looked at her watch, then back at Lars. "It's only four-thirty," she remarked, astonished that he was bidding her a good evening so early in the afternoon. "Is everything okay?" Martha had worked with Lars for over ten years, and knew him almost as well as she knew her own husband.

"Everything's fine. Why do you ask?" He felt a tinge of paranoia. Did Martha suspect him of dipping into the candy jar? He thought for a moment, mentally retracing his steps, knowing that Martha kept a tab on the prescription pads since she kept them in stock, but he had kept samples of the Oxy he'd gotten from his sales rep so there wouldn't be any suspicious prescriptions written. With his paranoia eased for the moment, he breathed a sigh of relief and responded before she could answer. "Thought I'd take off early for once."

"Oh, are you going to the beach this weekend?" she inquired, knowing that his wife was already there.

"Yeah. I want to get a jump on the traffic," he lied.

"Have a good weekend, and I'll see you on Monday."

Lars felt bad about lying to Martha, but she was beyond nosey and if he'd said that he was spending the weekend in the city, she'd want to know every single detail of his plans. "See you Monday," he simply replied, and headed out the door.

[15]

Lars wanted to run the few short blocks to the penthouse to get ready for his big evening, but he kept his cool and strolled down Fifth Avenue instead.

Once Lars was inside the apartment, he went straight upstairs to his large walk-in closet. All the way in the back, hidden behind his navy and khaki suits, were several pairs of black pants and various styles of black shirts. He snatched a pair of slacks from the hanger and grabbed one of many black T-shirts. He needed to shed his clean-cut, seersucker-wearing, doctor image in order to blend in with the club scene. The last thing he wanted was to look like was a pocket protector-wearing nerd.

Lars took a nap to energize his tired body for the long night ahead. After a few hours of sleep, he woke refreshed. He showered, shaved, and donned his all-black party gear. Lars checked out his image in the mirror and beamed at his reflection. The snug, jersey T-shirt hugged his muscular pectorals, showing off his toned upper body, usually concealed underneath a starched, white lab coat. Lars retrieved a tinted pair of

Aviators from the vanity drawer to complete the suave look. He then splashed his palms with Light Blue after-shave and lightly slapped his face with the scent. Now Lars was primed and ready to hit the town. He called a car service instead of tooling around town in his Benz so he wouldn't have to worry about drinking and driving. The last thing he needed was to get pulled over by the cops and be charged for a DUI. He trotted down the stairs to wait for the limo, but stopped dead in his tracks before reaching the landing.

"Shit," he said aloud. "How could I forget?"

He raced back up the winding steps, dashed into the bedroom, and riffled through the clothes he wore earlier, now lying in a heap on the floor.

"Eureka!" He found the OxyContin, popped one of the pink pills in his mouth, then rushed into the bath-room and chased it with tap water from the faucet. Though the drug had yet to take effect, he instantly felt the day's anxieties loosen their tight grip on him. He needed relaxing after the impromptu conversation with that nosey detective. Lars couldn't help but wonder if she knew about his recreational use of Oxy, but there was no way that she could know his secret. Nobody knew, not even his wife, and he planned on keeping it that way.

Lars stepped out of his building looking like a rock star dressed in all black as he slipped into the back of the waiting limo. He settled in the back of the car, took out his BlackBerry, and e-mailed the agent at Cyber-ierges, the personalized Internet concierge service. Cyber-ierges handled everything from securing sold-out tickets to Rolling Stones concerts, to booking first-class accommodations on a private island off the coast of South America, to practically any and everything that money could buy. The service was like having a 24/7 personal assistant in your back pocket.

He typed in his request for placement on the VIP list at three of the city's hottest clubs. The car pulled up in front of Spy club, and he peered through the tinted windows to get a read on the crowd. There were only five people standing on the opposite side of the velvet rope—not a very promising sign.

"Wait out front. I have a feeling it's slow in there tonight," he told the driver.

"Yes, sir."

Lars walked right past the partygoers, straight to the front of the short line. "Lars Braxton. I'm on the list," he said to the bouncer, purposely leaving off the haughty doctor title.

"Go on in," the bouncer said in a deep baritone voice after checking the guest list.

Lars walked inside and was unimpressed. The place was basically empty except for a few people sitting at the bar sipping drinks. There were more employees than customers in the spot. His BlackBerry vibrated indicating that he had a text, but Lars ignored it as he scanned the room, hoping there was at least one honey to cozy up with. The only two single women there looked like trolls straight from underneath a drawbridge. One woman had a shadow of a mustache so dense that even makeup couldn't conceal the dark skin above her lip. And her friend was equally unattractive, with an ill-fitting wig atop her enormous head. The woman's abnormally large head led Lars to believe that beneath all that synthetic hair was a man trying to perpetrate. The more he looked at the pair, the more they looked like transvestites. Lars wanted to get his freak on, but not with a pair of dudes with fake tits. He hightailed it out of the bar before he got hit on. In his haste to escape, he forgot to check his messages.

Back in the safety of the car, Lars instructed the driver to go to the 40/40 Club, hoping that he'd have better luck there. The black stretch rolled up in front of the club, and Lars couldn't believe the flock of people milling outside. Unlike the first stop, this place was jumping. His heart began to pump with adrenaline as he anticipated the possibility of meeting a willing candidate to fuck for the evening.

"You can park around the corner. I don't know how long I'll be. I'll call you when I'm ready," he told the driver.

Lars strutted up to the door and made his announcement to the bouncer.

The beefy doorman checked the VIP list, then spat, "You ain't on the list."

"Check again," Lars requested arrogantly.

"I said you ain't on the list," he responded, giving Lars a look that read, "And don't ask again."

Lars walked back to the curb, took out his cell, and called the driver. He then called Cyber-ierges instead of sending a text message.

"Cyber-ierges at your service, how may I help you this evening?"

"This is Dr. Lars Braxton," he said with authority. "I called earlier and requested to be on the guest list for Spy club, 40/40, and NV."

"Hold on, Dr. Braxton. Let me check your account."

Lars could hear the agent typing rapidly on her keyboard and within a few seconds, she came back on the line. "Yes, Dr. Braxton, I see your request."

"And?"

She hesitated for a moment, taken off guard by his rudeness, and then responded, "You are on the list for Spy and NV."

"What about the 40/40 Club?"

"Sorry, Dr. Braxton. There's a private party tonight at 40/40, and we—"

He cut her off. "Why didn't someone inform me of that? I'm standing outside the club at this very moment and can't get in. It would've been nice to have this information beforehand."

"I see in our records that we sent a text to your BlackBerry twenty minutes ago," she said efficiently.

Lars suddenly remembered the message indicator

sounding off at Spy. He took the gadget out of his pocket, and sure enough, there was an unread text from Cyber-ierges. "In the future, I'd appreciate a direct call when plans change," he said, trying to save face.

"Yes, sir," she said obediently. "Is there anything else I can do for you this evening, Dr. Braxton?"

"Please check to make sure I'm on the VIP list at NV," he said, softening his rude tone partially because he was embarrassed, and partially because the Oxy had begun to take effect, mellowing him.

Without hesitation, she answered, "Yes, sir, you're all set for NV, and for your inconvenience, I've reserved a private table with a bottle of Cristal on us."

"Thank you." Lars's dark mood brightened. Finally, his night was beginning to take shape. As he clicked off the phone, the limo rounded the corner. Lars got back in the car, leaned back on the black leather headrest, and closed his eyes as the car cruised toward the next destination. The OxyContin was now flowing through his bloodstream and he felt as if he were floating.

After sitting idle in front of the club for a few seconds, the driver finally rolled down the privacy window and announced, "We're here, sir."

"Oh, oh, okay," Lars said, coming out of his stupor.

He got out and drifted right up to the bouncer. This time he was granted access, and walked directly to the hostess podium. "I have a reserved table."

"Your name?"

"Lars Braxton."

She checked her long list and then said, "Right this way."

Lars subconsciously bounced his head to the pulsating music as they walked toward the back of the club. NV was alive with excitement. Bodies glistening with sweat were gyrating on the dance floor, and the bar area was three deep.

"Have a good time," the hostess said as she parked Lars at his table.

"I'm sure I will." He grinned, looking at the house full of scantily dressed beautiful people enjoying the music and each other.

No sooner had he sat down than a waiter came over with a champagne bucket and a chilled bottle of Cristal. He popped the cork on the expensive elixir and poured Lars a flute full of happiness. Lars sat back and sipped the delicious champagne. He was getting mellower by the second, and began to think about the last time he was at NV.

THAT NIGHT, LARS HAD A CHOICE TABLE and, from his vantage point, full view of the club. He spotted a trio of reed-thin women who appeared to be models. Their miniskirts exposed long, lanky legs that seemed to go on forever. From what he could discern, they each had bought boobs. The woman standing in the middle had the biggest breasts. The short midriff top she wore was cut extremely high, and stopped right underneath her assets. The majority of women with saline enhancements rarely wore bras, since their overripe breasts stood at attention all by themselves. This woman was no exception. Lars could clearly see her naked nipples through her sheer top. At the office, he was all business and treated the women who came through his door with complete professionalism, but though he worked with implants on a daily basis, it still excited him to see the end result in a social setting. "Showtime," he said to himself as he rose from his seat. Lars cut through the gyrating crowd, making his way over to his target.

Before he could make his move, a tall, blond, Eurotrash type approached the trio. The man stepped up to the woman in the middle, kissed her on the neck, and slipped his hand under her top, grabbing a handful of flesh. Lars watched as she giggled at his touch.

"Damn," he muttered and slunk back across the dance floor. At the edge of the sitting area, Lars stopped and looked around, dumbfounded. All the tables were occupied, even his. "What the..."

Sitting at *his* table and sipping *his* champagne was a chocolate-skinned honey with the face of a superstar. She sat there comfortably with her arm thrown behind the back of the chair as if she belonged.

"Why don't you make yourself at home?" Lars said sarcastically, approaching her.

"I already have."

Lars chuckled at her boldness. He extended his hand. "Hi, I'm Lars."

She looked him up and down, threw her long hair to one side, and then lightly shook his hand. "Hey, my name is Reece."

"Tell me, Reece, why did you pick this table?" he asked, curious as to her sudden appearance.

"All the VIP tables were taken, and I wasn't 'bout to stand up all night. Then when I saw you get dissed by them hoochies over there"—she nodded her head in the direction of the trio—"I thought you might need some company, since you was sitting over here all by yo lonesome. Plus, I was thirsty."

"Should I order another bottle?" he asked, choosing to ignore her comment about his embarrassing moment.

"Yep," she answered, sipping the champagne in her glass.

Lars checked her out on the sly. Though she was well proportioned, he could tell that she was young. Her skin was as smooth as a baby's cheek, and her vernacular was chock full of slang. "How old are you?" he blurted out. The last thing he needed was to get caught with an underaged teenager.

"Twenty-fo," she spat out. "Why you asking?"

"Making sure you're legal, that's all." He smiled.

"Trust me, I'm grown," she said, reaching for the bottle.

He was relieved that he hadn't picked up a teeny-bopper. He was tempted to ask her for proof, but he reasoned that she must be over twenty-one since the club checked IDs at the door. Lars poured himself another drink.

"Thought you was gonna order another bottle of 'pagne," she said, draining the last of the champagne.

Lars summoned the waiter without hesitation, wanting to impress his new friend with the obscenely priced champagne. He watched as she bounced to the music, and with each movement, her breasts jiggled up and down. *Good, no saline,* he thought. From what he could tell, she was au natural. "Do you want to dance?"

"Naw."

"So…?" he asked, trying to strike up a conversation. "You come here often?"

"Yeah, I come here all the—" Her phone buzzed before she could complete her sentence. Lars watched as she read a text message, smiled, and typed in a response.

The waiter appeared with another bottle and poured them each a glass.

Reece reached for the bubbly and sipped as she continued to text. She was in her own world, totally oblivious to her host.

Lars scooted a bit closer to her, hoping that she would take notice of him and stop texting, but she didn't.

Finally, after about five minutes, she put the phone back in her purse and poured herself another glass of champagne. "Thanks for the 'pagne." She turned the flute up to her lips. "But I gotta bounce."

"Come on, stay and have another drink," he said, trying to prolong the night. She was exactly what he was looking for—young, beautiful, and seemingly available—and he wanted to get to know her in a biblical way.

"Maybe next time, but I gotta go."

"I'd like to see you again. What's your number?" he asked point blank.

She cut her eyes at him and turned her mouth up on one side. "Why don't I call you?"

Lars didn't know what to say. He certainly wasn't going to give her his cell number; that was too risky. He didn't want to give out his office number either. Martha would have a gazillion questions if a non-patient began calling out of the blue. "I'm going to be out of town for the next few days, so it's best that I call you when I get back," he lied.

"Yeah, alright," she agreed, and rattled off her number. She got up and blended into the crowd.

He quickly logged her number into his BlackBerry under the code name "Ray." He smiled at the thought of seeing Reece again. "Next time, you won't get away so easily," he mumbled underneath the pulsating music.

THAT WAS AT THE BEGINNING OF THE SUMMER, and Lars had been true to his word and hadn't let Reece get away. Now he was beginning to question that decision. Reece was a handful, and he was starting to think that he had bitten off more than he could digest.

[16]

Liza went into town to do some light shopping, stopping first at the liquor store. She and Remi were having a girls' night in, and she wanted to make sure that they had enough libations for a leisurely evening. Her next stop was the gourmet deli to pick up two ready-made meals. Neither she nor Remi had any deep-seated culinary desires. Unlike the many people who had become enthralled with the cooking channel as of late, they preferred to dine out or have their meals prepared for them when dining in.

On her way out of the deli, Liza spotted a black Lamborghini cruising through town. The car stopped at the light and she squinted behind her shades, trying to see who was inside, but the windows were tinted. *I'll bet that's Donovan.* Liza hadn't seen him since the party. She stepped closer to the curb, trying to get a better view. The windows were too dark and she couldn't make out his face, but she waved anyway on the chance that it was Donovan. Before she could get his attention, the light changed and the car sped off. Liza had a good mind to jump in her car and follow him, but the Lamborghini was long gone. She had called him several times since the accident, but hadn't spoken to him. All her calls were sent to voice mail.

Liza walked to her car, went home, changed clothes, and then drove to Remi's.

"Hey, perfect timing. I just came back from the dock." Remi had gone to the yacht to make sure that there wasn't any evidence of her affair. She had checked underneath and around the bed for condom wrappers. Though they had a cleaning staff who maintained the boat, she didn't want any nosey maids in her business.

"I saw Donovan in town earlier," Liza said, walking into the house carrying an armload of packages.

"Really? What did he have to say?" Remi asked, taking a bag out of Liza's hands.

"I didn't get a chance to speak with him. He was in his black Lamborghini. That car is so sharp. It had blacked-out windows, definitely the type of car that a rapper would have."

"Yes, you're right. I can't imagine any of these stuck-up islanders driving around in a tricked-out sports car. Most of them are too conservative to have tinted windows," Remi said, putting the bag on the kitchen counter.

"I know. That's why I'm tired of dating these boring islanders, and Donovan is exactly the type of excitement I need." Liza took the wine out of the bag, uncorked it, and poured two glasses of chardonnay.

Remi couldn't really blame Liza. She was having her

own summer fling, and it was exhilarating! She wanted to share her secret with Liza, but that would be the kiss of death. Liza was a notorious gossip and couldn't be trusted with a secret this juicy. "If you must go to the other side of the tracks, be careful."

"Remi, he doesn't live on the other side of the tracks. Donovan lives in one of the most expensive estates on Coco Beach," Liza said, sounding a bit offended.

"I meant it metaphorically. Anyway, it's an afterthought now. Something bad has already happened. Maybe we should've never gone over to Donovan's house that afternoon," Remi said, picking up a glass of wine and taking a sip.

Remi thought back to the day they had driven over to Donovan's so that Liza could finally get her introduction to the rapper.

LIZA HAD PULLED UP IN REMI'S DRIVEWAY and beeped the horn of her Aston Martin convertible.

Remi came to the doorway wearing shorts and a T-shirt, holding a coffee cup in her hand. "Hey, what's with all the ruckus?"

"We're going over to TuSmArt's. Remember?" Liza yelled from the car.

"Tu who?"

"You know, Donovan Smart, the rapper."

Remi took a sip of coffee and said, "Do I really have to go?"

"You promised. Remember, we said that we were going

to show them little hoochies how to dress?" Liza had told Remi about her previous visit to Donovan's when Reece accused her of being a wannabe, and made Remi promise to go with her next time.

"Don't remind me." The last thing Remi wanted to do was to go over to some rapper's house. She wanted to call Troy and get fucked.

"Well?" Liza lifted her sunglasses. "Go get dressed. I'm dying to get over there and meet TuSmArt."

Remi exhaled. She realized that trying to get out of her commitment was pointless so she reluctantly conceded. "Okay, give me fifteen minutes."

Fifteen minutes later to the second, Remi came out of the house wearing a multi-colored Lilly Pulitzer sundress, with her hair slicked back and a pair of oversized shades perched on her tiny face.

"Why the hell are you wearing *that* dress?" Liza asked, turning up her nose.

Remi got in the car and smoothed down the front of the dress. "What are you talking about? This is a Lilly Pulitzer."

"Of course I know it's a Lilly Pulitzer, but I'm sure those girls over at Donovan's have no idea who she is. All they probably know is Baby Phat, Sean John, and the rest of those hip-hop designers. If we're going to show them how to dress, we need to wear designers that they're familiar with. That's why I'm wearing Gucci sunglasses, a Roberto Cavalli halter, and Miu Miu jeans."

"Aren't you a walking fashion show?" Remi chuckled.

Liza pulled out of the driveway. "Laugh all you want, but once they see me rocking all this designer gear, I'll get major kudos."

"Is that why you're driving the Aston Martin? To get major kudos?"

"They already saw the Bentley; now I want to show off the drop-top. I'm Liza Lord, after all."

"I can't believe how you're transforming into a hip-hop mama. One day you're the Princess of Island Protocol, and the next you're dressing and talking like some video vixen," Remi said, shaking her head.

"Look, I'm tired of these boring summers. I want some excitement in my life, and TuSmArt is my ticket to a different world. I'm sure you don't approve of me wanting to date a rapper. You have a perfect marriage with one of the leading plastic surgeons in the country, so I don't expect you to understand."

If only you knew. Lars and I have long since lost the lust that we once had for each other, Remi thought. "Trust me, Liza, I get it."

"Good. I don't need you judging me, too. Once TuSmArt and I are seen around town, the tongues are going to start wagging with a bunch of negative talk."

"You seem so certain that you two are going to be dating; I mean, you haven't even met the man yet. What if he already has a girlfriend?" Remi asked, trying to bring her friend back to reality.

"That is a possibility. I did read about him going out with some Broadway actress, but that was a while ago. From what I've read lately, he's single and free," she said optimistically.

"Since you are so determined, all I'm going to say is good luck." Remi was the last person to shoot down somebody's romantic prospects, especially since she had her own "romantic prospects" outside her marriage.

The ride to Donovan's was short, and soon they were pulling up in his driveway. Unlike before when there were a group of people partying out front, this time the place was quiet with no one around.

"I thought you said that the front of his house looked like a video shoot," Remi said, looking around at the stately grounds. She expected to see thugs with heavy gold chains hanging from their necks, and a fleet of Hummers with tricked-out rims. Instead, there was a gardener tending to a bed of roses, and parked in the driveway were a black Lamborghini and a milky white Jaguar.

Liza stepped out of the car and also took a glance around. "Wow, this is a completely different scene from before. If I didn't know better, I'd swear that the Wellingtons still lived here."

"You're right. This is not what I expected at all. Maybe this Donovan person is not the typical rapper," Remi said, following Liza up the walkway.

"Let's hope you're wrong. I want a roughneck, not some tamed version of a rapper," Liza whispered.

"You just want to get slammed up against the wall and fucked hard," Remi said in a low voice.

"Here's hoping," Liza remarked, and rang the bell.

After a few seconds, the door swung open.

"You ain't the pizza man. Who you?" Reece asked.

"Hi, I'm Liza Lord, and this is my friend Remi Braxton, and—"

"Hey, didn't you roll by here the other day?" Reece asked, cutting her off.

"Yes, I came by to see your brother, but he wasn't here. Is he in today?"

Reece studied them up and down before answering. She sucked her teeth, then said, "Ain't them the new Miu Miu jeans?"

Liza couldn't help but smile. She gave Remi a quick look as if to say, *I told you so.* "Yes, I ordered them from the store in Milan," she said proudly.

"What they cost you?" Reece asked without shame.

Before Liza could answer, Donovan walked up behind Reece. "Please excuse my sister. She has no tact." He stepped in front of Reece and extended his hand. "Hi, I'm Donovan Smart, and you are?"

Liza thought she was going to cream her panties. Donovan was finer in person than in magazines. Deep-set dimples pierced his chocolate cheeks, and his brown eyes were shaped into half-moons. He wore a cap-sleeved, white T-shirt that hugged his tight midsection, and a pair of faded jeans with rips at the knees. He looked so sexy that Liza unconsciously licked her lips. She wanted to jump him right then and there; instead, she shook his hand in return. "Hi, I'm Liza Lord, and this is my friend Remi Braxton. We came by to welcome you to the neighborhood." His grip was so firm and strong that she didn't want to let his hand go. She held it a little longer than she should have, and stood there smiling like a schoolgirl with a huge crush.

Donovan extracted his hand from hers. "Nice to meet you both, please come in." He stepped aside and turned to his sister. "Reece, can you go in the kitchen and get Maria?"

Reece sucked her teeth and rolled her eyes. She mumbled underneath her breath, "Why don't you go get the maid yourself," and then stomped off toward the back of the house.

They followed Donovan into the Great Room, which was exquisitely furnished with antiques, priceless artwork, crystal chandeliers, and imported rugs. "Have a seat," he said, motioning to an overstuffed, silk upholstered sofa.

Remi sat down and discreetly ran her hand across the fabric. She instantly recognized it as five-hundred-dollar-a-yard silk from France. She was considering the same fabric for her sofa. *This guy has great taste*, she thought.

A few minutes later, the maid entered the room. "Yes, Mr. Smart, what can I get for you and your guests?"

"Ladies, can I offer you some iced tea?"

"As long as you put some bourbon and a sprig of mint in it," Liza said.

"Maria, can you skip the tea and make up three mint juleps?"

"Yes, sir," she said, and headed back to the kitchen.

"Actually, ladies, I'm glad that you came by. I've decided to give a cocktail party, and I want to invite some of the locals."

Liza perked up. This would be a great opportunity to spend time with him. "Party planning is my specialty. Do you have a theme in mind?"

"I thought about an all-white party, but that's been done to death."

"Maybe you can put a spin on it." She hesitated a few seconds, trying to think of the perfect twist. "I know! How about a white and platinum party?"

Donovan put his hand to his chin. "Hmm, white and platinum? I like it."

"Oh good! We can do so much with that color combination, like using a silver carpet out front instead of a red one," Liza suggested, full of excitement.

Remi sat back and watched her friend go to work. Liza was easily drawing Donovan into her web, little did he know.

"I like the way you think." He smiled broadly. "I'll also need help with the guest list. Do you know most of the people in Coco Beach?"

"Most? I know them all. My family has summered in Coco Beach for generations," she said, sliding in her family history. Donovan nodded his head.

Liza continued. "I know who you should invite, and who should be omitted from the list."

"I don't want to offend anybody by leaving them off the guest list. I want this party to be fun as well as classy."

"Don't worry; the people who should be omitted wouldn't come anyway, so you won't be offending anybody."

Remi was getting bored with the two of them talking back and forth as if she wasn't there. Clearly they didn't need her input. This was a waste of her time, and she was ready to go so that she could try to hook up with Troy. Remi looked at her watch. "Liza, I need to get going."

Liza shot her a look that read, *Are you kidding me?*

"Don't leave yet; you haven't even had your drinks," Donovan said.

Liza didn't want to leave. She and Donovan were really beginning to gel, but one look at Remi's face and she could tell that her friend had had enough. Liza took her cell phone out of her purse. "What's your number, Donovan? I'll call you later, and we can discuss the party in more detail."

He rattled off his number.

Remi stood first. "It was nice meeting you."

"The pleasure was all mine," he said, standing up and shaking her hand.

Liza lingered on the couch a few more seconds before rising. Now she wished that she had come alone. One thing was for sure; the next time she saw Donovan, it would only be the two of them, with no third parties interrupting their flow.

DONOVAN AND LIZA HAD MET A FEW MORE TIMES before the party; they ironed out the details and little else. To Liza's chagrin, Donovan never made a move on her. He was the perfect gentleman. She had totally misjudged him. Liza thought that he would live up to the stereotype of a roughneck hound dog, but he proved her wrong. Now that the party was over, Liza hoped to at least invite him out for a drink, but he wouldn't return her calls. He was probably still upset about the drowning, and rightfully so. He had thrown the event to ingratiate himself to the community, only to end up the host of a death scene.

[17]

The event was finally here, and security was tighter than one of Dolly Parton's bustiers. Rap mogul Donovan Smart, a.k.a. TuSmArt, was hosting the sizzling soirée on *Lady Lord*, a multi-million-dollar yacht owned by the Lord family. This event was the hottest ticket in town, with a guest list boasting the names of A-List celebrities from both coasts, as well as a smattering of local notables.

The omnipresent menacing guards were on patrol to keep the uninvited—who tried to flirt their way into the party sans the platinum-trimmed invitation—at bay. Scantily clad groupies crowded the front of the marina hoping to either slither inside the gates, or at the very least get a glimpse of a famous face or two. But smoky tinted car windows protected the celebrated from the civilians as chauffeur-driven, six-figures-on-four-wheels—their occupants armed with the proper credentials—cruised past security into the land of the privileged. There were also valet attendants moving in tandem taking the luxury cars of guests who'd preferred to drive themselves.

Clinging to an open bottle of warm champagne, Reece stumbled and nearly tripped getting out of the passenger side of a black-on-black Hummer with customized rims.

"Girl, you'd better put that back in the truck before Donnie sees you," Chyna instructed, pointing to the bubbly.

"Chill out, Chyna." She leaned back on the truck and took a swig of champagne straight from the bottle. "I'm trying to get my party on," she slurred as she tossed the now empty bottle back into the truck.

Chyna shook her head. She was at a loss for words. Since Chyna was the designated driver, Reece took full advantage and began drinking early that afternoon. Now she was feeling no pain. Chyna thought back to their talk earlier that day, which obviously hadn't had any effect on Reece.

CHYNA WAS AT HER DESK, GOING OVER HER BUSINESS plan. Ever since she had arrived at the house she had been holed up in her room. She had two valid reasons for being in her room: one was that she wanted to work on the business plan for her boutique; and two, she didn't want to run into Reece. Chyna didn't know exactly what Donnie had said to his sister when he took her into his office, but she was sure that he had spoken to her about using drugs. Chyna was certain that Reece would think that she had told Donnie about the OxyContin, which she had, so she wanted to steer clear of Reece until the dust settled.

Chyna called down to the kitchen and asked the house-keeper/cook to bring her up a turkey sandwich, chips, and a Coke. After lunch, Chyna went back to work. She had found a prototype of a business plan on the internet, printed it out, and now was tailoring the plan to fit her needs.

Two hours later, Chyna decided to take a break. She moseyed over to the window and saw the groundskeeper mowing the lawn. He had gotten off the riding mower and was now pushing a smaller mower through a tight area of grass. He appeared to be Hispanic, and was young *and* buff. The sun was beaming down on his caramel-colored skin, causing him to break out in a sweat. The muscles in his forearms were glistening from the perspiration, making them look even more defined. His T-shirt was soaking wet and sticking to his chest. Chyna could clearly see his nipples and his abdominal muscles. She stood there nearly drooling. Watching his every move was making her hornier by the second. Chyna thought about going outside to introduce herself, but that would have been inappropriate. Donnie wanted them to act like they had class, which meant not fraternizing with the help.

"Damn! His ass is *fine*!" she said aloud.

As she was ogling the gardener, her cell phone rang. Chyna reluctantly walked away from the window, went back to her desk, and picked up her phone. She looked at the caller ID, but it said, "private call." Chyna thought about letting the call go to voice mail, but she had put in a few calls to real estate agents and thought that maybe one of them was calling her back regarding a retail space.

She pressed the call answer button. "Hello?"

"Hey, sweetness," a male voice whispered into the phone.

"Who is this?" she asked, annoyed.

"Somebody who wants to get next to you in a big way. You are one fine woman, and I can't stop thinking about you."

As he spoke, Chyna began to recognize the voice. It was Kalvin. "What do you want?" she asked, ignoring his lewd comment.

"I want you. I've been thinking that since you're looking for an investor for your boutique, I could float you the money and in return, you give up the snatch," he said tactlessly.

"You are such a pig! I don't need your money. If I gotta save until I'm a fucking hundred years old to have enough cash to open my boutique, then that's what I'ma do. The last thing I want *or* need is money from a lowlife like you!" When she had first met Kalvin, he seemed cool. They even went out to dinner a few times, but then he started getting frisky, treating her like she was an easy lay. Chyna ended their business dealings, and now the dude wouldn't stop calling her.

Chyna clicked the end call button before he could respond. "What an *asshole*!" she screamed aloud.

"Who's an asshole?" Reece asked, walking into the room.

Chyna spun around toward her. "Damn, Reece, haven't

you ever heard of knocking?" she asked, totally annoyed.

"I did knock, but you was so busy screaming that you didn't hear me. So what's up? Why you so mad?"

Chyna exhaled hard. "This dude I met through a friend of a friend wanted to invest in my boutique, but then I found out that he's a drug dealer so I turned him down. Now he keeps calling, trying to get in my pants."

"What kind of drugs is he dealing?" Reece heard the word *drug*, and her ears perked up. She was running low on Oxy and needed another connection. Lars was being stingy with his stash, and she was tired of begging him for more pills.

"Damn, Reece, is that all you can think about?"

"Hell, naw. I think about other stuff. But I like drugs. What's wrong with that?" she asked, with her hand on her slim hip.

Chyna shrugged her shoulders. "Whatever."

"So why you hiding out in yo room?" Reece asked, changing the subject.

"I'm not hiding out. I've been working," Chyna said without much fanfare.

"Working?" Reece cocked her head to one side. "On what?"

"On my business plan."

Reece rolled her eyes. "Yeah, whatever." She walked farther into Chyna's room like it was her own, and plopped down on the bed. "You been talking to Donnie about me?"

"What are you talking about, Reece?"

"You know damn well what I'm talking about. Did you tell Donnie that I've been using drugs?" she asked, looking dead at Chyna.

"Why would you ask me some dumb shit like that?" Chyna said, getting defensive.

"'Cause he acting all mad at me, and when Keisha and 'em was over he accused me of using, that's why. And don't nobody but you know that I indulge in Oxy and coke from time to time."

"Time to time? I'd say it's more than occasionally."

"So who died and made you my keeper?"

"Girl, you need to get a grip. Ain't nobody trying to be your damn keeper, let me alone!"

Reece hopped up from the bed and shouted, "Then stay the hell outta my business!"

Chyna exhaled. "Reece, what happened to us? We used to be best friends, now all we seem to do these days is argue."

"That's 'cause you changed. You acting like one of them snooty Coco Beach bitches."

"Don't be calling me no bitch! I might wanna be a businesswoman, but I'm still an around-the-way girl, and I'll kick your ass."

"You ain't kicking nobody's ass. All I'm saying is that you used to like to hang out and party. Now all you think about is opening up some stupid store," Reece said, crossing her arms in front of her chest.

Chyna took a deep breath. "It's not stupid to want to

have a successful business. Like I told you before, I plan on making my own money someday."

"Yeah, yeah, whatever! Stay out of my business, and don't go running yo mouth about me to Donnie," Reece said and stormed out without giving her friend a chance to respond.

Chyna stood there with her mouth open. She couldn't believe how far apart they had grown. When they were kids, you couldn't pry them apart with a crowbar. Now being in the same room was becoming painful. When Reece wasn't high, she was as mean as a snake, striking out with her forked tongue and inflicting injury with her hurtful words. Chyna was being patient because she knew that Reece had a problem, but Chyna wasn't going to take the verbal abuse much longer; she had too much on her mind.

"Where have you guys been?" Donovan asked, coming down the gangplank looking like he had strolled right off the pages of *GQ*. He wore a Tom Ford white linen suit, a silver silk tee, and a pair of white leather, open-toe woven slides. The theme for tonight's party was White and Platinum, a take-off on Sean Combs's annual White Party.

"Traffic was crazy getting through town," Chyna lied.

She wanted to say that Reece was lollygagging around trying to decide what to wear. Since her decision-making process was skewed from one drink too many, it was difficult for her to make up her mind. When Reece finally did decide what to wear, it was the same dress that Chyna was wearing. They had accidentally bought the same dress. Chyna started to change, but they were running late. Besides, it really wasn't a big deal since the dress code was white and silver, and everybody would basically be dressed alike anyway.

Donovan looked at his sister, giving her a hard stare. "Are you drunk?"

"Damn, D, why you hawking me like 'dat?" She *tsked* and rolled her eyes, "Naw, I ain't drunk."

"Yeah, right." He shook his head. "Whatever you say, Reece." Donovan knew better. His sister was a party animal who needed to be put on a short leash, but another lecture on her destructive habits would have to wait until tomorrow. He didn't want to make a scene tonight; there were too many important people milling about and causing an unnecessary altercation would be in poor taste, especially when the whole point of the party was to make a good impression. Besides, an argument with Reece would probably wind up in the tabloids, and bad press was something he could do without.

Donovan scowled in frustration, turned around, and walked back toward the yacht without saying another word.

Reece watched him disappear and said to Chyna, "Now come on and let's go check out this bad-ass yacht." Chyna began to follow her up the gangplank, but stopped in her tracks and did a double-take. She looked out toward the gate to the marina, into the parking lot, and could have sworn that she saw Kalvin, the guy who wanted to invest in her boutique but who turned out to be a stalker.

"What the hell is he doing here?" Before she knew it, Chyna had spoken her mind aloud.

"Who? Who you talking about?" Reece asked.

"That guy Kalvin."

Reece's eyes followed Chyna's, and she saw a guy standing next to a black two-seater Benz. "Is that him?"

Chyna squinted her eyes, trying to get a better view. "I don't know for sure." A chill ran up her spine. This guy was so slimy. Now she regretted ever meeting with him. Chyna continued on her way, and when she reached the entrance she looked back again, but Kalvin was gone. *Maybe that wasn't him*, she thought and breathed a sigh of relief.

A male server dressed in all silver with a wide white bowtie, holding a tray of chilled flutes filled to the rim with champagne, greeted her and Reece. "Welcome. Would you care for a glass of champagne?"

Reece didn't skip a beat. She picked up a flute, turned the narrow glass up to her mouth, and quickly drained the effervescent liquid. She placed the empty flute back on the tray, picked up a fresh one, and swallowed the champagne in one huge gulp. "Ahh," she said, and then belched. "Come on, girl, let's get our party on!"

Chyna blushed a deep crimson at the way Reece downed her drink. For a brief second she thought about hopping in her truck and driving back to the house, but dismissed the thought. Somebody had to keep an eye on Reece. Donnie was busy with the party, so unfortunately tonight that someone was her.

[18]

Kalvin Clarke had a menacing presence. His hardened demeanor had been purposely cultivated over the years. In his line of business—the drug trade—it was essential to strike fear in people so as not to be taken advantage of. Basically, in his industry the number one rule was survival of the fittest, and if nothing else, Kalvin was a survivor.

Born to a teenage mother and an absentee father, Kalvin was raised by his grandmother. Living in the roughest part of Brooklyn, he learned early how to carry himself so the bullies wouldn't pick on him.

His grandmother could barely make ends meet on her meager salary as a seamstress, so by the time Kalvin reached middle school, he decided to contribute to the household income by running drugs for the local dealer. It didn't take him long to catch on to the business. By the time he was in high school, he had runners of his own working for him.

While most teenagers were preparing for college, Kalvin was preparing to take over the neighborhood drug trade. Fast forward fifteen years, and he was now the kingpin of Red Hook. Not only was he dealing drugs, but he was investing in small businesses, trying to launder his money and slowly clean up his image.

A friend of a friend had introduced him to Chyna, saying that she was looking for an investor in a boutique she planned to open. The moment Kalvin laid eyes on her, he was smitten. Chyna was beautiful. He tried to maintain his cool and act professionally. They had an initial meeting at his office, and Chyna brought her business plan. She explained what she wanted to do with the store; how she wanted to use neighborhood designers to give them a chance. Kalvin admired her tenacity. He wanted to prolong their involvement, so he persuaded her to have dinner with him so that they could talk more about her plans.

He had made reservations at Five Points, a hip restaurant near NoHo. He had never been there before but heard the food was good. Kalvin wasn't much into the trendy scene. He didn't venture far from his comfort zone, preferring instead to stay in his familiar Brooklyn neighborhood where he was the "big fish." However, he had a feeling that someone like Chyna who was trying to get her act together would probably want to go someplace nice instead of one of his old dives.

Kalvin picked her up in his brand-new, two-seater Benz, one of his many cars.

"You look like two million bucks," he gushed when she got in the car.

"Thanks." Chyna noticed how Kalvin was eyeballing her, like she was a Happy Meal. She didn't like being stared at like an item on a buffet, but she didn't say anything. This was their first dinner meeting; she wanted to remain professional and not call him out, so she kept her mouth shut.

When they arrived at the restaurant, Chyna was impressed. The bar area in the front of the restaurant was filled to capacity. The crowd was mixed—black, white, Asian and Hispanic. Chyna had automatically assumed that since Kalvin was from the 'hood, he would take her someplace in Brooklyn. She was glad that she had underestimated him.

They walked up to the hostess's podium, Kalvin gave his last name, and the hostess promptly seated them at a choice table near the back. The dining area was open and airy, with stark white walls and black wood flooring.

A waitress approached their table once they had settled in. "Here are two menus. Can I get you something to drink?" the waitress asked.

"A bottle of Veuve." Kalvin had been drinking earlier and wanted to enhance his buzz, as well as impress Chyna by ordering champagne.

"Coming right up, sir."

Once the waitress was gone, Chyna said, "You didn't have to order champagne. I'm not much of a drinker."

"Really?" He found that odd, since most of the chicks he knew lapped up expensive champagne like it was liquid gold. "You want me to order you some bottled water instead?" he asked, wanting to please her.

"That's okay. I'll have a glass or two. Did you get a chance to look over my proposal?" Chyna asked, ready to talk business before he got tipsy. She had given Kalvin her business plan at their initial meeting.

"Naw, I ain't got a chance to look at it yet," he said, eyeballing Chyna again. Truth be told, Kalvin had no intention of looking at her business plan. He had already decided that he was going to drop more than a few grand her way. He hoped that money would buy him some "between the sheets" time with her.

"Oh." She sounded disappointed. "When do you think you're going to look at it? I really want to get started on this project, and if you're not interested, then I want to pass the plan on to another possible investor," she told him in her most professional manner.

"Don't worry about other investors. 'Cause my money is all you need."

It was apparent that he was hitting on her. She decided right then and there that she didn't want him involved in her business. "Look, Kalvin, I'm not for sale, and I don't need your money. If you think investing in my business will give you access to my goodies, then you are sadly mistaken."

Before he could answer, the waitress returned with the champagne. She opened the bottle and poured them each a glass. "Have you decided what you'd like for dinner?"

"I'ma have the chicken and the pork chops," Kalvin blurted out before Chyna had a chance to order.

"You want two entrees?" the waitress asked, a puzzled look on her face.

"Yeah. I'm starving."

She then turned to Chyna. "And what can I get you?"

Chyna was so turned off by Kalvin that she started to get up and leave, but now that the waitress was at their table, walking out would be totally rude. She took a deep breath to calm herself, and then spoke up. "I'm going to start with a Caesar salad, and for the main course I'll have the halibut," Chyna said, ordering like a pro. She might have grown up in the 'hood, but she had expanded her horizons beyond her meager upbringing.

Kalvin picked up his flute and guzzled the champagne in one gulp. He poured another glassful and drank it down just as fast as the first one. He then turned to Chyna. "Look, I know you ain't for sale," he said, raising his voice slightly and addressing her earlier comment.

"Let's talk about this later." She didn't want to get into an argument in public and embarrass herself.

Kalvin got up, went to the other side of the table, and sat next to Chyna. He put his arm around her and pulled her to him. "Oh, baby, don't be like that."

Chyna sat there stiff as a board. Her first thought was to elbow him in the side. "Can you please take your hand off me?" she said in a tight voice.

"Why? Don't you want some affection?" He leaned

in and slobbered all over her mouth, trying to force-feed her his tongue.

"Get off me! Are you drunk!?" She raised her voice slightly and pushed him back.

Kalvin wasn't used to being brushed off. Women fell at his feet all the time. He was used to the around-the-way girls from his 'hood who jumped at the chance to be with a baller. Obviously Chyna didn't care about his money.

He poured himself another drink. "Come on, baby, give me a chance. I'm really digging you."

"I'm looking for an investor, not a lover."

"Yeah, a'right," he said, sounding despondent.

The rest of the evening was a bust. Kalvin drank the remainder of the champagne and ordered another bottle. Chyna abruptly ended their involvement. In hindsight, Kalvin regretted having made a pass at her.

Kalvin tried to ask her forgiveness. He even showed up at her apartment, but she cursed him out before he had a chance to apologize. When he found out about the yacht party through some acquaintances, he showed up there hoping to change her mind.

[19]

Pulsating music greeted Remi and Lars as they made their way up the gangplank of the *Lady Lord*. Though the invitation to Donovan's White and Platinum soirée was addressed to Dr. and Mrs. Braxton, Remi had automatically assumed that she was going solo since Lars was back in the city. Remi was ecstatic about going alone. Troy would be at the party, and she had planned on flirting with him shamelessly. But to her disappointment, her husband had showed up unannounced earlier that afternoon with a garment bag draped across his arm, announcing that they were going to Donovan's party as if she didn't know anything about the event. Remi was curious how he knew about the party since the invitation had come directly to their summer home.

Remi had followed him upstairs to the bedroom to get some answers. She watched him unpack a crisp white linen suit, and as he hung up his clothes, Remi asked how he knew about the party. He told her that he heard about it from a friend. Remi thought that was odd. Most of Lars's friends were either boring or stuck-up and wouldn't be caught dead spending the evening at an event given by a rapper. She didn't press the matter. Lars was going and that was that.

"Welcome to Mr. Smart's White and Platinum soirée. Would you care for a glass of champagne?" the server asked once they reached the entryway.

Lars took two flutes from the tray and handed one to Remi. He touched his glass to hers. "Happy Summer." He smiled and took a sip.

Yeah, it would be happier if you were back in Manhattan, Remi thought. She returned his smile with one of her own, and then said, "Cheers."

"Come on, let's dance," Lars said, looping her arm through his.

Remi looked at him like he was a stranger. The Lars she knew would rather listen to Bach than Biggie. But Lars was bopping his head to the rap song that was playing. "You go ahead. I need to call Liza and see if she's here yet. With the music playing, I'm sure I won't be able to hear in there," Remi said, putting him off.

"Oh, okay." Lars kissed her on the cheek. "See you inside."

The second Lars made his way inside the yacht, Remi took out her phone and called Troy. "Hey there," she said once he answered.

"Hey, sweetcakes."

"Are you at the party?" she whispered.

"No, I'm still at the restaurant. I'll be there in a few. I can't wait to grind up against you on the dance floor."

Remi looked over her shoulder, making sure that Lars was safely inside. She didn't see him, so she continued talking. "That's not going to happen."

"And why not? Don't you want my dick against your fine ass?"

"I'd love nothing more, but Lars is here. He came from town unexpectedly," she said, her voice full of frustration.

"Now that the cat is no longer away, I'm guessing that the mouse won't be playing." He chuckled.

"I'm glad you find this funny, but I'm not amused. Maybe I can sneak away tomorrow, when he's—"

Troy cut her off. "I don't think so. Fucking around when your husband is in Manhattan is one thing, but doing it practically right underneath his nose is suicidal, and I'm not ready to die."

Remi rolled her eyes to the sky. "Why do you have to be so dramatic? Lars is clueless. He thinks I occupy my time with gay decorators trying to choose color palettes."

"And I want to keep it that way. So before you insist, we will not, I repeat will not, be fucking around when your husband is in town. Is that clear?"

"Whatever!" Remi said, and punched the end call button. "Men!" she huffed.

"What about them?"

Startled, Remi swung around at the sound of the familiar voice. She hoped the person hadn't heard her entire conversation. "Hey, Liza. How long have you been standing there?"

"I just came above deck. I was in my stateroom getting ready. Like my outfit?" she asked, spinning around.

Remi checked out Liza's white silk halter gown, which she wore with a thin silver belt wrapped around her slim waist. The belt buckle was encrusted with diamonds, which complemented the large, teardrop diamonds dangling from her earlobes, neck, and wrists.

"Wow! Aren't you iced up!"

"You think the diamonds are too much?"

"They are a bit over the top," Remi told her.

"I want to be blinged out to catch Donovan's attention. You know how rappers love diamonds." Liza's scheme to seduce Donovan wasn't working according to plan. Even though they had met several times before the party to iron out the details, he hadn't given her a second look. He was all business. Tonight Liza wanted to show him that she was a party girl and not a stuck-up Hamptonite.

"He won't be able to miss you with all that blingage,'" Remi said, putting her fingers up to make air quotes.

"I hope to at least get a dance out of him, and hopefully a kiss or two. You didn't tell me that Lars was going to be here," Liza said, switching gears.

"I didn't know he was coming into town either. I thought he would be staying in the city this weekend," Remi said, sounding disappointed.

Liza raised her eyebrow. "Sounds like you don't want him here. Is there trouble in paradise?"

If there is, you'll never know, Remi thought. She was glad that she hadn't mentioned their blissless marriage. Liza was all too ready to dig into Remi's dirt, even though she didn't have a shovel. "Oh, no, girl. I'm thrilled that my husband is here. I've missed him terribly," Remi said, putting on a phony smile. She wanted to get Liza off her case, so she turned the tables. "Come on; let's go find our men before they get hit on."

"Good idea." Liza wasn't about to let some hoochie put her hooks into Donovan. This was her yacht, and as far as she was concerned, Donovan was her date tonight, even if he didn't know it.

Liza and Remi entered the party and each went their separate ways. Liza set off in search of the rapper, and Remi did her best to avoid Lars. She wasn't in the mood to shake her rump on the dance floor. She was still pissed that Troy had blown her off, and she had some choice words for him. Remi went to the bar and waited for Troy. Their conversation was far from over.

[20]

Lars inched his way across the crowded dance floor, maneuvering among the gyrating bodies grooving to the beat. Although the room was dimly lit, he saw a few familiar faces, but not the face he was looking for. He couldn't believe that some of the local snobs were actually mingling with the hip-hop bunch. Coco Beach residents were so uppity, especially the ones who had a long history of family wealth. Most of them regarded people with new money as tacky and ill-bred—a common misconception. He and Remi were initially shunned when they moved into the community, and it wasn't until Liza embraced them that their fellow neighbors followed suit. Now they were considered part of the elitist bunch.

"Hey there, Lars; haven't seen you around in a while. How's it been going?" asked Michael Lord, Liza's brother. Michael was a rich socialite like his sister who did nothing more than hang at the country club playing golf all day, and carouse around town at night. He was a ladies' man and had women all across the country. As he was often fond of saying, "I can have as many women as I can afford." With his money (or better yet, his family's fortune), he could manage a stableful.

Lars slapped him on the back. "Hey, man. I can't complain. Business is steady, and that's a good thing."

"As vain as women are, I'm sure you'll be slicing and dicing for a long time to come." Michael laughed.

"Yeah, you got a point there. Some of my patients are so conceited that they are addicted to cosmetic surgery. Luckily for me, growing old gracefully is a thing of the past."

"I don't know how you work with fine women every day." Michael stepped closer and whispered, "Come on, man, tell me." He looked over his shoulder, making sure no one was eavesdropping. "Have you ever slept with a patient?"

"I swear, Michael, you are such a dog." Lars shook his head. "Don't you know I could lose my license for such inappropriate behavior?"

"Yeah, yeah, I know. But aren't you ever tempted?"

Lars wanted to tell him that it wasn't the patients who had him horny, but the hot young honeys that he met at the clubs. "No. Never," he said, adamantly.

"Oh, come on, man." Michael nudged Lars on the shoulder. "You can tell me the truth."

Lars was tempted to tell him about Reece, but thought it best to keep his mouth shut. The last thing he needed was for Michael to slip and tell Liza, and she would no doubt blab to Remi. No, this secret would be kept to himself. "Mike, I love my wife and would never dream of cheating on her," he said with a straight face.

"I hear you, man," Michael said, and then winked as if he didn't really believe him. "Come on, let's go to the bar and get a drink."

Lars glanced over at the bar area and saw Remi standing there. "Go on ahead; I'll meet you over there. I need to go to the head," Lars said, putting him off. He wanted to steer clear of his wife. He was on the hunt for a woman, but Remi wasn't the one.

"Oh, okay," Michael said, and walked away.

Lars slipped off down the hallway out of sight. He peered into one of the staterooms and saw a group of people mingling and sipping cocktails. With everyone dressed in white and silver, it was hard to tell who was who. He thought he saw Reece standing in the crowd, but when the woman turned around, it wasn't her.

Lars continued down the hall until he came upon another large stateroom. A couple was walking out as he came in. The room was exquisitely furnished, with a round king-sized bed draped in a fluffy, snow white duvet. There was a sitting area with four silver leather, low-back chairs situated around an art deco cocktail table. Lars was the only one in the room, so he decided to use the opportunity to get high. Cruising the yacht looking for Reece was making him feel anxious, and he wanted to mellow out. He had brought OxyContin with him; a tablet or two that would do the job nicely. He reached into his pants' pocket and took out the small envelope, which contained enough Oxy to last the weekend. He didn't have any water to take them with, so he crossed the room, heading toward the bathroom. When he reached the door, it opened.

"Well, well, if it ain't the good doctor," Reece said.

He pulled her to him. "Where have you been? I've been looking all over for you."

In the city they had partied often like celebrities until the wee hours. Lars had learned on their second date that Reece was an Oxy head, and he promised her some to lure her out on a third date. That night they were both feeling horny, but instead of taking her back to his penthouse, Lars booked a luxury suite at the Royalton Hotel. They couldn't get in the door fast enough before he started ripping her clothes off.

Reece began unbuckling Lars's belt, feeling him up at the same time. She ran her hand up and down his crotch. He was so big that she couldn't wait to see his rod up close and personal.

"I wanna suck yo dick," she had panted.

Lars unbuttoned his pants and let them slide to the floor along with his underwear. He grabbed his erect shaft and swung it back and forth. "Is this what you want?"

Reece had licked her lips. "Yep." Big dicks made her salivate, and her mouth watered with desire as she looked at the bulbous head on his cock. She dropped to her knees, kissed the tip of his head, and then wrapped her full lips around his dick. She held on to his naked ass as she sucked the length of him in and out of her juicy mouth. Her mouth was so wet that saliva oozed from the sides. Reece was sucking hard and making loud, nasty noises with the spit. The sounds were a natural aphrodisiac.

"Damn, girl…, where…did you learn…how to suck a dick?" Lars had managed to say, his words coming in spurts.

Reece hadn't responded. She kept sucking and licking, trying to make him cum. Lars pulled her to her feet and led her to the bedroom. He wasn't ready to bust a nut so soon.

Reece lay on the bed and spread her legs wide, allowing him to fit perfectly in between her thighs. She reached down and guided his dick into her slippery opening. At first his huge cock was having a hard time penetrating her, but after a few deliberate thrusts, he was in, and it felt good. Her canal was deep, and his long cock filled her perfectly.

Lars reached underneath and took hold of her butt, hugging her in tighter. Reece grabbed him around the shoulders and the two of them rocked back and forth, grinding deeper and deeper into each other until they were on the verge of climaxing.

Lars made an ugly face, scrunching up his mouth and tightening his eyes, and then he blurted out, "I'm cumming!"

"Me toooo!" Reece sang.

After their heated climax, they both lay dripping in each other's sweat, silently trying to recover. Lars had been the first to speak. "My God, that was awesome."

"Yes, yes, it was." Reece was extremely satisfied. She hadn't had sex this explosive in a long time, and it felt good.

"I'VE BEEN LOOKING FOR YOU, TOO," Reece said, giving him a deep kiss.

Lars pulled her in closer so that his cock was pressing against her crotch. Sneaking around on Remi while he was in New York was exciting, but doing it right under her nose would be totally exhilarating. Lars was a thrill seeker; that was one of the reasons why he had started taking OxyContin. "I was thinking about the night we were at the Royalton, and how good you sucked me off. Come on and show me some more of your skills." He pulled her hand, leading her to the bed.

"I will, but first I need some Oxy. You got some?" Reece's buzz from the liquor was wearing off, and now she was ready to reach a higher stratosphere.

Lars didn't want to feed Reece any more Oxy. He had already broken one of his rules by giving her the drugs in the first place. Lars gripped the envelope in his hand. "No, I don't have any tonight," he lied.

"Damn!" She plopped down on the bed, folded her arms, and pouted.

"You want a drink?" he asked, walking over to her.

"Yeah, I wanna damn drink, *and* some Oxy!"

Lars could tell that he wasn't going to get any head unless he gave up the drugs. He tossed the package of Oxy on the bed. "Surprise!"

Reece glanced down at the envelope, picked it up, and looked inside. "Now you talkin!" She grinned. Reece popped two pills in her mouth and swallowed them without the benefit of water. She tossed the envelope on the bed, with the remaining pills, and crooked her finger at him. "Come here, Big Daddy, and let Mommy show you some appreciation."

Lars walked to the door and closed it so that they could have some privacy. He then went over to Reece, leaned down, and began kissing her frantically. He eased her back on the bed, and lay his body on top of hers. He started grinding into her twat. He was getting ready to reach down, unzip his pants, and unleash his cock, when he heard someone yell out his name.

"*Lars!*"

[21]

Remi abandoned her position at the bar. She got tired of waiting for Troy; besides, after belting back a few glasses of champagne she needed to go to the restroom. The yacht had swelled to capacity, and the party was now in full swing. The local islanders had left their haughty attitudes on the dock and were letting loose with the hip-hoppers. Remi was shocked that everyone was gelling so well.

She elbowed her way through the packed dance floor and made her way to the other side of the room. Remi sauntered down the hallway in search of an empty bathroom, but they were all occupied. She had been on the yacht several times and was familiar with its layout. She went back to one of the more private staterooms and saw that the door was closed.

"Good; there's probably nobody in here," she mumbled as she twisted the doorknob.

Remi couldn't have been further from the truth. Not only was the room not empty, but her husband was on the bed grinding on top of some skeezer.

"*Lars!*" she screamed at the top of her voice.

Lars froze. The sound of his wife's shrill voice made him stop cold. He scrambled off Reece, zipping his pants at the same time. He started to talk, but the words were caught up in his throat. "Uh, uh, it's not, uh—"

"*Shut up, Lars!* Don't even try to lie. I saw you with my own eyes on top of this, this"—she pointed her finger at Reece—"hoochie!"

"Who the hell is you calling a hoochie?" Reece shot back, sitting up in the bed.

Remi glared at her. "You, that's who!"

Reece scooted to the edge of the bed and stood up. "Okay, bitch, I got yo hoochie. You the one who come storming in here, busting in on me and my man, and now you got the nerve to be calling me names."

"Your man? Is that right?" Remi said, putting her hand on her hip. She then turned to Lars. "Sooo, since you're *her* man, I guess that would mean that you've been cheating on her with *me*?"

"No, baby. It's not what it looks like. I've had a little too much to drink, and Reece and I were just—"

"'Baby'? Why the hell you calling her 'baby'?" Reece asked, butting in.

"Reece, please be quiet," Lars told her.

"He's calling me 'baby' because I'm his wife, and not some tramp trying to snag a married man!" Remi said vehemently.

Reece jerked her head around to Lars. "Married? You

didn't say nothing about being married. Ain't that a bitch!"

"Oh yes, he's quite married." Remi held up her left hand and wiggled her ring finger, showing off her five-carat diamond engagement ring and platinum wedding band.

"Obviously that ring don't mean shit, 'cuz he's all over me like a fucking rash!" Reece spat out.

Lars could see that this back-and-forth banter wasn't leading anywhere. He needed to separate the women before they came to blows. He turned to Reece and said in a low voice, "Reece, can you please give us a few minutes alone?"

Reece rolled her eyes and sucked her teeth. "Whatever!" She walked past Remi and leered at her. She recognized Remi from her coming to the house with Liza. Remi was one of them stuck-up Coco Beach bitches, and she wanted to smack the smug expression off Remi's face, but didn't want to start a fight. Donovan would be pissed if she turned his party out, so she restrained herself.

Once Reece was gone, Lars smoothed his clothes, trying to compose himself. He attempted to clear his thoughts. He didn't know exactly how he was going to talk his way out of this mess, but he sure as hell was going to try. He walked over to his wife and took her by the arm. "Remi, sit down."

She snatched her arm out of his grip. "I don't want to sit down on the bed where you had your whore!"

"She's not my whore. Remi, this is a complete misunderstanding."

"What's there to misunderstand, Lars? I come in here and you're in bed on top of another woman, getting ready to screw her brains out. I would say that's pretty cut and dried," she said, as if she were as virginal as a saint.

"I wasn't getting ready to screw her, or anybody else for that matter. I had too much to drink and fell over on the bed," Lars lied, trying to sell her on the idea.

"Yeah, right. Don't insult my intelligence. I'm not stupid, Lars. I know what I saw. Instead of standing there lying to my face, why don't you go find your whore? I want to be alone."

"Remi, please—"

"I've heard enough. Now will you please leave me alone? I need to collect myself before I go back to the party. This is not the place to discuss your infidelity. We'll deal with this at home," she said, putting her foot down.

Lars hung his head. He didn't know what to do. He had been caught not only with his hand in the cookie jar, but with the cookie in his mouth. At this point, all he could do was concede. "Okay, Remi, whatever you want. I'm going to go home and wait for you." He slunk out of the room with his ego bruised. No man wanted to be busted red-handed with another woman. Now he would have hell to pay, at the very least. Although he loved womanizing and drugs, he wasn't willing to lose his wife over his indiscretions.

Once Lars was gone, Remi sat on the bed and thought about what had just happened. She wasn't hurt by her husband's unfaithfulness. Quite the opposite: Now Remi could use this as leverage. A huge smile spread across her face. "Perfect timing!" she sang aloud.

Remi went into the bathroom, freshened up, and rejoined the party. Although she was still pissed at Lars, their talk would have to wait until they got home. She wasn't about to ruin the party by having an altercation with her husband. Remi was much too refined for that type of drama.

[22]

"Liza, you really outdid yourself. This party is exactly what I wanted. My neighbors seem to be accepting my crew," Donovan said. He and Liza were out on the deck watching the guests through the sliding doors.

Liza leaned back on the railing and let the night breeze flow through her long hair. She arched her back slightly, causing her nipples to protrude against the sheer fabric of her dress. Liza wanted to entice Donovan. He was looking so fine in his white suit, and she wanted to take him home and fuck his brains out. "You're more than welcome." She stepped closer to him and rubbed his arm. "The pleasure was all mine."

Donovan was no dummy and knew when a woman was trying to seduce him. Liza Lord was pulling out all the stops. He could barely keep his eyes off her titties. The outlines of her areolas were showing through the dress, and her rack looked good enough to eat. Up until now, he had been strictly businesslike with her. Since he didn't know her well, he wanted to remain professional. Donovan was still trying to ingratiate himself into the community and didn't want to make any waves. The Lord family was a big deal in Coco Beach, and the last thing he needed was to screw around with Liza and have their affair go sour. Liza had proven that she was connected and could make or break his reputation. But at the same time, he didn't want to refuse her advances. Donovan knew that a woman scorned could be dangerous; therefore, he had to walk a fine line.

"And I appreciate all of your hard work, Liza. I couldn't have pulled this event off without you. I'm going to have to take you out to dinner to show my appreciation," Donovan said warmly.

"I'll pass on dinner." Liza moved in closer. "I know a better way for you to show your appreciation." Before he could respond, she put her arms around his neck and began kissing him.

Liza's tongue entered his mouth with ease. Donovan's mind was in protest, but his body was responding like that of any red-blooded heterosexual. Her soft lips meshed with his perfectly, and he could feel his jimmy responding to her kisses. Donovan wanted to pull back, but his manhood wouldn't let him. Instinctively, he started grinding his growing penis into her pelvis. He hadn't been laid in a while and the heat between them was too much to withstand.

"*Ahem!*" Donovan heard someone clearing their throat and turned toward the sound.

"Excuse me. I don't mean to interrupt, but I need to talk with Liza," Remi said, clearly upset.

Liza looked at Remi like she had lost her mind. Liza was finally getting somewhere with Donovan and didn't want to stop. She was horny and wanted to get fucked. "Can't it wait? I'm rather busy," she said, her arms still around Donovan's neck.

"No! This is really important," Remi said, standing there with her hands on her hips, refusing to move.

"Remi, I'm sure your crisis can wait." She cocked her head in Donovan's direction. "Can't you see I'm busy?"

Donovan used this opportunity to extract himself from Liza's embrace. He had let himself get carried away, but now wasn't the time nor place. "Ladies, please don't let me interrupt. Liza, I'll talk with you later," he said, and went back inside.

"Your timing couldn't have been worse." Liza rolled her eyes. "We were really getting into a groove." She sighed hard out of frustration.

"I'm sorry that I ruined the moment, but I just caught Lars with another woman!" She was still upset, and wanted to vent.

"Ohmigod!" Liza threw her hand to her mouth. "You're kidding! I thought you guys had a solid relationship. Who is she? Do you know the other woman? What are you going to do? Are you leaving him?" Liza asked, bombarding her with a slew of questions.

Suddenly Remi regretted running to Liza and shooting off at the mouth. She should have known that Liza would be full of annoying questions. She had only recently told Liza that she and Lars were blissfully happy. Now she'd have to dispel the myth. "No, I'm not going to leave my husband. I'm over-reacting. Lars even said that it's nothing, and that he had had too much to drink," Remi said, trying to lessen the seriousness of the incident. To further downplay the scene, Remi thought it best not to mention that the woman she caught with Lars was Donovan Smart's sister.

"And you believe him? Men will lie even when the evidence is undeniable. If you need the number of a good divorce attorney, let me know."

Divorcing Lars wasn't an option. Since they didn't have any children, her settlement wouldn't be as generous, and she wasn't about to downsize her lifestyle. Besides, Remi loved the cachet that came from being the wife of a renowned plastic surgeon. "I'm sure I won't need an attorney. Lars and I will have a good talk when I get home," she said, trying to sound convincing.

"Don't be a fool. Now that you know he's cheating on you, you need to cover your bases and call an attorney. Have you given any thought to the possibility of him leaving you for the other woman?" Liza asked.

Remi hadn't considered that possibility. *Oh shit, what if Lars leaves me for that tramp?* Remi's body started trembling, and it wasn't from the night breeze. It was from the thought of being abandoned. The scandal of Lars leaving her for an ill-bred hip-hop chick would have the tongues in Coco Beach wagging for a long while, and living through that shame would be torture.

"That's not going to happen. I've invested too much time in my marriage to let some stranger come along and destroy everything we've built." Remi was ready to take action. She wanted to talk to Lars immediately. Remi needed to make sure that her marriage was secure and that his affair was nothing serious. Although she wasn't deeply in love with Lars anymore, there was no way she was going to lose him *and* his money.

[23]

"Where the hell have you been?" Chyna asked Reece. She hadn't seen Reece since they'd arrived an hour ago. She had started to get worried, since Reece had been drinking all day. "Are you all right?"

"Yeah, I'm okay. I was fucking around with this dude I know," she said candidly. Reece had been outspoken all of her life. Even as a kid, she spoke her mind. She thought small talk was a waste of time.

"What dude? Is he one of Donovan's friends?" Chyna asked excitedly, thinking that Reece had met a nice guy.

"Naw, he ain't no friend of Donnie's. He's this doctor that I met at a club back in the city. We've been kicking it for a minute."

"Wow, a doctor? I didn't think you were into the smart type," Chyna said. Reece normally went out with Rollie-wearing thugs.

"I'm into all types. As long as they know how to throw down, and ain't stuck up." When Reece first met Lars at NV, she thought that he was a little nerdy, especially after seeing him get dissed by that model and her crew.

She soon found out that Lars was anything but a nerd. He could fuck his ass off, *and* he did Oxy, which was a real bonus. He even gave her free pills so she no longer had to buy Oxy on the black market. He was older than most of the men she dated, but she didn't care. All Reece cared about was keeping her pipeline to the drugs open. Dating Lars was like dating an all-night pharmacy, and she planned to do whatever it took to keep him around.

"Where is he? I'd like to meet him," Chyna said, looking around the party. She was curious to see the man who had captured her friend's attention. Chyna wondered if he was rough around the edges like Reece.

Reece hunched her shoulders. "I dunno where he is. Probably still talking to his wife."

"Wife? He's married?" Chyna asked, shocked.

"Yep. Sure is," Reece answered cavalierly.

"Damn, Reece, ain't nothing sacred to you? How can you mess around with a married man? What about his wife?" Chyna had never been married, but she held marriage in high esteem nonetheless. Her parents were happily married for years until her dad died, and she admired the commitment they had shared. Her mom took care of her father until death parted them. As far as Chyna was concerned, the vows of holy matrimony were to be cherished.

"What about his wife? I don't know the bitch. I take that back. I met her once. She and Liza Lord came to the house to talk to Donnie, but I didn't know she was his wife," Reece said, rolling her neck.

"Is she here at the party? I thought when you said, that he was talking to his wife that you meant on the phone."

"Yep, she's here!" Reece nodded.

"Wait a minute. I'm confused. You mean to tell me that he introduced you to his wife like it was no big deal?"

"Not exactly. We was getting our freak on in one of the bedrooms when his wife came busting in on us, like this is her damn boat." Reece was beginning to get mad all over again, thinking about what had happened.

A waiter was passing by. Chyna stopped him and took a flute of champagne from his tray. After hearing Reece's shocking news, Chyna decided that she needed a drink to help her digest the in-formation. She was also still feeling nervous and paranoid about the possibility of Kalvin being at the party. She took a sip, then refocused her attention on Reece and her drama. "His wife caught you guys making love?"

Reece also took a glass. "Naw, we wasn't fucking—at least not yet. We was only on the bed kissing and stuff," Reece said as if that were an innocent act.

"Damn, Reece, why you got to mess around with a married man when all of these fine single dudes are here?"

Reece shrugged her shoulders. "I didn't even know he was married until tonight."

"Yeah, right! I find that hard to believe." Then Chyna realized the real reason Reece was dating the doctor. "Is he supplying you with drugs?" Chyna asked knowingly.

"Yep, but now he's starting to slack off. I swear if he

doesn't start back giving me Oxy on the regular again, then I'ma have to drop a dime and have his license revoked for giving out medicine illegally."

"Damn, that's cold. You mean to tell me that you'd ruin his career because he won't feed you more Oxy?" Chyna shook her head. "How can you be so heartless?"

Reece drained the last of her drink. "It's not heartless. He should've never given me Oxy in the first place. He knows it's against the law to dole out meds without a script. So it ain't my fault if he gets busted."

"Girl, you're a trip."

"I ain't a trip. *He's* the trip. You should have seen the way he practically threw me out of the room. He said that he wanted to talk to his wife *alone*. I'm sure he told her a bunch of lies. Like he's been telling me," Reece said, getting madder by the second.

"What lies did he tell you?"

"For starters, he didn't mention that he was married. He was always blowing up my phone and what not, like he's free and single. Now I know he was playing me to get the booty. I hate to be played for a fool. But I'ma get that muther fucker back, trust me," Reece said, sounding like the scorned woman that she was.

"Now I understand why you'd drop a dime on him. You're pissed that he chose his wife over you, but still doesn't mean it's right to turn him in to the police," Chyna said.

"Yeah, I'm pissed. He used me to get some ass, but he ain't getting away with it," she huffed.

As they were talking Reece saw Lars cutting through the crowd. She nodded her head in his direction. "There he is," she said, pointing him out to Chyna.

"He's a handsome man. Looks like the rest of these respectable islanders," Chyna said, taking in Lars's appearance.

"Yeah, that bastard is anything but respectable. That's a front." Reece rolled her eyes. "Where's that waiter? I need another drink."

"Me, too." Tonight Chyna was drinking more than she had in her entire life, but it was nothing compared to Reece's consumption. Chyna wanted to take the edge off. Kalvin was probably at the party. She didn't want to hear anything he had to say, and now Reece had dropped a bomb on her about screwing a married man.

As Chyna and Reece looked around for the waiter, they had no idea that someone had been eavesdropping on their conversation. Reece had said a mouthful, and now that the information was out, it could be detrimental—and not only to Lars.

[24]

The yacht's galley was bustling with cooks and servers working frantically to keep up with the demand for booze and hors d'oeuvres. They were opening more cases of champagne and replenishing trays of ahi tuna, beef tartar, mini quiche, and shrimp cocktail. Everyone was so busy doing their jobs that no one noticed the out-of-place guest who had no business being back in the kitchen amongst the help. They also didn't notice when the guest dumped a heaping spoonful of crushed OxyContin into a glass of champagne, waited until the drug dissolved, and put the flute on a tray all by itself.

"Excuse me."

The server stopped in his tracks and said to the guest, "Yes, can I help you?"

"Come with me." They walked out of the kitchen, but stopped before entering the main room. "See those two women over to the side talking?"

"Yes."

The guest handed the server the tray. "Can you make

sure that the one on the left gets this drink? It's a special champagne, just for her."

"Sure, no problem." The waiter took the tray and, without any questions, made his way across the room.

An hour later, Donovan was at the microphone speaking to his guests. "I'd like to thank everyone for coming out tonight. Many of you may only know me by my songs, and what you've read about me in the media, which are half-truths. That's why I wanted to throw this party, so that I could personally introduce myself and my family to the community. Rappers often get a bad rap—pardon the pun." He chuckled. "So I want to dispel the myth that we're all knuckleheads who like to drink forties and cause a ruckus. Don't get me wrong. I love a good party, but getting unruly and disturbing the peace is not my idea of fun. Rest assured that there will be no upheaval at my estate. Not only am I a rapper, but I'm also a businessman, and I understand the importance of maintaining property values. The Wellington estate, which is now my home, will remain as pristine as it always has been. In time, I hope you come to accept me and my family as your neighbors. Thank you."

The guests applauded, and Donovan smiled. Everything was going better than he had expected. Now that the evening was almost over, he could relax. The locals seemed to be nice enough. He had mingled throughout the evening and had spoken to every guest. They were all quite engaging and didn't turn up their noses at him—

at least not to his face. Everyone seemed to be having a good time, and Donovan was beyond pleased.

Donovan saw Liza in the crowd and began making his way over to her. He wanted to thank her again for helping him organize the event, and also to make plans to finish what they had started out on the deck. She had gotten him all hot and bothered, and he wanted more. She seemed really cool, so he put his paranoia about dating her out of his mind. Now that his acceptance into Coco Beach society seemed imminent, hooking up with Liza wouldn't be a bad thing. She was well-connected and he could benefit from her clout. But before he could reach her, Donovan heard someone yell.

"Oh my God! Somebody's in the water!"

Donovan turned toward the sound of the voice and pushed his way out to the deck. He looked over the railing, and sure enough, a woman was floating face down in the bay. From where he stood, he couldn't see who it was. He began to panic.

Donovan raced down the steps to get a better look. He peered over the railing, but still couldn't make out the woman's identity. She had on a white dress and silver shoes, like nearly every woman at the party.

Donovan's heart began pounding loudly, and felt like it was going to jump right out of his chest. The first person he thought about was his sister. All he could think about was her getting wasted and falling overboard.

"Oh my God, she can't swim!" Donovan shouted.

He raced out to the dock, quickly took off his jacket, and kicked off his shoes. Donovan was getting ready to dive in when someone grabbed his arm.

"Stop! Don't go in the water. We'll handle it from here," a uniformed policeman told him.

Someone had called the cops and they were there pronto, taking charge of the scene.

Nearly all the guests had migrated outside, gawking at the woman's body. Donovan stood on the dock in shock. Moments earlier he was preaching that he and his crew were civil and there would be no upheavals. Now someone could be dead. Talk about a cruel twist of fate.

"Okay, people, back inside. Nobody leaves this boat until we've talked to them," the police officer said, trying to get the crowd under control so they could do their jobs.

A plainclothes officer came on the scene, and Donovan assumed that she was a detective. He watched the detective and the officer clear away the people from the decks. A few minutes later Liza came outside and talked with the detective. They didn't talk long before Liza went back inside.

Once all the guests were back inside waiting to be questioned, a team of divers brought the woman's limp body out of the water. Donovan stepped closer, trying to see who it was, but her wet hair covered her face.

The divers lay the woman's lifeless body on the gurney, and her hair fell to the side. As they were getting ready to zip up the black plastic body bag, Donovan got a glimpse of her face.

"Oh...my...God," Donovan said slowly before falling to his knees.

He keeled over and cried like a baby. He prayed that this was a bad dream, that he would wake up any minute and everyone he loved would be alive and healthy. But as he watched them carry her away, he knew that she was gone from this life forever.

[25]

Theo had a body, but still no clues as to who gave the victim an overdose of OxyContin. So far through her investigation she had learned that the victim didn't do drugs, and with the lethal amount of Oxy found in her system, Theo concluded that someone must have slipped her the drugs, either in her food or drinks. But who? Whoever drugged her was probably the same person who pushed her overboard. Theo sat at her desk and read over her notes again for the umpteenth time, hoping that something would jump out at her. It had been five days since the drowning, and she was still searching for clues.

"Excuse me, Boss La—I mean Theo," Officer Rodgers said, poking his head in her door.

"Yeah, Rodgers, what is it?" she asked, not bothering to look up.

"You wanted me to remind you when the funeral for the victim starts. The services are set to begin in about an hour," he informed her.

"Thanks." Theo wanted to attend the funeral not only

to pay her respects, but to survey the crowd to see if anybody stood out as a suspect. From her experience, she knew that most murder victims actually knew their attacker. Theo had wondered why the funeral was being held in Coco Beach instead of the city, but she'd yet to ask the person organizing the services. If she got a chance, she planned on asking him today.

"You want me to go with you?" Rodgers asked. He had a slight crush on his boss and took any opportunity he could to be in her presence.

"No, that won't be necessary. I don't want the family to think that the cops are intruding on such a private and somber occasion. I plan to slip in the back of the church and quietly observe." Theo preferred working alone these days. She had a partner back in New York whom she'd trusted with her life, but he'd had a heart attack and died in his sleep. Since then, she hadn't found anyone with whom she felt comfortable.

"Okay, sure, no problem," Rodgers said and went back to his desk.

Theo gathered up her notes, put them back in the folder, and stuck the folder in her tote bag. She took a compact out of the bag, looked in the mirror, ran her hand over her hair, and then dotted her nose with translucent powder. Now that her face and hair were together, she stood up and adjusted the belt around her waist. Knowing that today was the day of the funeral, Theo had dressed in a black cotton, short-sleeved dress and a pair of black Tory Burch ballerina flats. She wanted to blend in with the crowd of mourners and not stand out as a cop. Theo took her shades out of her tote and walked out of the station to the parking lot.

She drove the short distance to St. David AME Zion Church, one of the town's oldest landmarks. Theo parked across the road from the cemetery and waited. She had arrived early so that she could see the mourners as they filed into the sanctuary.

Thirty minutes later, a procession of black cars came rolling slowly down the street. The hearse pulled up in front of the church. Theo watched as six handsomely dressed men in black suits got out of a limo, walked over to the back of the hearse, and stood at attention as a white-gloved attendant opened the hatchback and pulled the casket forward. The men each took hold of a handle and carried the silver casket into the church.

Donovan Smart got out of another limo, along with three women. The ladies each wore large, black straw hats with wide brims and sunglasses. Theo couldn't make out their identities from where she sat. She watched as the four of them locked arms and somberly made their way into the building.

Theo waited until at least seventy more mourners gathered inside the quaint church before she went in. There were beautiful floral arrangements lining the front of the sanctuary, and a spray of white roses sat atop the foot of the casket. The wooden pews were filled to capacity, so Theo stood in the back and watched as people passed by the open casket to say their goodbyes. An organist played an old spiritual, and the sad hymn had all eyes in the house teary, including Theo's.

The minister approached the pulpit, and stepped to the podium. "Once the service begins, we will close the casket, and it will not be opened again. So if there is anyone who wants to say their final goodbye, please do so at this time."

One of the women who had walked in with Donovan went up to the casket and began wailing. "Oh, my baby, my baby! Lord, why did you take my baby from me?" She threw her body over that of the deceased.

Donovan came up and put his arms around her. "Come on." He eased her upright and handed her a handkerchief. "It's going to be all right." He cradled her in his arms and led her back to the front pew.

Once the lid was closed, the minister began the eulogy. "God, we thank you for this day, and we thank you for the life of Chyna Jones. She was a bright young woman who had dreams and aspirations. Though her passing was unexpected, her spirit will live on through her many friends and family."

As he spoke, Theo watched the front pew. Donovan and his sister, Reece, were clearly grief stricken. They held on to each other and cried uncontrollably. Obviously, the loss of Chyna had affected them deeply. She looked around the church and wondered if the killer was in the room. Somebody was responsible for Chyna's death, and Theo planned on finding out who that some-one was.

After the minister finished his eulogy, the choir sang an uplifting song as everyone filed out. The service, although sad, had ended on an upbeat note, reminiscent of a New Orleans–type funeral.

People were milling around out front, hugging and comforting each other. Theo walked up to Donovan and the woman she assumed was Chyna's mother. "I'm so sorry for your loss."

"Thank you," they both said.

"Did you know my baby?" Chyna's mother asked.

"No, ma'am, I didn't." Theo thought about telling her that she was investigating her daughter's death, but didn't think it was appropriate at the time.

Donovan whispered in Theo's ear. "Can I talk to you for a second?"

"Sure."

They walked over to the side, away from the crowd. "Do you have any suspects yet?" Donovan asked. He knew from the autopsy report that Chyna's mother shared with him that Chyna had lethal amounts of drugs in her system. He also knew that she would never take drugs, therefore her death was no accident.

"No, not yet, but I'm working on it."

"Let me know if I can be of any help. This has really been hard on Chyna's mother, as well as my family. Chyna was like a sister to me." Donovan still couldn't believe that someone had killed Chyna. This was all so surreal. Seemed like only yesterday when they were talking about her plans to open a boutique; now she was dead. It didn't make any sense. Chyna didn't have any enemies that he knew of.

"There is one thing, I was wondering why you had her funeral in Coco Beach?" Theo asked.

"Because neither I nor her mother wanted a media circus because of my fame. We knew that if we had the services in Manhattan every tabloid under the sun would be there trying to get pictures of me and my family, so we put together a low-key ceremony with only her close friends and family," he explained.

"Oh, I see."

People had started to get into their cars. Donovan looked over at his limo, where everyone was waiting for him. "Look, I gotta get going, but please call me the second you find out anything. And it doesn't matter if it's early in the morning or late at night. I'm anxious to find out the truth, so that we can all have some closure."

"Sure thing."

Theo watched as everyone piled into their cars and headed off toward the cemetery. Theo went back to her car. She didn't pull off right away; she took out a pad and jotted down some notes on what she observed. A young life had been snuffed out, and it was her job to find the culprit. There was a murderer running loose on Coco Beach, but not for long.

[26]

Liza and Remi were lounging poolside underneath a huge blue-and-white striped canvas umbrella, sipping Long Island Iced Teas and munching on finger sandwiches. Remi would've been at home relaxing by her own Olympic-sized pool, but the pool boy was there performing his weekly cleaning duties and she didn't want to get in his way.

"So what did Lars have to say for himself?" Liza asked, referring to Lars's indiscretion at the party. It had been nearly a week since the party, and she and Remi hadn't had a chance to talk about what happened and Liza wanted an update.

"When I finally got home from the party he was asleep, and when I woke up the next morning he was gone back to the city. He had an early morning surgery. I've called him, but I keep getting his voice mail." She hadn't spoken to her husband in a couple of days. She picked up her glass, placed the straw between her lips, and took a long sip of the ice-cold drink.

"So have you decided what you're going to do?"

Remi looked out at the aqua waters of the pool and thought for a minute. Lars and his bimbo were the furthest thing from her mind. She had other things to deal with. She still hadn't heard from Troy. They had crossed paths at the party, but didn't get a chance to talk. There were too many people around.

"I'm not leaving him, if that's what you mean. All couples go through rough patches, so I guess it's our turn now," Remi said, downplaying the incident.

"You call rolling around in the bed with another woman a rough patch?" Liza said, looking at Remi like she was crazy.

Remi bristled. She didn't like Liza's implying she was clueless. "No offense, Liza, but you've never been married, and don't know the complexities between a husband and wife."

"I don't have to be married to know that when a man cheats on me, it's over. O.V.E.R.!"

As the two women were bantering back and forth, Remi's cell phone rang. She snatched it off the glass-top table and looked at the caller ID. She didn't recognize the number and started to let the call go to voice mail, but she wanted the distraction. The con- versation with Liza was becoming irritating.

"Hello?" she barked into the tiny phone.

"Is this Remi Braxton?" a female voice asked.

"Yes, this is Mrs. Braxton. Who's calling?" she asked, using her upper echelon tone.

"Detective Pratt. I talked to you briefly the night of the party, but I have a few more questions for you. Can you come down to the station?" Theo asked, getting right to the point.

"What type of questions?"

"Just a few brief ones; it won't take long. I really don't want to get into this over the phone. Can I expect you in an hour?" Theo was direct and didn't plan on taking no for an answer.

Remi thought about putting the detective off, but she could tell by her tone that it wouldn't be a good idea. Besides, she didn't have anything to hide. "Make it two hours instead," Remi said, trying to exert her own authority.

"Okay, see you then," Theo said, and hung up.

"Who was that?" Liza asked, full of questions as usual.

"Detective Pratt. She wants me to come down to the station. She said that she has a few more questions to ask me."

"I swear that woman is a bulldog. She practically strong-armed me at the party, demanding that I stay on the yacht until she gave me the Spanish Inquisition."

"I guess she was only doing her job."

"You want me to go with you?" Liza offered.

Remi knew that Liza's offer was anything but genuine. Liza only wanted to go with her to be nosey, and nothing more. "No thanks. I'll be all right." Remi got up and gathered her belongings. "I'll call you later," she said before leaving.

Remi drove home, took a leisurely shower, and changed into a white-and-beige seersucker pantsuit, exchanging her straw tote for a tan Birkin bag. Her look was polished and sophisticated. She wanted to portray the image that she was an upstanding member of the community.

Instead of the convertible Thunderbird, Remi drove the more respectable four-door Benz. On the way to the station, she thought about the questions the detective might ask her—questions that she already had answered. That night on the yacht, Detective Pratt had asked Remi if she knew the victim, to which Remi had answered no. She also asked if Remi had seen anything out of the ordinary. Again Remi answered no. Remi didn't have any more details to add, and wondered why she was being called down to the station now. She started to call her attorney, but that would make her look like she had something to hide.

Before long, Remi was pulling into the parking lot. She was beginning to get nervous, and could feel her underarms getting moist. Remi kept telling herself that she had nothing to hide. She got out of the car, held her head up high, and strolled into the station.

"Mrs. Braxton to see Detective Pratt," she announced to the desk sergeant.

"Just a moment, ma'am." He picked up the desk phone and dialed Theo's extension. "A Mrs. Braxton is here to see ya. Oh, okay." He hung up and said to Remi, "She'll be right out to get ya. Have a seat on the bench."

He pointed to an old wooden bench that looked like it had seen better days.

"No, thank you. I prefer to stand," Remi said, turning her nose up at the relic of a seat.

A few minutes later, Theo came out into the waiting area. Remi noticed for the first time how attractive the detective was. That night on the yacht Remi had been too shaken up to pay much attention to the detective. Theo didn't look like a hardened cop. Her features were delicate and extremely feminine. She was tall and lean. Her hair was a little past her shoulders, and her complexion was flawless. With the right clothes and makeup, she could easily blend in with the upper-crusty ladies of Coco Beach.

"Please come back to my office," Theo told Remi.

Once they entered Theo's office, she shut the door. "Please, have a seat." She gestured to a brown leather and wood chair. "Would you like some water or maybe a glass of iced tea?" Theo offered.

Remi reluctantly sat down. "No, thank you. Over the phone, you said that you have more questions for me," Remi said, ready to get this unpleasant encounter over with.

Theo went behind her desk, sat down, and opened a file folder. She read over a few notes, and then looked up at Remi. "Someone heard you arguing with Reece Smart the night of the party. Is that true?"

Who the hell heard us? Remi wondered, and then remembered that when she busted Lars, she had left the door open. "Reece who?" she asked, pretending not to know the hussy's name. Remi knew exactly who Reece was. She had met her at Donovan's house.

"Reece Smart, Donovan Smart's sister, who is also the best friend of the deceased."

"Oh her. Yes, we had a few words, but nothing serious, just a misunderstanding." Remi thought about lying, but didn't want to put herself in a trick bag. Obviously someone had heard them talking, so really there was no use trying to lie her way out of it.

"What were you arguing about?" Theo asked, pinning Remi with a hard stare. Of course, Theo already knew what they were arguing about.

Remi sighed. "Detective, this is really embarrassing, but I caught my husband with Reece. I lost my head for a moment, until my husband calmed me down and told me that it was nothing."

"And you believed him?" Theo asked. She wasn't buying Remi's explanation.

Here she goes, sounding like Liza. "Why wouldn't I? He's never cheated on me before. He had too much to drink and got caught up in the moment. I've totally forgiven him." Remi put on a phony smile, trying to convince the detective that it was all a big misunderstanding.

"I see." Theo nodded. She then asked, "Have you spoken to Reece since?"

"No, I haven't," Remi answered quickly.

Theo had a hunch that Remi was holding something back, but she had no evidence to prove her theory so she didn't press the issue. "Okay. Thanks for coming down, Mrs. Braxton. That'll be all for now."

Remi was glad that this interview was over. She hated that someone had overheard her argument, but she was smart enough not to deny the truth. Being caught up in a lie during a murder investigation would make her look like a suspect, and Remi didn't want any fingers pointing her way.

[27]

After Remi left, Liza finished her cocktail and after an hour of lounging around eating and drinking, she began to get bored. Her thoughts drifted back to the kiss with Donovan. She had finally cracked his hard exterior and was getting her groove on when Remi interrupted them. Liza thought about calling him again, but didn't want to be sent to his voice mail, so she decided to pay him a pop visit instead. He had been feeling her that night, and she wanted to see if the chemistry between them was still there.

She left the pool side and went indoors. The coolness of the house was a stark contrast to the heat and humidity outdoors. The air conditioning felt good against her skin. Liza made her way through the solarium, up the winding staircase, and through the double doors of her bedroom suite. She peeled off her swimsuit and took a nice cool shower. Afterward, she changed into a black Ralph Lauren sundress and a pair of gold Roman sandals. Liza went back downstairs, grabbed her purse, left the house, and got in her car.

As she was driving up the entry to Donovan's estate, she saw a row of black limousines parked in the driveway, along with a host of other luxury cars. Liza then remembered that today was Donovan's friend's funeral. She thought about turning around and leaving, but the road was too tight for her to whip a U-turn, so she continued driving. The mood seemed somber, even on the outside. Liza knew that this wasn't the right time to proposition Donovan like she had planned. Even though she was horny, she wasn't heartless. *I'll pretend like I came by to offer my condolences*, she thought as she rang the bell.

A few moments later a uniformed maid opened the door. "Hello, miss. Come on in; everyone is in the parlor. Follow me."

Liza was surprised that the woman didn't even ask her name and had openly invited her into the house. Then it occurred to Liza that the repast must be taking place. *That's why all those cars are out front.* Liza was glad that she had worn black instead of a bright color. At least now it would seem as if she were indeed there to express her sympathy.

The maid opened the double doors to the parlor and Liza stepped inside. There was chamber music playing softly in the background, and people were talking in small groups. She glanced around and saw a host of unfamiliar faces. There was no one from the community. *These must all be Chyna's and Donovan's friends*, she thought.

As she stood there feeling totally out of place, a butler came up to her. "May I get you a drink?" he asked.

"Sure. I'll have a double shot of Patrón, rocks, with two limes." She wanted a stiff drink to help calm her nerves. The butler disappeared through the crowd.

Liza began shifting from one leg to the other. It wasn't often that she felt out of place, like now. *I think I should go.* She turned around to leave, and nearly bumped into Donovan's sister.

"Oh excuse me," Liza said, and braced herself. She remembered Reece from before and was ready for one of her smart remarks.

"No problem." Reece looked Liza up and down. "Hey, aren't you that chick who came by with the Miu Miu jeans on? And the one who helped Donnie throw the party?" Reece had been out of the house the few times Liza and Donovan met, and had only seen Liza twice. She had seen Liza at the party, but they never got a chance to talk.

"Yes. Liza Lord," she said, reintroducing herself.

Reece extended her hand. "I'm Reece."

Liza looked shocked. Reece was actually being civil. "I'm so sorry about your friend."

Reece looked down at the floor. She still couldn't believe that Chyna was dead. She partially blamed herself. Reece and Chyna had been talking about Lars, and Chyna got upset that Reece was seeing a married man. Chyna told her that she needed some air, and went out on the deck. Reece stayed behind and went to the bar instead. Now Reece couldn't help but think that if she had only followed Chyna outside, her friend would still be alive.

"Thanks. If you're here to see Donnie, he's in his office. He's so shaken up that he's not talking to many people."

"I probably shouldn't bother him."

"Naw, it's okay. I'm sure he won't mind. Come on. I'll show you the way," Reece said.

Liza followed Reece down a long hallway. She waited as Reece knocked on the door, and went inside. After a few minutes, she came out with a funny look on her face.

"Sorry, but he doesn't want to see anybody."

"Is he okay?" Liza asked, concerned.

"Naw. He's in there crying like a baby. Damn, this is really fucked up. Chyna's dead, and Donnie is falling apart." Reece was scared. Donovan had always been the rock of the family, someone that she counted on. Now he was a mess and she didn't know how to help him.

"Is there anything I can do?" Liza offered.

Reece shook her head. "Naw. Ain't nothing but time gonna make him feel better. I mean, I'm tore up too, but somebody's gotta keep it together." Reece was finally stepping up to the plate. Too bad it took Chyna's death to help her grow up.

Liza reached in her purse, took out a pen and pad, and wrote down her cell and home numbers. "Here, take my number. Don't hesitate to call me if you need anything. I'm right up the road."

Reece took the paper and put it in her pocket. "Thanks." She walked Liza out.

Liza got in her car and sat there for a moment. She still

couldn't believe how nicely Reece had behaved. The nasty-mouthed girl that she met a few weeks ago was now acting like an adult. Although Liza had been there to see Donovan, she was glad that she and Reece got a chance to talk. Getting close to his family was definitely one sure way to cozy up to Donovan. Liza decided to give him some time to grieve, but not too long. She was a woman with needs, and the sooner she satisfied them the better.

[28]

After Liza left, Reece went up to her bedroom. People were still downstairs in the parlor eating, drinking and sharing their personal stories about Chyna. Reece couldn't bear to listen to any more of them. She still felt guilty for leaving Chyna alone. Maybe if she hadn't been so self-centered, talking on and on about Lars, then Chyna would be alive today instead of buried six feet deep in some dark, cold grave.

Reece walked down the long, second-floor hallway, and when she neared Chyna's room, she slowed her gait, remembering the last conversation they'd had in that room. Chyna had warned Reece about using drugs. At the time Reece was being bullheaded and didn't want to hear Chyna's words of wisdom, but after Chyna's death Reece finally wised up.

The day after Chyna drowned, Reece quit taking Oxy. She went cold turkey and even cut out cocaine and champagne. The first few days without the drugs were really hard. She had night sweats and couldn't sleep. The daytime was equally as bad. She didn't have an appetite, was shaky, and worst of all, she couldn't even concentrate long enough to help Donovan with the funeral arrangements. Chyna was her best friend, and she couldn't even plan her home-going celebration. She felt lower than low.

Reece went to a doctor who gave her a prescription for methadone. Taken once a day, it was helping her cope with the Oxy withdrawal. She was determined to beat the hold that the drug had on her. Chyna had refocused her life and decided to become a businesswoman, and Reece knew that she could do the same. It was time for her to finally grow up and become a responsible adult.

Reece decided to honor Chyna by turning her life around. No more drugs or booze, and no affairs with married men. She was on the straight and narrow and was determined to make Chyna proud. Even if Chyna wasn't there in person, Reece knew without a doubt that Chyna was in heaven looking down on her.

Now that Chyna was gone, Reece regretted lashing out at her. She realized that Chyna had been trying to be a good friend by looking out for her. Reece couldn't have asked for a better friend. A tear slipped down her cheek, followed by an onslaught of waterworks. Reece went into Chyna's room, threw herself across the bed, and boohooed. She was never going to see Chyna again, and that sobering fact hurt her to the core.

[29]

Lars was back in the Hamptons. After he'd finished his work week, he went home, packed, jumped in his Jag, and fought the traffic on the Long Island Expressway on his way to Coco Beach. Remi had been surprised to see him (as usual), and didn't welcome him with open arms, but rather an uptight attitude. He didn't take her lack of enthusiasm to heart. He wasn't in town to see her anyway, but to hook up with Reece. He hadn't seen Reece since the party and he wanted to get laid. Lars knew that he'd have to contend with his wife and her annoying questions about getting busted with another woman, but he didn't care. All he cared about was getting in between Reece's slim thighs.

Lars told Remi that he was going to take a walk on the beach, planning to call Reece as soon as he left the house. He had called her on his way into town, but had gotten her voice mail. Lars was hoping to cook up a plan for this evening.

I'll take her to Nipit/Tuckit. *The yacht will be better than meeting at the town inn. Remi never goes near that boat, so it'll be safe*, Lars thought. He had no idea that his wife used their yacht for her own personal pleasures. The phrase "love boat" had definitely taken on a new meaning.

The more he thought about fucking Reece on the yacht, the more excited he became. He could feel his dick twitch at the thought of being inside her warm, wet canal. Lars took out his cell phone and dialed her number. After a few rings, she picked up.

"What up?" she spoke into the phone.

She was so unlike his stuck-up wife. Lars loved the homegirl in Reece. She was down to earth and didn't put on any pretenses. With Reece, he could say exactly what he wanted without the sugarcoating that he had to use with Remi.

"Hey, Reece. It's Lars. I'm here in Coco Beach and thought you could meet me on my yacht and finish what we started at the party," he said eagerly.

"Naw, that ain't happening."

"Why not?" Lars knew about the drowning, but he didn't know that the victim was Reece's best friend.

"'Cause my friend Chyna died that night, and since then, I'm trying to do the right thing. And that mean I ain't fucking around with married men no more," she told him.

"Oh, I'm sorry to hear about your friend. Since you're feeling down, I have the perfect thing to make you feel better," Lars said, referring to the OxyContin he had in his pocket. He had totally dismissed her claim of not screwing married men anymore.

"I ain't doing drugs either," Reece said, knowing exactly what he was getting at.

Damn! Lars thought. Based on how much Reece had enjoyed Oxy in the past, he had automatically assumed that she would have jumped at the chance to get high. He had one more trick up his sleeve. "I have a case of Cristal on the yacht. I'll order dinner from Café Coco, and we can chill out. I'm sure you could use a nice relaxing evening," he said, refusing to take no for an answer.

"I ain't drinking champagne either." Reece was determined to stay true to her word, even though Lars was making it hard for her to decline his offers. Sex, drugs, and champagne, three of her favorite things. However, Reece had made a promise to Chyna's spirit that she would straighten up and act right, and she wasn't about to go back on her commitment to getting her life in order.

"Oh, I see," Lars said, sounding defeated. He was trying to think of another ploy to lure Reece out, but she ended the conversation before he came up with another plan.

"Look, Lars, I gotta go," she said, and hung up.

Lars kicked his feet in the sand like a spoiled kid who hadn't gotten his way. He assumed that he would be getting Reece into bed tonight, but he was sadly mistaken. He put his phone in his pocket, turned around, and headed back home. When he walked through the sliding glass doors, Remi was sitting perched on one of the counter stools.

"Guess your little whore couldn't see you tonight, huh?" she said with a smirk on her face.

"What are you talking about, Remi?" Lars asked. He kicked his sand-covered shoes off, walked into the kitchen, opened the freezer, and took out a bottle of vodka. He knew that he would need something strong to help him deal with Remi and her accusations.

"You know damn well whom I'm talking about. Don't play dumb," Remi shot back. She and Lars had yet to talk about his indiscretion. He had left so early in the morning the day after the party that Remi didn't get to express her true feelings.

Lars took a glass out of the cabinet and poured himself a double shot of vodka. He turned the glass up to his mouth and downed the clear liquid in one swallow. He wanted a quick buzz to dull the pain of his wife's ranting. "Look, Remi, I told you at the party that it wasn't what you thought you saw. Reece and I were not making love. I had had too much to drink, and had fallen over onto the bed, and—"

Remi cut him off. "And you so happen to fall on top of her, I suppose?"

"Can't we forget it ever happened? Reece means nothing to me. So drop it," he said forcefully.

Remi rolled her eyes, and twisted her hand around in the air. "Whatever, Lars!"

Lars took a deep breath. He realized that trading words with Remi was useless. It was doing nothing but giving him a headache. "Honey," he said, lowering his tone, "can we please call a truce?"

"Yeah, Lars, whatever you say." Remi could've given Lars more grief, but she wasn't in the mood. Lars had caught her by surprise by popping up out of the blue. She had planned on calling Troy and seeing him, but now that plan was a wrap. All she could do now was go with the flow.

"Let's go out to dinner. I'm in the mood for the Chilean sea bass at Café Coco," he said, pouring himself another double shot.

"All right, let me go change. I'll call Liza and Michael and see if they want to join us." Remi wasn't in the mood to have dinner alone with Lars. She turned and left the kitchen. She wanted to look good in case she got a chance to see Troy.

Lars sat down and finished his drink. He was glad that Remi had dropped the Reece incident. Now that Reece was history, he needed to find a replacement—and soon. Unfortunately, sex with his wife was no longer thrilling, and one thing Lars thrived on was thrills. He took an OxyContin tablet out of his pocket, laid it on the counter, and crushed it with the back of a spoon. He scooped the powder up and poured it in his drink. Lars sipped the concoction and took a deep breath. The drug-and-vodka cocktail was exactly what he needed to ease the sting of losing his lover.

[30]

Business at Café Coco hadn't skipped a beat since the murder. The police were doing their best to keep the details of the homicide hush-hush. They didn't want to cause panic among the summer tourists and the local residents. Most people assumed that Chyna had drowned accidentally. They had no idea that she had been drugged and the OxyContin in her system caused her to become disoriented, which was probably when the killer took the opportunity to finish her off by attacking from behind and pushing her over the railing into the bay. The local newspaper didn't furnish very many details. The brief article merely stated that a woman had drowned. The mayor made sure that Chyna's death was downplayed. He didn't want to lose one penny of summer revenue. Besides, Coco Beach had a pristine image to uphold, and being associated with a murder wouldn't bode well for the island's reputation.

The dinner crowd was beginning to settle in. The bar area and the main dining room were alive with Saturday night energy. People were eating, drinking, and enjoying themselves. The younger set took up residence at the bar, with men trying to pick up women and vice-versa. The sound of ice rattling around in a martini shaker was background noise to the constant chatter of the guests. The silver shaker never stopped moving. As soon as the bartender shook up a cold one, somebody else would order another drink. And the more they drank, the friendlier everyone became.

With the kitchen staff under control, Troy took the opportunity to check on the patrons. His favorite part of owning the restaurant, aside from cooking, was meeting and greeting the customers. He was so personable, and made everyone feel like they were his special guest.

Troy's first stop was the meat market, a.k.a. the bar. He wanted to see if he could stir up any trouble. He was feeling randy and wanted a new play toy for the evening. He smiled and spoke to several people he knew as he made his way to the bartender.

"Hey, Joe, I'll have a Maker's Mark on the rocks," Troy said, nearly screaming over the loud noise.

"Coming right up, boss."

Troy stood back and scanned the crowd, but he didn't see any potential victims. Most of the women in the room he had either already slept with or had no interest in fucking. As Troy sipped his drink, he saw an unfamiliar face. He studied the guy from across the room. The man was tall, coffee-bean black, on the husky side, and was dressed in all black. From his attire, Troy could tell that the dude wasn't a regular on the island. The regulars abandoned Manhattan black in lieu of colorful summer colors, and when the islanders did wear black, it was in a lightweight fabric like cotton or linen. But this guy seemed to have on a knit top. *He must be burning up*, Troy thought.

Troy made his way over to greet the stranger. "Hey, man!" Troy smiled. "Welcome to Café Coco. I'm Troy Hamilton, the owner."

"Kalvin," he said, without a smile or a last name.

"Are you visiting the island on vacation?" Troy wanted to know who the stranger was who had infiltrated his playground. He didn't like competition.

"No, I'm not on vacation. I came to town for a funeral," Kalvin said, even though he had been in town since the party.

So that explains the all black, Troy thought. "Oh. Sorry for your loss. Let me buy you a drink," Troy offered.

"Thanks, man, but you don't have to do that," Kalvin told him.

"I know I don't have to, but I want to."

"In that case, I'll have a double-shot of Hennessy, straight up."

"No problem." Troy turned and made his way back to the bar.

Troy ordered the cognac, and as he waited for the bartender to pour the drink, he looked down the bar and saw the lady detective. Troy nervously ran his hand through his curly hair. Suddenly, he began to feel anxious. The last time he'd seen Theo at the station, she was less than friendly. Troy took a deep breath and walked toward her. He was going to take another stab at trying to win her over.

"Hey there, Detective," he said, his eyes lighting up. He looked at the half-empty drink sitting in front of her. "I see you're enjoying another glass of our homemade lemonade."

Theo looked up from her book. She was trying to read, but it was too noisy in the bar area. "Yes, I am," she simply said.

He signaled for the bartender. "Since you're almost finished, I insist on buying you another glass of lemonade. And I'm not taking no for an answer." He smiled a broad, charming smile.

Theo sighed. "All right, but can you send it over to my table in the dining room? I have a reservation. The bar is too crowded." She got up, leaving her drink on the counter and Troy standing there in her wake as she went over to the hostess.

A few minutes later, the hostess was seating Theo at a quiet table. Theo put the novel in her tote and glanced around the room. It was second nature for her to check out her surroundings. Sitting in a nearby booth was a group of elderly women, all dressed in jewel-toned dinner suits. They were drinking what appeared to be sherry, and chatting quietly.

Her eyes then landed on a choice table near the window, and there sat Dr. Lars Braxton and his wife, Remi. They were both staring off into space. Neither one was talking; there seemed to be an awkward tension between them. Theo turned her eyes toward the door, and in walked Liza Lord and her brother, Michael. They headed directly over to the Braxtons' table.

Liza leaned over and air-kissed Remi, then spoke to Lars. Her brother said his hellos and they both sat down. Lars summoned the waiter over and spoke to him briefly. The waiter disappeared, returning quickly with a bottle of wine. He poured Lars a sample, waited until he got the okay, and then poured glasses all around.

Remi's eyes wandered around the room and landed on Theo. Remi nodded a polite hello before turning her eyes away. She then excused herself from the table. Theo assumed that she was going to the ladies' room.

Everyone in the dining area was enjoying cocktails, wine, tea, or lemonade. Theo was getting thirsty watching them, and wondered where her drink was. She sat there for another five minutes, and as she was getting ready to call for her wait-person, a waitress came forward with a tall glass of lemonade on a silver tray. "Here's your drink, and a menu. Tonight's specials are listed on the right side. I'll be right back to take your order."

"Thank you." Theo took the menu and perused the specials. The lobster mac and cheese with truffle oil sounded delicious, as did the Chilean sea bass with garlic mashed potatoes and French string beans. Theo picked up her lemonade and drank it while she pondered the menu. She was torn between the mac and cheese and the pan-fried trout. The waitress was taking forever. By the time she came back, Theo had finished her drink and was ready for another one.

"Have you decided yet?" the waitress asked.

Theo looked at the menu again. She studied it for a moment, but the words were becoming blurry. She blinked her eyes, but the words were still fuzzy. She closed the menu. "I'll have the sea bass, and another glass of lemonade."

"Sure thing. Would you like to start with a salad?"

"Yes, I'll have a Caesar salad with extra croutons."

"Sure thing," the waitress said again.

I must be coming down with a summer cold, Theo thought. She was beginning to feel lightheaded. She looked in her tote for an aspirin, but she was all out. By the time the waitress brought the salad, Theo felt like she was going to pass out. She took one bite and stopped. The food seemed to be getting caught in her throat. She signaled for the waitress.

"Can you have my dinner wrapped up? I'm not feeling good. I have to go." Theo was feeling weaker by the second, and all she wanted to do was to go home and lie down.

"No problem," the waitress said, taking the salad away. "Do you still want the sea bass?"

Theo nodded her head yes. She didn't even feel like opening her mouth to talk.

Five minutes later, the waitress came back with a doggie bag and the check. Theo put down two twenties. Not wanting to wait for her change, she got up, leaving the waitress a handsome tip.

Her legs felt like limp noodles as she walked to the door. It took all she had not to pass out right there in the restaurant. As she walked through the parking lot to her car, her vision became more and more clouded. She pointed the car remote, unlocked the door, and fell inside. She was so weak that she could barely close the door.

What the hell is happening? was Theo's final thought as she slumped over the steering wheel.

[31]

"*Somebody help me! I need help!*" Troy yelled as he bolted through the double doors of the emergency room with Theo cradled in his arms.

A nurse rushed up to him. "Come this way," she said, hurrying over to an empty bed. "What happened?"

He gently lay Theo down. "I don't know. I found her passed out in her car," he said shakily. Troy was panicked, but at the same time was doing his best to remain calm.

The nurse lifted Theo's eyelids and looked at her pupils with a small flashlight. She checked her pulse, heart rate, and then touched her forearms and forehead. "Go get Dr. Richards, STAT," she barked to one of the orderlies.

"What's wrong with her?" Troy asked.

"I can't be sure, but it looks like a drug overdose. Her pupils are like pinpoints; her heart rate is weak; and her skin is cold and clammy."

Troy was shocked. Theo didn't seem like the type to use drugs. She was a cop, for God's sake!

"What seems to be the problem?" the doctor asked.

"Looks like a drug overdose," the nurse replied.

"Have you taken any blood yet?" asked the doctor.

"No, not yet."

"Let's get a blood sample. In the meantime, start an IV." The doctor turned to Troy. "You're going to have to wait outside in the waiting area."

Troy looked at Theo, who was still unconscious. She looked so helpless, and he didn't want to leave her side, but he knew that she was in good hands. "Oh, okay."

Troy was too anxious to sit down, so he paced back and forth. He then remembered that no one at the restaurant knew where he was. He had simply left the café to get his briefcase out of the car. He took out his cell phone and called the restaurant.

"Café Coco, Pam speaking. How may I help you?"

"Pam, it's Troy. I had to run out. I won't be back tonight, so tell the manager to close up."

She heard the urgent tone in his voice. "Is everything okay?"

"Yeah, everything is fine." He didn't want to get into any details since he really didn't know exactly what had happened.

"All right. Uh, Troy, why don't I come over tonight after work?" Pam suggested, remembering how he had rocked her world the last time they were together.

"Not tonight. I don't know what time I'm getting home."

"It doesn't matter. I can wait in my car until you get there. I don't mind," she said desperately.

"Not tonight," he said again, but this time more forcefully. "Talk to you later." He pressed the end call button and put the phone back in his pocket.

Troy continued pacing. He didn't know Theo well, but he was worried nevertheless. He started to call the police station and let them know that she had been taken to the hospital, but decided against it. He didn't want to get her into any trouble. If she was indeed using drugs, she could possibly get fired from the department. Troy wanted to talk to her first before he made any rash decisions.

After what seemed like hours when in actuality it had only been a few minutes, the doctor finally came into the waiting area and walked up to Troy.

"What relation is she to you?"

"My wife," Troy said quickly. He didn't want to chance not being able to see Theo. He knew that hospital staff were extremely guarded and didn't release information to mere acquaintances.

"We gave your wife an injection of Narcan. She had an overdose of OxyContin in her system, and the Narcan counteracts the effect of the drug. She's going to be fine. How long has your wife been taking OxyContin?"

This question threw Troy for a loop, but he was a quick thinker. "For about a month." He started to elaborate and say that Theo had had an accident and was prescribed the painkiller, but he didn't want to get caught up in too many lies.

The doctor looked at him sternly. "Did you know about her addiction?"

"She's not addicted. I'm sure she accidentally took too many pills, that's all. Can I see her now?" he asked, switching subjects, ready to end the inquest.

"Sure, right this way." The doctor led Troy down the hall and into a room.

Theo was sleeping peacefully. Troy tiptoed into the room and sat down in a chair beside her bed. He didn't want to wake her, so he sat quietly and watched her sleep.

Theo finally blinked and opened her eyes. She slowly looked around the room and saw the white walls, IVs, monitors, and a bed tray. Instantly she realized that she was lying in a hospital bed, but had no idea how she had gotten there.

"What—what happened?" she asked in a weak voice.

"I came out to the parking lot to get something out of my car and saw you passed out in your car. At first I thought that you'd had too much to drink. Then I remembered that you were only drinking lemonade. I tried to wake you up, but you were stone cold out of it. I didn't want to waste any time, so I carried you to my car and drove you to the emergency room," Troy told her.

She thought for a second. "It's sort of coming back to me. I remember eating my salad and suddenly starting to feel sick. My head started hurting, and then my vision became blurry. I remember asking for a doggie bag. I paid the bill, and when I was walking to the door, my legs became really, really weak. I could hardly make it to my car. The last thing I remember is opening the door and getting inside," Theo said, with a faraway look in her eyes.

"I found you slumped over the steering wheel. Luckily you hadn't locked the doors, so I was able to get you out in time."

"What do you mean 'in time'?" She looked puzzled. Theo was still feeling groggy and hadn't put two and two together yet. She didn't know that she had been drugged. She was thinking that maybe she had been brought to the hospital for food poisoning.

"The doctor said that you had an overdose of Oxy-Contin in your system. Did you accidentally take too many pills?" Troy asked softly. He didn't want to imply that she was a drug addict.

"*OxyContin!* Are you kidding me!?" she said, raising her voice. "I don't take drugs!"

"Then how do you explain it being in your bloodstream?" he asked, wondering if she was telling the truth.

"I don't know." Theo's head was cloudy and she couldn't think straight. She was quiet for a moment, trying her best to get her faculties together. "OxyContin. That's the same drug that was found in the murder victim," she said, more to herself than to Troy.

"Are you sure?"

"Of course I'm sure." Her senses were returning, and she was beginning to feel like herself again.

"Maybe you're getting too close to solving the crime and the perpetrator is trying to send you a message," Troy said, offering his assessment.

"Good point. I have been questioning a lot of people, and it stands to reason that the killer would also want me dead, thinking that would stop the investigation. Whoever did this obviously put the drug in my lemonade," she said, remembering that she had had two tall glasses of lemonade.

"I don't know how that's possible. I trust everyone on my staff," Troy said, getting a little defensive.

"I'm not saying that it's somebody who works at your restaurant. It could've been one of the guests. All it takes is a few seconds to slip a powdered substance into a drink. The lemonade could've been sitting at the bar waiting to be picked up by the server. The drink could have been left unattended for just a moment, plenty of time for somebody to come along and slip me a Mickey," Theo explained.

Troy nodded. "Yeah, that's true."

The doctor walked in, holding a chart in his hands. "How are you feeling?" he asked, looking at her intently.

"Much better," Theo said. "Doc, just so you know. I don't do drugs. Never have and never will. Somebody tried to kill me tonight," she said, clearing up any doubts in the doctor's mind. She then went on to explain what she had told Troy.

The doctor accepted her explanation and didn't see any reason to keep her overnight. "Since you're feeling better, your husband can take you home," he said.

"My husband?" Theo looked at him strangely.

Troy spoke up before she blew his story. "Yes, honey. I'll take you home now. Come on, let me help you," Troy said, walking over to the bed.

Theo didn't say a word. She followed his cue until the doctor left the room. "What was with the married act?"

"I knew that the hospital wouldn't release any information to an acquaintance, so I told the doctor you were my wife. Also, I didn't want them calling the station and possibly getting you into any trouble. At the time I didn't know if you were on drugs or not, so I thought it best to keep this to ourselves," he explained.

"Good thinking." Theo eased out of bed with Troy's help. "Can you hand me my clothes?"

"Sure. You need any help?"

She looked at him, and raised her eyebrow. "No thanks, I can manage."

"I'm not trying to get fresh. I'm just trying to help."

"I appreciate it, but like I said, I can manage." Theo went into the bathroom, and changed.

As they were walking to the car, Theo stumbled and Troy caught her.

"Are you okay?" he asked with genuine concern.

"I'm still feeling a little lightheaded."

"I don't think you should be alone tonight. I'm taking you to my place." Troy saw the skeptical look on Theo's face, and then said, "Don't worry. I have a guest room with a lock on the door. I'm not trying to get into bed with you. I'm only concerned about your safety."

Theo thought about it for a moment. She had to admit that she really didn't want to be alone tonight. Her head was still a little fuzzy. Besides, there was a lunatic on the loose who had tried to kill her. She wasn't one hundred percent yet, and until she was, being with another person was comforting, even if that person was Troy Hamilton.

[32]

"How do you take your coffee?" Troy asked Theo as she walked into his well-appointed kitchen the next morning wearing a pair of his cotton pajamas and a terrycloth robe.

Theo took a seat at the counter island. "Black, with a little half and half if you have it."

"Of course I have half and half. I hope you like French vanilla coffee beans," he said, pouring a mug full of the steaming brew. He opened the fridge, took out the cream, poured in a few drops, and handed her the mug.

Theo took a deep whiff, and sighed. "Oh, I love the smell of coffee, and French vanilla happens to be one of my favorite flavors."

"Good. I'm glad." Troy stood directly in front of her and stared as she drank her coffee. He couldn't believe the detective was actually in his house, wearing his pajamas. Talk about a pleasant turn of events. He wasn't glad that she had been assaulted, but rescuing her had worked out in his favor.

Theo peeked over her mug and caught Troy giving

her the eye. She began to feel uncomfortable. She put the coffee cup down and pulled the collar of the robe up around her neck. "Look, I'd better get going."

"Don't hurry off. I'm sure you're still weak from last night. I mean, you did have a lethal amount of drugs in your body. What you need is a good hearty breakfast," he said, moving over to the Viking stove. Now that he had softened her resolve, Troy wanted to get to know Theo better.

She took another sip of coffee. The truth was, Theo didn't want to leave yet. She was indeed still weak from the drugs and needed to collect herself before returning to work. She had called the station when she got up and told them that she was taking a sick day. Until she had some hard evidence, Theo planned to keep what happened last night to herself. She knew that the chief would be on her back, pressing her for answers. He was desperate to get this case wrapped up and so was she.

Theo had to laugh to herself. The one person whom she had shunned and been cold to had turned out to be her savior. Life was ironic that way. Troy hadn't tried to put the moves on her. Last night he had been a total gentleman, offering her a clean set of his PJs and the use of his comfortable guest room. He wasn't even full of useless conversation. He simply told her to yell for him if she needed anything. He then closed the bedroom door and let her get some rest. Now Theo looked at Troy totally differently. He wasn't the single-minded hound dog that she thought he was. He was turning out to be a pretty nice guy.

"I guess you're right. I am starving."

"What'll it be? Blueberry pancakes with honey smoked bacon or an everything omelet and home fries?"

"Hmm, they both sound delicious. How about the omelet and home fries?"

"Coming right up." Troy was in his element. He swung open the refrigerator and took out a carton of eggs, onions, green peppers, tomatoes, and cheese. He cradled the ingredients in his arms and carried them over to the counter. He then returned to the fridge and took out a wedge of Canadian bacon and a couple of potatoes. He started slicing and dicing and before long was plating up breakfast. He carried the two plates to the counter, set one in front of Theo, and sat down beside her with his own plate.

"Wow! This looks amazing," she exclaimed, glancing down at the perfectly folded omelet. "I haven't had a home-cooked breakfast in eons." Theo was good at solving crimes, but lacked any type of culinary skill. She even had a hard time making toast. She always burned it to a crisp.

"Thanks." Troy smiled.

They chowed down in silence. Theo finished every last bite. "That was delicious," she said, wiping the corners of her mouth with a napkin.

Troy got up and cleared the plates. "Thanks. I'm glad

you enjoyed it." He reached for the coffee pot and refreshed their mugs.

"Do you think I could get a reservation list? I want to see who had dinner at Café Coco last night," Theo said. Now that she had refueled, her brain was working properly again and she was ready to get back on the case.

"Sure, no problem. I can tell you that last night we basically had the regular crowd." Troy knew almost everyone who was at the restaurant. He thought about seeing Remi and her husband when they came in, but he wouldn't dare admit that Remi was his lover, or rather his ex-lover. Troy had decided that if he wanted to have a chance with Theo, he would have to sever all romantic ties to Remi.

"Since you know nearly everyone on the island, who do you think might be capable of poisoning somebody with drugs?"

Troy thought for a moment, quickly scanning the list of people he knew from the island in his mind. He shook his head. "Nobody. I can't think of a single person who could have done this."

"Are you sure?"

"Wait a minute. There was a strange guy in the restaurant last night. I've never seen him before. He said that he was here for a funeral," Troy told her.

"He must have been here for the victim's services. Did you get his name?"

"Uh, let me think…Kevin? No, that's not it. Keith? No." Troy scratched his head. "Kalvin. Yeah, that's it, his name was Kalvin."

"Did you get his last name?" Theo asked, now in full detective mode.

"No, I didn't."

"Wait a minute; let me go get my tote." She got up, rushed into the bedroom, and came back to the kitchen. She sat down, dug in her bag, and took out her notepad.

"What did he look like?"

"Tall and dark. He was on the husky side, and had a menacing look about him," Troy told her.

"Uhmm." She nodded, and jotted down his description. "Is there anything else you can remember?"

Troy thought for a moment. "He had on a fall-looking outfit, and wasn't very friendly. That's about it."

"Thanks, Troy; this is good. I need to go home and change. I have to pay somebody a visit. Now that I have a lead, I want to follow it up ASAP," she said, getting up from the table.

"No problem. Glad I could be of help."

Theo disappeared into the bathroom, took a quick shower, and was soon ready to leave. Troy was in the kitchen stacking the dishes in the dishwasher when she came back.

"You look refreshed," he said, admiring her beauty.

"Better than last night, I'm sure. And speaking of last night, Troy, I want to thank you again for saving my life. I owe you, and thanks for your hospitality," she said sincerely.

"My pleasure, and you don't owe me anything." He walked up close to her and put his hand on her shoulder.

"Be careful. The closer you get to solving this case, the more dangerous it's going to get."

Troy had a point. Whoever this psycho was, he wanted to stop her from finding out the truth. "Don't worry. I'll be careful. And you can best believe I'll be keeping a close eye on my beverages from now on." She chuckled, trying to make light of the situation. "Thanks again, Troy."

"No problem. Stop by the café this afternoon and I'll get that list to you."

"Okay, I will." And with that, Theo was out the door.

A few seconds later his doorbell rang. It was Theo.

"I forgot that my car is still in the parking lot at the restaurant. Can you give me a lift?"

Troy was so smitten with her that he had also forgotten. "Sure thing." He grabbed his keys, and they took off. Troy was elated that he had at least a few more minutes to spend with Theo, even if it was just a short drive. For the first time in a long while, he wanted to do more than fuck. Unlike the other women he had loved and left, he wanted to get to know Theo and possibly have a lasting relationship with her.

[33]

The mid-morning sun was shining brightly. It was another perfect day in the Hamptons. The murderer was feeling extremely chipper today. Last night had been a successful one. It wasn't hard to slip a healthy dose of OxyContin into that nosey detective's drink. With little prompting, the chatty waitress had disclosed that the detective had ordered a glass of lemonade. After the bartender poured the drink and set it on the service end of the bar, it was easy to unobtrusively drop in the crushed drug, which had been prepared earlier in the event an opportunity such as this arose. The timing was perfect! Almost as soon as the drink had been tainted, the waitress swooped it up and carried it off to the intended target.

The detective was getting too close to the truth and needed to be dealt with. From a vantage point across the room, it was easy to tell the drug was taking effect, and soon the detective was leaving the restaurant on wobbly legs. It would only be a matter of time until she passed out and died from the overdose. Then it would be good riddance. It couldn't be soon enough!

Although the murderer had been listening to the news all morning hoping to hear about the untimely death of one of Coco Beach's finest, nothing had been reported yet. They were probably keeping the news on the down low since that would be two deaths in less than a month.

Leaving to run errands, the murderer hopped in the car and promptly turned the radio to the news channel in case the story about the detective's death broke. But no such luck.

The murderer drove to the local market, parked, got out, and went inside to pick up a few items. It didn't take long, and soon the murderer was back in the car, with the radio on full blast. The news covered the usual stuff—the stock market, weather, and boring political news, but nothing about the death of that annoying detective.

After pulling out of the lot and waiting for the light to change, the murderer had planned on running more errands, but an unpleasant surprise changed that agenda.

"What the fuck?" Luckily the windows were up, and nobody heard the loud curse words or the beating of the steering wheel. The source of this angst was sitting in the car across the street.

Heading in the opposite direction was that nosey-ass detective being driven by Troy!

"She's supposed to be dead!" The murderer didn't understand how the detective was still alive. There had been enough drugs in her drink to kill a horse, but yet there she was chatting away like nothing had happened.

"I bet Troy helped her! Yeah, that has to be it!" The murderer was talking aloud as if someone else was in the car.

The light changed, and there was an immediate change of plans. Instead of running errands, the murderer headed back home to rethink what should happen next. The detective must know that someone had tried to poison her, and she would be on the case harder than ever, since it was now personal.

"Shit! I fucked up!"

And then there was an echo in the murderer's mind. "No you didn't. Now calm down and think of your next move."

With that thought in mind the murderer began to take deep breaths. Ms. Hotshot Detective may have won this round, but the game was far from over!

[34]

After Troy dropped Theo off at her car, she drove home, changed, and headed back out. She wanted to talk to Donovan, hoping that he could shed some light on this Kalvin person. Theo finally had a viable suspect, and she wanted to get as much information on him as possible so that she could bring him in for questioning.

Theo nearly sped along the long tree-lined driveway that led to Donovan's estate. The entrance to his home was impressive with its finely manicured lawns and beautifully arranged flower beds. But the opulence of his stately white mansion with Corinthian columns was lost on Theo. Her only concern at the moment was talking to the rapper.

She parked her Crown Victoria beside a highly polished black Bentley. Her dirty black car looked gray in comparison to the shiny luxury vehicle. Theo got out, went up to the door, and rang the bell.

"Good afternoon, miss. Can I help you?" asked the uniformed maid.

Theo took out her badge and flashed it. "Detective Pratt here to see Mr. Smart."

"Please step inside. I'll see if he's available." The maid left Theo standing in the marbled entranceway while she went to find her boss. A few minutes later she reappeared. "Please follow me."

Theo trailed the maid into a handsomely furnished library. The room had floor-to-ceiling bookcases on one wall filled with leather-bound books. The other three walls were covered with rich mahogany paneling. A huge, aqua-blue world globe balanced on a brass stand occupied one corner of the room, and a professional-looking telescope sat near the window. There was a handsome wooden desk facing the door, and two over-stuffed brown leather sofas facing each other in the center of the room.

"Have a seat. Mr. Smart will be with you momentarily," the maid said before exiting.

Theo didn't sit; instead she walked around the room, inspecting its contents. She ran her hand across a row of books and noticed that they were classics from the likes of Bronte, Dickens, Keats, and Shakespeare. She thought it odd that a rapper would have a literary collection of this magnitude.

"They belonged to the previous owner, who was an avid reader."

Theo swung around, and Donovan was standing in the doorway.

"I thought the books gave the room class, so I paid the owner a ton of cash to keep them," he explained, as if reading her mind.

"Yes, they do add a certain *je ne sais quoi*. However, I didn't come here to talk about your impressive library. I came to ask you a few questions," Theo said, getting right to the point.

Donovan entered the room and sat behind his massive desk. "Sure thing. Like I told you after the funeral, I'm here to help in any way that I can." Donovan had finally come out of his grief-induced depression, having realized that secluding himself in his office wasn't doing anybody any good. He knew that Chyna wouldn't want him crying his eyes out day and night. Besides, there was a killer on the loose, and he needed to pull himself together in order to help solve the crime.

Theo sat in one of the chairs facing him. "Does the name Kalvin ring a bell?"

"Hmm, Kalvin?" Donovan thought for a few seconds. "No, that name doesn't ring a bell. Does he have anything to do with her death?"

"I don't know yet; that's what I'm trying to find out."

"Maybe my sister knows him. She and Chyna were best friends and talked about everything, so if there's one person who might know, it'll be Reece." Donovan took out his cell phone and called his sister, who was somewhere on the estate.

"Yo, D, what up?" Reece asked after she picked up.

"Come to the library. I need to see you," he said urgently.

"Can it wait? I'm getting ready to have my first tennis lesson." Now that Reece had vowed to turn her life around, she decided to occupy her time with constructive activities to keep her mind off the drugs and booze.

"No, it can't. Detective Pratt is here, and she needs to ask you some questions about a friend of Chyna's," he told her.

"What friend?"

"Look, Reece, come inside and talk to the detective."

"Yeah, alright."

Five minutes later, Reece came bouncing into the room in her tennis whites. Donovan did a double-take. He was used to seeing his sister dressed like a homegirl in street clothes, but today she looked like she belonged to a country club, dressed in the proper tennis attire. Even her hair was tied back in a ponytail.

"Reece, this is Detective Pratt," Donovan said, making the introductions.

"I know. We met the night Chyna died, or should I say she interrogated me that night," Reece said, speaking her mind as usual.

"It wasn't an interrogation. I only asked you a few questions, like every other guest," Theo said, clarifying Reece's statement. "Do you know if Chyna had a friend named Kalvin?" Theo asked, getting right to the point and ignoring Reece's smart comment.

"I don't think so."

"Are you sure? Think hard, please, this is important," Theo said, probing.

Reece was quiet for a moment, and then said. "Wait a minute, yeah, now I remember her telling me about some dude named Kalvin who wanted to invest in her boutique, but she ended up kicking him to the curb."

"Do you know why?"

"She said that he tried to snatch the booty, but she wasn't having none of that so she drop-kicked him," Reece said in her colorful way.

By now Theo had her notepad out and was recording Reece's statement. "Do you know his last name?"

"Naw, she only called him by his first name."

"Do you know the last time Chyna saw him?"

"She thought that she saw him the night of the party, but she wasn't sure. She said that he had been stalking her. I had looked out in the parking area and saw a dude standing next to a Benz, but I don't know if that was him," Reece added.

"What type of Mercedes?" Theo asked.

"A black two-seater. It was hard to tell from where I was standing, but the car looked new. I'm into dope whips, that's why his car caught my eye," she explained.

Theo jotted down the information in her notepad. "Do you remember seeing a tall, dark, husky guy dressed in heavy clothing at the funeral?" Theo asked, recounting the description that Troy had given her.

Donovan wrinkled his brow in deep thought. "Wait a minute; I do remember seeing somebody dressed like that. It struck me as odd that someone would have on heavy clothing in this hot weather. I had never seen him before, but it didn't alarm me since I didn't know all of Chyna's friends."

"You think he killed her?" Reece asked.

"I don't know, but I plan to find out. He was at Café Coco last night. If he's still in town, I'll find him and bring him in for questioning." Theo put the notepad back in her tote and got up. "Thanks so much for your help."

Donovan also stood up. "No problem. Our priority is to bring Chyna's killer to justice, so feel free to drop by anytime."

"Yeah, we gotta catch that bastard!" Reece chimed in.

"Don't worry; we will. You can be sure of that," Theo assured them.

Donovan walked her to the door. "Thanks, Detective, and let me know your progress. Chyna was like a sister to me, and I won't rest until her killer is found."

"I feel the same way." Now that the murderer had tried to kill Theo, she had a personal interest in finding the perpetrator.

Although Theo had called in sick, she headed to the station. If this Kalvin guy was still in town, she needed to track him down before he left Coco Beach. She didn't have too many clues to follow, but she was resourceful and good at her job. If Kalvin was the killer, he would slip up—they always did—and Theo would be there to slap the cuffs on him.

[35]

Kalvin was still in town, trying to make sense of Chyna's death. He had come to Coco Beach the night of Donovan's yacht party after hearing about the party from a friend. He was well-connected and had finagled an invitation to the event of the season. He even wore the required white. His linen suit was tailor made, and his shoes were Italian. The only silver he wore was a Cartier diamond and platinum chain with matching bracelet. Kalvin loved designer clothes and expensive jewelry. Being a fast-money millionaire, he could more than afford the luxuries of life.

He had come to the party, hoping to get a chance to apologize to Chyna for making an ass out of himself at dinner. He knew that she didn't want to see him so he stayed in the shadows, trying to figure out a way to approach her without her going off on him like she had done before.

Kalvin had followed her nearly all night and saw her talking to several people. At one point, she was wandering around the boat as if she were looking for someone.

And then he had noticed that she looked relieved when she caught up with Donovan's sister. As Kalvin watched them have an intense conversation, it occurred to him how much they looked alike. Their features were similar, they even wore identical dresses, and their hair was styled basically the same. If he didn't know any better, he could've sworn that they were sisters.

After Chyna finished her conversation with Reece, she went out on the deck. Kalvin started to follow her, but got distracted by a woman who came up to him and wanted to dance. He tried to brush her off, but the woman insisted. She was drunk and talking loudly, so he reluctantly agreed instead of making a scene.

As soon as the song was over, Kalvin ditched his drunken dance partner and hurried off the dance floor. He had finally figured out what to say to Chyna so he set off to find her. She was still on the deck, but was talking to someone else. From where he stood, it looked like they were having a heated argument. Chyna was pointing her finger, as if she were upset. The other person seemed to be trying to remain calm, but Kalvin could see frustration registered all over the person's face. Kalvin didn't know the other person, and decided to go to the restroom until they finished their conversation.

By the time Kalvin returned, Chyna was nowhere in sight. He had searched the yacht for her, to no avail. Between the time when he'd gone to the bathroom and come back, Chyna had disappeared. He then heard someone yell, *"Somebody's in the water!"*

When Kalvin heard that gut-wrenching scream, his stomach sank. He had an eerie feeling that the person in the bay was Chyna. He had been around death so often in his life, and when someone he cared about died, he felt it in his soul.

That night, he didn't find out for certain whether Chyna had died. He got the official word a few days later, when news spread that Donovan Smart's sister's friend had drowned. He then thought back to the person he saw with Chyna out on the deck, and had a sneaking suspicion that that person was somehow responsible for Chyna's death. It didn't add up that a grown woman would fall over the railings of a yacht that was docked. It wasn't like the boat was out on the open seas and had hit some bad weather, causing her to lose her footing. The only other explanation was that the other person had pushed Chyna overboard, but the question was why?

Kalvin regretted not keeping a closer eye on her. Had he watched her every move, he would have been able to stop the murderer. Fortunately he had gotten a good look at the person whom Chyna had been talking to when she was out on the deck. Now he was doing some detective work of his own.

Kalvin had followed the person to Café Coco the night before and watched the suspect intently. The person was laughing and having a good time like nothing had ever happened. It was pissing him off that the killer wasn't acting remorseful, but was carrying on with life when Chyna's life had been snuffed out.

He started to go to the police with his suspicions, but he didn't have a good rapport with the law. Luckily, the night of the murder, he was able to slip off the boat before the cops arrived in order to avoid questioning. With his record, he knew that the police would be looking at him as a suspect, and he wanted to stay off their radar.

Kalvin had been extremely rude to Chyna, but he never got the chance to express his regret for acting like an ass. Now that she was gone, he felt the least he could do was to make sure the person responsible for her death paid, one way or the other. Kalvin was a thug and didn't think twice about taking the law into his own hands. He knew that the wealthy could buy their way out of mostly anything, including murder, and he wasn't about to let that happen.

Kalvin had been trailing his suspect all day. The morning started off early, and now he was sitting in his car across the street from the person's house waiting for the suspect to make another appearance.

He turned off the engine to conserve gas, since he was running low. He rolled down the windows, and before long he was sweating bullets in the summer heat. He had had one of his lackeys drive out to Coco Beach and bring him something to wear for the funeral, but the idiot brought winter clothes. Kalvin had been trailing the suspect so closely, that he hadn't had time to go shopping for more appropriate clothing.

I should've worn the linen suit from the party, he thought, wiping a thick coat of sweat from his wide forehead.

To take his mind off the heat, he took out his cell phone, switched to the game menu, and began playing an electronic version of Solitaire. But it didn't take long for him to become bored.

Kalvin looked across the street at the house. His first thought was to go up to the front door and confront the person. He had his ever-present Smith and Wesson strapped to his leg and was prepared for a possible altercation. He then reconsidered, thinking that a shootout in broad daylight wasn't the answer. If he needed to avenge Chyna's death, he would use another method like sneaking into the house in the wee hours of the morning, screwing on the silencer, and popping the person one time in the middle of the forehead.

As he sat there thinking of clever ways to commit murder, Kalvin realized that time was ticking by and it was getting later and later. He got tired of waiting around. Obviously the person was in for the evening, so he left.

As he drove to the Inn on Main Street, he had no idea that he was now being followed. He pulled into the parking space in front of the inn and got out. He walked inside, totally unaware that his every move was being studied.

[36]

As luck would have it, the detective gods were smiling down on Theo when she turned onto the main road after leaving Donovan's house; she spotted a black Mercedes two-seater. Theo used her expert tailing skills and dropped back two cars so she wouldn't be spotted as she followed him.

This was a town filled with luxury cars, and Theo couldn't automatically assume that the Benz belonged to Kalvin. To be one-hundred-percent certain, she trailed the car in order to get a read on the license plate.

The Mercedes pulled into the parking lot of a local market. Theo also pulled into the lot a few cars away and waited for the driver to get out, but no one did.

Theo dug into her tote, took out her shades, and put them on. She got out of the car, and discreetly walked to the entrance of the store. She went inside, grabbed a free newspaper that was sitting near the door, and waited for a few seconds before coming back out.

She walked toward the car, trying to see who was inside, but the windows were tinted. Theo couldn't see the driver, but she had a clear view of the plates. She made a mental note of the plate and quickly walked back to her car, where she took out her pad and wrote down the number. The identity of the car's owner wouldn't be a mystery much longer. With advanced technology, it would only be a matter of minutes before she found the information she needed.

She punched the plate number into her car's mobile data system, waited, and voilà…his name, address, and info on outstanding warrants or parking tickets appeared on the small screen.

"Kalvin Leroy Clarke," Theo said, reading his full name. He had no outstanding warrants, and his driver's license was clean. She read further and saw that he did have some prior offenses, nothing major though. Theo wanted to detain him right then and there and haul him in for questioning, but she didn't have just cause, at least not yet. The only thing she could do at this point was trail him and hope he did something careless, like run a red light.

Fifteen minutes later, the Benz pulled off, and Theo followed suit. There was a line of cars waiting at the exit for the light to change. As Theo waited, she thought it odd that Kalvin had driven into the market but hadn't gotten out of his car. She trailed him back out to the residential section of town, where the stately mansions were surrounded by exquisite acres of lawn. This was the same neighborhood where Donovan lived. Theo thought Kalvin was going to see the rapper since they both came from Brooklyn, but he suddenly pulled over and parked.

She looked ahead and saw that the car ahead of Kalvin's had pulled into the driveway of a palatial estate.

Looks like he's following somebody, Theo thought.

She hung back and parked a couple of cars down. She slouched down in the seat so her head wouldn't be visible if he looked into his rearview mirror.

Hours went by, and soon the sun was setting, casting beautiful shades of amber mixed with muted blues across the evening sky. The Benz finally pulled away. Theo waited a few seconds, revved up her engine, and followed him.

Kalvin drove back into town, parked in front of the Inn on Main Street, and went inside.

Obviously he's staying there.

Theo had partial information on Kalvin. But she didn't know why he had stayed after Chyna's funeral. He didn't seem like the Hamptons type, more like the Rikers Island type.

Theo sat in the car across the street from the inn, trying to figure out why Kalvin was following a prominent member of the community. It didn't make sense to her. And then she remembered Reece saying that he had been stalking Chyna.

This guy must have picked out a new victim.

Once Theo came up with a seemingly plausible explanation for why Kalvin was still in town, it made sense that he would be at the restaurant last night. He probably had followed his intended victim there.

"Oh shit!" she said aloud. Theo was so preoccupied following Kalvin that she'd forgotten to go by Café Coco earlier to pick up the reservation list. She didn't have Troy's cell number, so she called the restaurant.

"Hello, may I speak with Troy Hamilton?"

"I'm sorry, but he's gone for the day," said the hostess.

"Thanks," Theo said, sounding disappointed. She'd had a pleasant time with Troy and was kind of looking forward to seeing him again, even if it was only for a few minutes.

"Do you want to leave a message?"

"No, thank you." Theo thought about asking the hostess if he had left the reservation list, but she didn't want to raise any suspicions. The hostess might ask why she needed the list, since it wasn't a normal request. Theo found the best way to conduct an investigation was to remain low key and keep unnecessary people out of the mix.

She wanted the list, however, so she decided to go by his house since she knew where he lived. However, she didn't want to leave Kalvin unsupervised in case he decided to go back out and continue stalking his prey.

She called the station and ordered a car to sit outside the inn.

"Hey, Rodgers, it's Theo. I have a lead on the case." She quickly filled him in.

"Okay, I'm on it," he said, and hung up.

Theo waited until the car arrived, then took off. On the way over to Troy's, she began to get nervous, thinking he might not be at home, but then again, what if he was? Would he be alone? He was an eligible bachelor, and it was highly likely that he could be entertaining tonight. She didn't want to interrupt his groove.

She approached his block, turned the corner, and drove down his street. Theo saw Troy's car parked in the driveway, and she caught herself smiling at the thought of seeing him again.

Before she got out, she dug into her purse and retrieved a tube of lipstick. She flipped down the visor, looked into the mirror, and applied a thin coat of the pale pink color to her lips. She took her hair out of the ponytail and let it cascade over her shoulders. Troy had seen her look her worst last night, and now she wanted him to see a spruced-up version.

Satisfied with her quick transformation, she got out, locked the door, and made her way up the walk. Theo's palms were sweating as she reached for the doorbell. She felt like a nerdy teenager with a crush on the captain of the basketball team. Theo hadn't felt this way since she first met her ex-husband. Her feelings for Troy had done a complete one-eighty. The fact that he had saved her life was a major brownie point, and now she was drawn to him like a bee to a sunflower.

She rang the bell. Her heart was pounding loudly,

and felt like it was going to jump right out of her chest. A few seconds later, she heard footsteps approaching the door. Suddenly she got cotton mouthed and wanted to turn around and get back in the car, but it was too late to escape. Troy had opened the door and was standing in front of her with a huge grin painting his face.

[37]

Troy couldn't believe that Theo was standing on his porch. When she didn't show up at the restaurant to pick up the reservation list, he assumed that she had been too busy working to stop by. She seemed like the workaholic type. He recalled that during their initial meeting she was all business, and hadn't cracked a smile even when he had made a lame joke.

"Well, well, well, what did I do to deserve an evening visit?" Troy asked, smiling broadly from ear to ear.

Theo looked at his handsome face and admired his straight white teeth, which were so perfect that he could have been in an advertisement for toothpaste or invisible braces. She felt herself grinning, but stopped. Theo didn't want him thinking that she had fallen victim to his charms.

"I was tied up earlier and didn't get a chance to come by the restaurant to pick up the reservation list. I called, but was told that you had left. I figured I'd drop by and pick it up. That is, if you brought it home with you." It then occurred to Theo that Troy might have left the list at the restaurant. After all, what reason would he have to take it home? "You know what, I'll come by the restaurant tomorrow morning and get the list," she said, trying to cover up her faux pas. She turned to leave so as not to further embarrass herself.

"Wait a minute." He reached out and lightly touched her arm. "Don't leave. I brought it home, in case you dropped by." He stepped aside, allowing her to come in. Troy had actually brought the list as a lure, on the off chance that she called the restaurant after he had left. He'd hoped she'd drop by his house to pick it up. Troy silently thanked his lucky stars that his wish had come true.

"Great!" Theo said, with more enthusiasm than she intended.

"Are you hungry? I brought home takeout from the restaurant. How about some Chilean sea bass and garlic mashed potatoes?"

Theo hadn't eaten since breakfast and was starving. "That sounds delicious." She followed him into the kitchen and parked herself on the same stool where she had sat that morning, putting her purse on the granite countertop.

"How about a glass of wine?"

"Sure, why not? I'm off duty."

Troy brought over a bottle of chardonnay and two wine glasses and poured them each a glass. He clinked his glass to hers. "Here's to summer, the best season of the year."

"I'll drink to that. I love summer. But it's too short. By the time you get in the groove, fall is here, with winter waiting impatiently to storm in." Theo took a sip of wine. "Hmm, this is yummy. It's so rich and buttery." She swirled the wine around in her glass and took a sniff. "I smell hints of vanilla and pear."

"Wow! I'm impressed. You're absolutely right. Who knew you were a wine connoisseur?"

Theo blushed. "I'm not an expert, but I've spent some time in Napa and Sonoma Valley. I love the wine country. It's so relaxing. That's where I go to unwind. I usually spend at least two weeks there every year, sampling wine, lounging around in mud baths, and having massages." Theo omitted the fact that her first time in Sonoma was on her honeymoon. Her ex-husband was a wine nut and got her involved in the nuances of wine tasting.

Troy liked her more and more. Not only was she pretty, but she was smart and easy to talk to. He showed her the label on the bottle. "This is a French white that I picked up when I was in the south of France last summer." He went over to the stove and heated their dinner.

"That's one place that I've always wanted to go. I hear it's breathtaking."

"Yes, it is. And the quaint cafes in the countryside serve some of the best food you've ever tasted," he said, sounding like a true chef.

"Have you always wanted to be a chef?" Theo asked, curious to know more about Troy.

"Yes, for as long as I can remember. When I was young,

I would destroy my mother's kitchen trying to invent different recipes. I've always liked mixing ingredients and seeing what the outcome would be. I've had formal training, but the best dishes are the ones that I created. Like this Chilean sea bass dish," he said, presenting her with a plate and taking a seat next to her.

Theo tasted the fish; it melted in her mouth. "Oh my, that's really good."

"And it's simple to make. The basic ingredients are sea bass, shallots, plum tomatoes, and some seasoning. The dish wouldn't be complete without potatoes on the side."

"You make it sound like anyone could throw this dish together," she said, taking another bite.

"Anybody can. All it takes is the desire to want to cook. Cooking is all about love. You have to enjoy it; otherwise, it's a chore," he said, sounding quite passionate.

"I can't cook a lick. I can't even boil an egg without it coming out runny, or make toast without burning the bread." She laughed.

"Oh come on. You're not that bad, are you?"

"Yep. Worse!"

"Tell you what. I'll give you the recipe and even give you a demonstration, so you won't mess the dish up. I'll have you cooking in no time," he said, taking a bite of mashed potatoes.

"That'd be a miracle!"

As they were chatting, his cell phone rang. Troy started to ignore the phone, but he didn't want Theo thinking that he was avoiding some woman, a logical assumption when men didn't pick up their phones while in the company of another woman.

He looked at the caller ID before answering. "Hey there," he said.

"Hey, lover," Remi purred into the phone. "I saw you at the restaurant last night, and you sure looked good," she said.

"Oh yeah?" He had seen her *and* her husband, but didn't want to say that in front of Theo and have her think that he was talking to a married woman.

"Seeing you at the restaurant made me horny. Why don't I come over so you can scratch my itch?"

He looked at Theo, who was eating. "No. That's not a good idea."

"Why not? Don't you want to stick that big dick of yours in my tight pussy?"

"Sorry, but I won't be able to do that anymore," he said, making his response short and to the point.

"Why not?" she asked, sounding pissed. "The night of the party when I talked to you on the phone, you talked about grinding with me on the dance floor. Don't you remember?" she asked, trying to jog his memory.

"Yep. But that wasn't all that was said."

"Don't remind me," Remi said, thinking back to his comment about not fucking around with her while Lars was in town. "If you're worried about my husband, don't. I can handle him."

"I'm sure you can." He noticed that Theo was nearly

finished with her dinner, and he didn't want to be rude. "Sorry to cut the conversation short, but I have company," he said, hoping that she'd get the hint.

"So that's why I can't come over, because you're screwing somebody else?" Remi said with venom in her voice.

"You got it. Okay, have a good evening," he said and disconnected the call. Troy hoped his frankness was enough to get rid of Remi. Even though he had enjoyed their affair, he knew that it had to end, especially if he had any chance with Theo. Theo didn't seem like the type of woman who would tolerate infidelity. Troy didn't mind ending his fling with Remi; it had been only temporary anyway. Being a player was getting old, and he was ready to settle down. Theo was somebody he could see having a future with.

After they finished their dinner, Troy poured more wine and led Theo into the living room. He wanted to get a little more comfortable. The wine was loosening her up, and he was glad. When she had first come in, she seemed a bit uptight. Now she was laughing and enjoying herself.

Troy threw a few pillows from the sofa onto the floor and sat down. Theo followed suit.

"So, what made you want to become a cop?" he asked, crossing his legs Indian style.

"My dad was a detective, and growing up, I thought he was the coolest person I knew. He wore this black leather jacket, carried a gun, and caught bad guys. He was my superhero. So I guess you could say that I followed in his footsteps," she said, taking another sip of wine.

"Is he still on the force?"

"No, he retired a while back, but he'll always be a cop at heart. He calls me on a regular basis to get updates on my cases and to offer his advice, which I often take to heart."

As she was talking, Troy scooted a little closer, until his knee was touching hers. He didn't want to make any bold moves and scare her off, so he took it slowly. Theo wasn't just some chick he wanted to bang. There was something about her that was different from all the other women he had dated. For starters, she wasn't desperate, willing to take whatever he dished out, and he liked the challenge she presented.

Theo felt his leg rest against hers and wanted to melt. She hadn't been this close to a man in a long time. Sure she worked with men every day, but this wasn't the same thing. She was extremely attracted to Troy, even though she had tried to deny her feelings. Theo could feel a surge of heat rise up from her toes, filling her body with desire. The wine didn't help matters either; it was making her even hornier. She finished talking about her dad and looked down into her lap. She was afraid to look into Troy's eyes for fear she would fall under his spell.

The silence between them was heavy with lust, and they could both feel the tension. Troy decided to take his chances, so he leaned in and kissed her lightly on the lips.

Theo didn't object. She kissed him back.

This was exactly the signal he needed. Troy's kisses became deeper and deeper until his tongue was dancing with hers. He then eased her down onto the pillows and gently covered her body with his muscular frame. He pressed his rising cock against her groin and began slowly grinding.

Theo wanted to object, but her body was all too willing and not listening to her mind telling her to stop. She threw her arms around his neck and opened her legs, drawing him in closer.

Troy began unfastening her blouse, but before he could get to the goodies, he heard the faint ring of a cell phone. He knew it wasn't his because the ringtone was different. He continued working her buttons, hoping that she would ignore the phone, but no such luck.

"Wait a minute; I think I hear my phone." Theo got up and ran into the kitchen where she had left her purse.

A few minutes later she was back, and in a completely different mood. She had transformed back into cop mode. "That was one of my co-workers. I've got to go. We may have a break in the case."

Damn it! Troy thought, but remained cool. "Oh, all right."

Theo buttoned her blouse, straightened her clothes, and ran her hand through her hair. She glanced down at Troy, who was still lying on the floor. "Thanks for dinner. I really had a good time."

"Anytime. Too bad you have to leave so soon, but I understand." He stood up and walked her to the door.

Theo dashed to her car and was gone in a flash.

Troy stood in the doorway, watching the red taillights of her car disappear into the darkness. "Next time, Ms. Detective, you won't get away so easily," he said into the night air, looking forward to their next heated encounter.

[38]

After a day of running errands Lars was back home enjoying the pool, something he rarely had a chance to do. He had done a series of laps before settling into a comfortable recliner. Remi was also out running errands, and he thought about using this opportunity to call Reece. Their last conversation hadn't ended as he had liked and he wanted to give it one more try.

He got up, went inside, and took his cell phone out of his jeans pocket. Lars found her code name, Ray, in his contact list and hit the send button.

"What up?" Reece answered, using her typical ghetto greeting.

"Hey there, it's Lars," he said.

"Yeah, I know who it is. What up?" she asked again.

"I was calling to see how you're doing." Lars had a huge smile on his face, thinking about the possibility of fucking Reece.

"I'm alright." Reece wasn't giving up much conversation.

Lars noticed her dry tone. "Sounds like you could use some cheering up. How about I take you shopping? I'll pick you up in the morning, and we'll drive back to Manhattan. First we'll stop by Manolo Blahnik for some shoes, then Gucci for a new purse. From there we'll head over to Prada for a couple of outfits," Lars said, knowing that it was one hell of an offer, and she couldn't possibly refuse him now. He was no dummy; he knew all the right buttons to push to get her to say yes. Since the drugs and booze hadn't worked last time, he'd pulled out a major trump card. The shopping spree would cost him a bundle, but it would be worth every penny to get Reece back in the sack. She was one hell of a good lay and he was jonesing for her in a bad way.

"Damn, you got it like that?" she said, referring to the amount of money he was willing to spend on her.

Lars chuckled at her terminology. He found her slang amusing. "Taking you shopping will be my pleasure," he said with a smile on his face.

Reece sighed hard into the phone. "Man, you making it hard for a sistah to say no."

"Then don't. Come on; it'll be fun. Afterward, I'll take you to dinner wherever you want to go," he said, dangling one more carrot.

"As good as all that sounds, I gotta say no. I told you before that I ain't messin' around with married men no more. Chyna didn't want me fucking around with you. She told me so the night she died. She was upset that I had been sleeping with you, and now that she's gone, I gotta honor her last wishes. So the answer is no, I ain't going."

Damn that Chyna bitch! Lars thought. He was glad she was dead, but she still had a hold on Reece. And no matter what Lars tried, he couldn't break through. "If you don't want to go shopping, how about we go away on vacation? Have you ever been to Saint Barts?"

"No, I ain't been to no Saints Bart, whatever it's called. Look, Lars, I ain't going on yo boat. I ain't going shoppin', and I ain't going to no Saint whatever! I ain't going no place with you. Get it? What we had is over. Don't call me no mo!" she said forcefully and hung up in his face.

Lars stood stunned in the middle of the kitchen with the phone still up to his ear. No one had ever spoken to him like that before and it threw him for a loop. With all his money, he couldn't even buy the booty.

I need a drink, he thought, shaking his head. Lars set his phone on the counter, opened the freezer, and took out a chilled bottle of Grey Goose. He didn't bother getting a glass. He opened the top, tilted the bottle up to his mouth, and took a big gulp, followed by several more until he felt a buzz coming on. He wanted to take the sting of Reece's rejection away.

As he was drowning his sorrows, he heard Remi coming through the front door. Lars put the vodka back in the freezer, then took a bottle of Fiji water from the refrigerator and began to drink. He didn't want Remi seeing him drinking vodka straight from the bottle. She would have a fit. She was Ms. Manners, and detested when he drank from the orange juice carton. She could barely stomach him drinking from an individual bottle, let alone one that they shared.

He heard her heels clicking across the floor as she made her way to the kitchen.

"Hey there, how was your day?" Lars asked, trying to sound like everything was right with the world when in actuality, a piece of his world had just crumbled.

"It could've been better," she said, putting a bag of groceries on the counter.

"Sounds like you could use a drink. You want me to make you a martini?" he asked.

"Sure. Why not?"

Lars took the vodka back out of the freezer and a container of blue cheese-stuffed olives out of the fridge. He took the shaker off the shelf and filled it with ice, vodka, and a little olive juice. He shook the ingredients vigorously, taking his frustration out on the shaker. He retrieved two glasses from the freezer—they always kept martini glasses chilled and ready to use—and poured the dirty martini in the glasses, finishing the drinks off with three plump olives.

He handed Remi a drink. "Cheers," he said, clinking her glass.

Lars drank the martini quickly, as though he hadn't had alcohol only moments before. The buzz was mellowing him out, exactly what he needed in order to cope with his wife. His hectic work schedule had made him an absentee husband, and when he was free, she always seemed to have something else to do that didn't include him. Lars had gotten used to them living separate lives, and had used the time to cultivate outside relationships. At this point he and Remi were married in name only.

"How about I throw some steaks on the grill?" he said.

"Sure." Remi didn't feel like going out. She was in a foul mood; still mad at Troy for blowing her off over the phone, among other things.

Lars made another shakerful of martinis, then gathered the ingredients to grill their dinner. He was happy for the distraction; at least it would keep his mind off Reece.

An hour later, dinner was ready. He peeked through the glass sliding doors and called Remi outside. It was a nice, warm night, and he had set up dinner out on the patio.

Remi walked out and looked at the candles and place settings. "Everything looks nice." Lars had not only grilled steak, but thrown a couple of ears of corn on the grill along with some asparagus. She sat down and poured herself another martini from the shaker that was sitting in the middle of the table.

They ate in silence. The only sounds came from the chirping crickets and other nocturnal creatures.

Remi didn't feel like making small talk. She wanted to eat and then go to bed. Her day had been full of unexpected surprises, and she wanted to put an end to it as soon as possible. She picked up an asparagus spear and bit the tip off; she ate half of her steak, and all of the corn. "Thanks for cooking dinner. It was tasty." She got up, leaving her plate on the table. "I'm turning in early tonight. Good night."

Lars was still eating, but didn't mind her leaving him alone. "Okay. Good night."

Once she was gone, he polished off his meal and finished the rest of her steak. He then drained the last of the shaker contents. Lars was full to the brim and a little tipsy. He cleared the table, made another batch of martinis, and went back outside.

The pool was lit and the aqua water looked so inviting. He thought about taking another swim, but he was too full to make the effort so he sat in a lounge chair and gazed out at the water. He still couldn't get Reece's rejection out of his mind. She had been cold, and firm in her decision not to see him anymore.

Guess I'll have to find another lover, he thought as he sipped his drink. Lars knew that wouldn't be a problem, especially with the lure of money and drugs. Most of the girls he ran across at the clubs loved OxyContin, and he was more than willing to toss them a few pills in order to get into their panties. Lars knew using Oxy was a dangerous game, but he loved the thrill of living on the edge.

He polished off the pitcher of martinis, and before long had nodded off into a light sleep. Thirty minutes later Lars woke up and stumbled upstairs to stretch out in the comfort of his bed. Their bedroom door was closed, a sign that Remi didn't want to be disturbed. Sighing, he went down the hall to the guest room instead of crawling into a bed where he wasn't wanted.

Drunk from too many martinis, Lars fell into bed fully clothed. He immediately dozed off, and began snoring loudly. In his stupor, he had forgotten to lock the patio doors. Little did he know that his carelessness had created the perfect opportunity for murder!

[39]

Once Kalvin returned to the inn, he went directly up to his room. There was a quaint restaurant right off the lobby that specialized in seafood, but he wasn't in the mood to sit in a room full of strangers. Instead, he ordered room service along with a bottle of Hennessy. After dinner and a few drinks, he took a shower and went to bed. He was exhausted from driving around town all day following Chyna's murderer.

He settled underneath the crisp white sheets of the king-sized bed and quickly dozed off thanks to the booze. But his sleep was interrupted by a series of disturbing images, causing him to toss and turn uncontrollably.

In one dream, Chyna was having a heated argument with her assailant. They were on the deck of the yacht screaming back and forth at each other, trading one nasty word for another. From where he stood inside the boat, Kalvin could see that the argument was escalating, and he tried to make his way through the crowded dance floor to intercede, but before he could reach Chyna, she had been violently pushed overboard.

The next dream was even worse! Chyna was fighting for her life, flaying her arms in the dark waters of the bay, thrashing around, trying to keep her head above water. Kalvin was standing on the dock watching her struggle, but powerless to help as she called his name over and over again. He could clearly see her, but was paralyzed and couldn't move. *Kalvin! Help! Kalvin, please help me!* Chyna had said repeatedly, reaching out for him.

He woke up in a cold sweat with the sheets twisted around his body like a toga. Chyna's cries of distress were ringing in his ears, even after he was awake. Although it was only a dream, the vision of her struggling to stay alive was stamped in his mind's eye.

"Damn it!" he yelled and slammed the down pillow with his fist. Chyna had been murdered and the killer was walking around free without a care in the world.

The police don't seem to have a clue; either that or they are being paid off by the rich motherfucker, he thought.

Kalvin was getting madder by the second. Since the police were not concerned with her death, he had no choice but to avenge her murder. Although he and Chyna had gotten off on the wrong foot, Kalvin truly cared for her. The killer had ruined any chance at a future that he and Chyna could have had. Now it was time to get even.

He tore the sheets from around his body, got up, and put his clothes back on. Instead of strapping his gun to his leg like he normally did, Kalvin put the firearm in the waistband of his pants in case he needed to access it quickly.

Kalvin walked the two flights down to the lobby, which was quiet. The restaurant was closed and no one was around except the desk clerk, who was nodding. He went through the doors, clicking the remote to his car to unlock it. Kalvin got in, revved up the engine, backed out of the parking space, and drove back to the residential part of town where he had been earlier that day.

The winding roads were dark, with only the headlights from his car guiding the way as he sped toward his destination. Kalvin didn't know these roads and nearly drove over the edge a couple of times, but he was an experienced driver and was able to swerve to avoid hitting a tree.

When he neared the killer's house, he turned off the lights, slowed his pace, and parked near the corner. He got out of the car and quietly closed the door, but didn't lock the car. He didn't want the *beep-beep-beep* from the alarm to sound. He looked behind him several times as he crept down the block toward the house.

This area of town wasn't brightly lit like downtown, and he welcomed the cover of darkness. Dressed in all black, he blended in with the night perfectly.

Kalvin was soon upon the house, and his heart began to beat a little faster. He stood behind a tree across the street and peeped out at the house. From where he stood, he didn't see any lights on inside. It was late, and he assumed that the person inside was fast asleep.

He looked up and down the street, making sure that the coast was clear before he dashed out. There were no cars driving by, and no signs of life. Kalvin quickly walked across the street, went directly to the side of the house, crouched down, and crept along the side until he reached the back. There was a wrought-iron gate, but fortunately it wasn't locked. He entered the backyard, which was massive, with an in-ground, Olympic-sized pool, huge electric grill, and exquisite lawn furniture. The pool was lit, and the cerulean water looked inviting. Kalvin admired the pool, but hated the fact that the lights caused him to cast his large shadow. He crouched down even lower, until his knees were almost touching the ground.

Kalvin made his way to the sliding glass doors, praying that they were unlocked. His heart was beating wildly as he put his hand on the door and tried to slide it open. *Bingo!* he thought as the door slid open. Kalvin waited for an alarm to sound before entering, but there wasn't one. He couldn't believe how careless some rich people were, as if their community was too exclusive to be invaded.

He crawled inside, closed the door behind him, and looked around. Though it was dark inside, the light from the pool illuminated enough of the room for him to see that the kitchen was top of the line. The appliances were stainless steel, and the countertops were black marble.

Kalvin stood up and eased his body along the wall

until he reached the doorway to the living room. He peeped around the corner of the wall and looked in the humongous living room; no one was there.

They must be asleep, he thought.

There was a wide staircase that curved in a semi-circle, leading upstairs. He took two steps at a time, quickly arriving at the top. He looked down the long hallway, and couldn't decide which way to go. There was no light peeking from underneath any of the doors. He decided to go to the right.

Taking the gun out of his waistband, Kalvin released the safety and tiptoed down the hall. He turned the knob on the first door that he came to and gently opened it, but it was a powder room. He closed the door, and continued searching for his suspect.

Kalvin opened door number two, but it was a linen closet.

This must be the bedroom, he thought as he came to door number three. He turned the knob, peeped inside, and sure enough someone was in bed sleeping. He raised his gun, and eased toward the bed.

He stood at the foot of the bed, where his suspect's head was nearly hanging over. Kalvin began to squeeze the trigger, ready to blow the guy's brains out right then and there, but he wanted some answers.

Kalvin poked the side of Lars's temple with the gun, but Lars didn't move. He poked him a little harder, but he still didn't budge. Lars began snoring louder, totally oblivious to the fact that his life was in grave danger.

"Wake up, motherfucker!" Kalvin leaned down and said into Lars's ear.

Still no movement.

Kalvin exhaled. If he hadn't wanted to question Lars so badly, he would have shot him in his sleep. But he had to know why Lars had pushed Chyna overboard.

"I said, wake the fuck up!"

This time, Lars blinked his eyes open. There was a stranger standing over him. Lars thought that he was dreaming. He blinked again, but the image didn't go away.

"Who the hell are you?" Lars asked, trying to sit up.

Kalvin pushed him. "Lay the fuck back down."

"What do you want? If it's money, all I have is a few thousand dollars."

"I don't want your damn money. I wanna know why you killed Chyna."

"What? What are you talking about?" Lars asked with a puzzled expression on his face.

"Don't play dumb with me, asshole." Kalvin raised his gun and pointed it directly at Lars's head. "Tell me now, or I'ma blow your fucking brains out!"

"Stop! Police! Drop your weapon!"

Suddenly the lights came on. Kalvin looked over his shoulder and saw a female cop dressed in plainclothes, and a team of uniformed cops standing next to her.

"I said, drop your weapon!" Theo repeated.

Kalvin eased the gun down on the bed and put his hands in the air. He knew the routine all too well.

The uniformed police ambushed him, threw him on the bed, bound his wrists with plastic restraints, and then read Kalvin his rights.

"Are you all right?" Theo asked Lars.

"Yeah," he said, watching the cop haul away the intruder.

By now Remi had rushed into the room. "What happened? Who is that man?" she asked, pointing at Kalvin.

"He came through the back door. We won't know what he was doing here until we question him," Theo told her.

Lars stood up. "Do you need for us to come down to the station?"

"Yes. I'm sure you'll want to press charges," Theo said.

"We sure do!" Remi chimed in. "We'll be right there after I put on some clothes." She turned to leave the room, and then turned back. "Do you think that man had something to do with the yacht murder? I'll bet he's the killer and is terrorizing the island," she said.

"I don't know, but I plan to find out," Theo said, and left.

Theo had gotten the call that Kalvin's car was gone. The cop watching him had dozed off, but woke up in time to see Kalvin drive away. He tailed Kalvin, making sure to stay a good length behind and calling for backup en route. Theo and her crew were a few minutes behind the officer. But thankfully, they arrived in time to prevent another killing. Theo had her man.

[40]

Adrenaline was pumping through Theo's veins as though someone had given her a hit of speed. She had caught Kalvin in the act with a gun in his hand, ready to unload a deadly bullet directly into Lars's skull. Luckily for Lars, Theo and her backup had arrived in time to save his life and possibly his wife's, too.

This was the break in the case that Theo had been looking for, except she hadn't thought it would come wrapped up so neatly, the suspect poised with the weapon in his hand and his finger on the trigger. Even though it seemed cut and dried, Theo had to question Kalvin nonetheless, and hopefully extract a confession. She was eager to put this case to bed and ease the minds of the residents of Coco Beach, and also to get her boss off her back.

As Kalvin was being processed, Theo was at her desk with the case notes spread out in front of her. She perused them for the umpteenth time. She knew the facts of the case inside and out, but there were still some missing pieces to the puzzle, and she hoped that Kalvin held those pieces.

She picked up the phone and hit the speed dial to the front desk.

"Hey, Hank, it's Theo. Is Kalvin Clarke processed yet?" she asked the desk sergeant.

"Yep. He's in the interrogation room with Rodgers. They're waiting for you."

"Thanks, I'll be right there." Theo hung up, gathered her notes in the folder, and headed out of her office. She walked briskly down the corridor, stopped at the two-way mirror, and peered into the dull-gray interrogation room.

Kalvin was sitting at a metal table with his hands secured behind his back with plastic restraints. He was looking straight ahead with no expression registered on his face. Theo tried to get a read on him before she entered the room so that she could plan her strategy better, but Kalvin was a blank slate. He sat erect with his shoulders squared back and his legs cocked slightly open. His body language was that of a confident man who didn't have a care in the world, instead of an attempted murder suspect who had been caught in the act.

Theo inhaled and exhaled hard. She turned the knob and walked into the room.

"Rodgers, how's it going?" she asked her fellow detective.

"He's not talking. Says he wants to wait for the boss, and since the chief isn't here, you're next in line," Rodgers told her.

Theo sat in the silver metal chair next to Rodgers, scooted close to the table, and looked directly into Kalvin's eyes. "So, Mr. Clarke, you wanted to talk to me?"

He nodded his head and said, in a deep voice, "Yeah."

"So, you're going to tell me why you killed Chyna, and why you were getting ready to pump a bullet into Lars Braxton," Theo said, taking the direct approach.

"I ain't kill Chyna! That bastard did; that's why I was about to off his ass," he spat out with venom in his voice.

"And how do you know that?" Theo asked calmly.

"Cuz I saw his ass arguing with her out on the deck of the yacht the night of the party."

"Having a disagreement with someone is a far cry from killing them," Theo said.

"Yeah, I know that, I ain't stupid. But the dude was giving her the look of death as they traded words. I been around the streets a long time, and I know when someone is pissed enough to kill. Let me tell you, that Lars dude had murder written all over his face. Chyna must've said something to set him off, cuz he was mad as hell."

"Do you know what they were arguing about?"

"Naw. I couldn't hear from where I was standing. But trust me, whatever they was talking about was serious. I could tell that by their body language."

"Okay, but what makes you think that Dr. Braxton pushed her overboard?" Theo said, challenging his claim.

"Look, I didn't see him push her, but my gut is telling me that he's responsible for her murder. I watched their argument, but ran to the bathroom for no longer than a few minutes. When I came back, Chyna was missing, and that dude was nowhere in sight," he said, raising his voice.

Theo could see that he was passionate about what he was saying, and it made her wonder about his connection to Chyna. "So tell me, how do you know the victim?"

Kalvin held his head down for a second. He was still embarrassed about the way he had treated Chyna, and wished with all of his heart that he could change the way he had behaved. "I know her from around the way," he said, purposely omitting the fact that she had come to him to finance her boutique. Kalvin didn't want the cops digging into his business, so he gave limited information.

"You know her from the neighborhood?" Theo asked, trying to get clarification.

"Yeah, we're both from Brooklyn."

"Did she invite you to the party?"

"Yeah, I was her guest," Kalvin lied. He didn't want to admit that he had come to the party to apologize to Chyna. He knew that his past behavior would paint him as a suspect, and he wanted the police to focus on the real killer and not him.

Theo didn't say a word, just nodded. She was digesting what Kalvin was saying, trying to make sense of it all.

Kalvin looked at Theo and could see that she didn't quite believe his story. After all, why should she? He was the one caught with the gun, getting ready to blow someone's head off. "Look, I know you don't believe me, but you need to ask that dude why he was arguing with Chyna."

Theo thought back to her previous conversation with Lars. She had asked him if he knew Chyna and he told her no. Now Theo wondered why he had lied. Obviously, Lars had something to hide. "Yes, I will speak to him. However, I'm not finished with you yet," she said, pinning him with a death stare. "So you were going to kill Lars as retaliation?"

"Hell, yeah! His ass was walking around like he ain't done nothing. And he needs to pay for what he did," Kalvin said with certainty.

"Okay, you need to calm down, Mr. Clarke. Whether or not Dr. Braxton killed Chyna, it isn't your responsibility to avenge her murder. You can't go around taking the law into your own hands."

"I had to, cuz y'all wasn't doing nothing," he shot back.

"Mr. Clarke, you are not privy to our investigation, so you don't know what progress we've made on the case," Theo said, setting him straight.

He shrugged his shoulders. "Yeah, whatever."

"I suggest you call your attorney, Mr. Clarke. Even if you're not Chyna's killer, breaking and entering, and attempted murder are crimes," she said.

Theo had heard enough. She got up and left the room. Once back in her office, she couldn't help but wonder why Lars had lied about knowing Chyna. If he lied about that, there was no telling what else he was hiding. Lars and his wife were coming into the station to press charges against Kalvin, and Theo planned to have a nice chat with the good doctor.

[41]

Lars was still shaken from having his life threatened by an intruder. He had been so wasted from the martinis that when he fell into bed, he'd drifted off into a deep sleep. At first Lars thought he was dreaming when he woke up to the barrel of a gun, but the man pointing the weapon in his face was no mirage. He was as real as they come. Lars didn't recognize the gunman and had no idea why he was the target of a killer. However, he planned to find out once they went down to the police station.

Lars had fallen asleep in his clothes, so he didn't bother to change. He went into the bathroom, splashed some cold water on his face to help wake up, and went downstairs to wait for Remi. While he waited, he made a pot of coffee to further aid his sobering. Soon the coffee had finished brewing, and he was on his second cup, but his wife hadn't come downstairs yet.

"What the hell is taking her so long?" he said aloud. He was ready to go and was getting antsy.

Lars made his way out of the kitchen and was heading

upstairs to find Remi when she appeared at the top of the staircase looking like a million bucks. She had on a white Juicy Couture jogging suit, a pair of silver sequined sneakers, and was dripping in diamonds from her ears to her wrist. Her short hair was styled to perfection, and her makeup was flawless. She could have easily done a quick wardrobe change into an evening dress, and been ready to attend a black-tie affair.

"Why are you so dolled up?" Lars wanted to know.

"I'm not dolled up. I only have on a jogging suit," she said, shrugging her shoulders.

"A jogging suit and a million dollars' worth of jewelry, not to mention your hair and makeup look amazing," Lars said, blown away by her transformation. At dinner, her face had a shine from the humidity; her hair was hidden underneath a plaid Burberry scarf; and she looked tired from running around all day. Now she was refreshed, as if they were going to a friend's house for dinner instead of to the police station.

"Thank you. I want to show that Detective What's-Her-Name that we are upstanding members of the community with means, and not some run-of-the-mill commoners," Remi said, as she made her way down the stairs.

"I don't think she'll have a problem recognizing our net worth, since you're wearing enough precious jewelry to give Elizabeth Taylor a run for her money." Lars chucked and shook his head. No matter how much wealth they attained, Remi was always trying hard to prove that she wasn't poor any longer. Unlike Liza, who had old family money and was secure in her wealth, Remi clung tightly to her status like it would be snatched away at any given moment.

Remi ignored his comment, walked to the door, and said, "Let's go."

Lars's Mercedes was parked in the driveway. He opened the door for his wife, helped her inside, went around to the driver's side, and got in.

He cruised toward town, all the while wondering why a stranger had broken into their house.

Maybe word got out that I have OxyContin, and the burglar was looking for drugs, Lars thought. No sooner had that thought left his mind than another one entered. *Maybe that detective knows about me dispensing drugs without a prescription!*

Lars's palms began to get clammy as he considered this possibility. He took a deep breath and tried to remain calm. Lars then realized that if the cops knew about his illegal drug activities, they would have arrested him right along with the intruder.

I have nothing to worry about, he told himself as they neared the police station.

Lars pulled into the lot, and he and Remi got out. They walked inside the small building and Lars approached the desk sergeant.

"Dr. and Mrs. Braxton to see Detective, uh, uh…" Suddenly Theo's last name escaped him.

"Detective Pratt," the sergeant said, completing Lars's

sentence. "Wait right over there." He pointed to the same wooden bench that Remi had shunned before.

"No thank you, we prefer to stand," Remi said, again refusing to sit on the relic.

After a few minutes, Theo came out and led them back to her office. She shut the door and offered them a seat. After they were all seated—Theo behind her desk, with Lars and Remi in front of her, Theo began speaking.

"Dr. Braxton, why did you lie about knowing Chyna Jones?" she asked, staring directly at Lars, daring him to lie *again*.

Oh shit! Lars was caught totally off-guard. He hadn't expected to be blindsided with a loaded question. He thought that they were coming to the station to press charges, not to be investigated. Lars started to again deny knowing Chyna, but he took one look at the detective's face and knew that he had better come clean. The only problem was that his wife was sitting next to him, and he didn't want Remi to hear what he was about to say.

"Can we speak privately?" Lars asked Theo in a low voice, as if Remi wasn't there.

"I'm not going any damn where! Whatever you have to say, you can say it right in front of me. I already know about your tacky affair, so what else do you have to hide?" Remi said, blasting Lars with a mouthful.

"Dr. Braxton, how do you know the victim?" Theo asked again.

"Technically, I didn't know her. We only met the night of the party. She came up to me when I was out on the deck getting some air."

"What did you two talk about?" Theo asked. She wanted Lars to know that she knew about their heated conversation so he wouldn't try to backpedal his way out of telling her the truth.

"Basically, she told me to leave Reece alone," he said, giving her the abbreviated version.

"Really? Is that all?" Theo asked, not buying his short answer.

"Yes." Lars omitted the fact that Chyna had threatened to turn him in to the police for giving Reece Oxy without a prescription. He'd tried to deny any involvement with drugs, but Chyna wouldn't let up. Their conversation became heated, with Lars lying through his teeth. Finally he walked off, leaving her standing on the deck.

"I've heard enough! I'm going home. Lars, take a taxi home, or better yet, call your girlfriend to come and pick you up," Remi said, and stormed out.

Theo and Lars watched her leave. Lars was actually relieved that his wife had gone. He was sure that hearing about Reece and Chyna was bringing up unpleasant thoughts for her, and he wanted to spare her more embarrassment.

"Okay, now that your wife is gone, you want to tell me what really went down out on the deck between you and Chyna?" Theo said, leaning on the desk with her elbows.

"I told you, we argued about me and Reece." Lars was determined to stick to his story. Chyna was dead, and nobody else had heard their conversation, so he had nothing to worry about.

Theo flipped through her notes, studied them for a moment, and then turned her eyes back to Lars. "Didn't you two argue about drugs? OxyContin, to be precise?"

Holy shit! *How does she know about that? It must be in her notes somewhere. I bet somebody overheard us after all!* Lars thought. His palms began sweating again, and he could feel the perspiration spreading all over his body.

Theo took one look at him and knew that she had him on the hot seat. He was visibly nervous, exactly the response she was going for. Now all she had to do was press him into confessing. "Well, Dr. Braxton? Is this true or not?"

Lars hung his head in shame. He had taken a solemn oath to help heal the sick, but he had abused his profession for his own pleasure. "Yes, it's true, we argued about me supplying Reece with OxyContin," he said, in a small voice.

Bingo! Theo wanted to shout. She had bluffed Lars into thinking that she had notes on his conversation with Chyna, when she had actually been reading an interview with another guest that had nothing to do with their conversation. He'd bought her ruse without question.

"So you were giving her drugs without a prescription?" she asked, making sure she had the story right. Theo had set her tape recorder before Lars and Remi entered her office and had been taping their entire conversation to use as evidence.

"Yes."

"Did you also slip Chyna an overdose? Trying to shut her up, and keep her from telling your dirty little secret?" she said, surmising his motivation for murder.

"No!" Lars jumped to his feet. "I didn't kill Chyna!!"

"Please sit down, Dr. Braxton." Theo hit the intercom button on her desk, and called Rodgers into her office.

"Rodgers, book Dr. Braxton on one count of homicide."

Rodgers began reading Lars his rights, at the same time putting the customary plastic restraints on his wrists. He led Lars out of Theo's office, without a fuss. Lars was stunned into silence. He couldn't believe that he was being booked on murder.

Once they were gone, Theo leaned back in her chair and breathed a sigh of relief. She wrote up a briefing for the chief to get him up to speed on the recent events. She had thought about calling him at home, but it was late. Besides, there was nothing he could do at this point.

Although Lars had denied killing Chyna, Theo wasn't buying his version of what happened. Like the little boy who cried wolf, Lars had lied so many times, and now no one believed his story. Least of all her.

[42]

Theo was on a natural high. Catching the murderer had her feeling totally elated. After Lars was booked, Theo cleared her desk and headed home. She could barely sleep from the adrenaline coursing through her veins, and was up bright and early the next day. Her first order of business was to call Donovan and tell him the good news.

She reached for her cell phone, looked through her recent call list, and found his number.

"Hello?" Donovan said in a groggy voice, answering on the fourth ring.

"Good morning, this is Detective Pratt. Sorry to wake you so early, but I have some excellent news!" she said, sounding excited.

"I hope you're calling to tell me that you caught Chyna's killer."

"That's exactly why I'm calling. Last night, in a twisted turn of events, we arrested her suspected killer," Theo said, giving him the abbreviated version of what happened, leaving out the detail about catching Kalvin trying to blow Lars's head off, and the identity of the murder suspect.

"What do you mean 'suspected killer'? Sounds like you're unsure that it's the right person," Donovan said, quizzing her.

"I'm sure it's the right person. However, he hasn't confessed. But he had motive and opportunity. This morning I'm going to issue a search warrant for both of his homes as well as his office. I'm sure we'll turn up some hard evidence that will aid in convicting him." Theo hoped to find the OxyContin that had killed Chyna. There were different strengths of the drug, and she hoped that the strength found in Chyna's blood-stream would match up with what Lars had. Since he had admitted to giving Reece Oxy without a prescription, Theo was certain that he had loose pills at home. She planned on finding them and sending them straight to the lab. If the findings came back as a match, that would be one more nail in Lars's coffin.

"Oh, I see. So who did you arrest?"

"I am sorry, but we're not releasing the name as of yet."

"Why not?" Donovan asked, sounding upset.

"He's been detained on circumstantial evidence, and could easily walk if we don't find the smoking gun, if you will," she explained.

"You keep saying 'he.' I take it that the suspect is a man," Donovan said, trying to extract any information that he could.

"Yes, the suspect is a man, and that's all I'm saying."

"Okay. Please let me know the second you find the evidence that will lock him up for the rest of his life. That's the least he deserves for killing Chyna. She was a smart girl who had her whole life in front of her. She even had plans for opening a business," Donovan said sadly, remembering his friend.

"Don't worry; you'll be the first person I call. Have a good day, and I'll speak with you soon," she said and hung up. Her next call was to the station, so that they could start the paperwork on the warrant.

Theo got out of bed, did her customary morning stretches, and then took a shower. Afterward, she dressed in a pair of khakis, a white shirt, and a pair of tan espadrilles. She was starving and had a taste for an omelet, but not just any omelet. She wanted a Troy special. After their passionate kiss, she couldn't get him off her mind. Now that she had the prime suspect behind bars, she could relax for a moment and at least take an hour or two to enjoy a nice breakfast.

With that thought in mind, Theo grabbed her tote bag and keys and jetted out of the house. She was anxious to see Troy. Although she couldn't reveal too much about the case, she wanted to at least share with him that she had arrested a suspect. Troy was easy to talk to, and Theo enjoyed being in his company.

She cruised through the country roads, which were quiet this time of morning, with only an occasional car or two. Theo had the windows rolled down and she inhaled the fresh air, scented with hints of lavender and wild flowers.

As she neared his house, Theo began to rethink her impromptu visit. What if he was still asleep, or worse, in bed with someone else? She started to turn the car around and head to the station, but remembered that he had welcomed her with open arms before.

Troy's car was parked in the driveway, and Theo pulled in behind it. She turned off the engine, stepped out, and made her way to the front door. Theo reached for the bell, held her breath, and pressed it. She waited, expecting him to open the door smiling like he had done before, but there was no answer. She rang the bell again and waited.

Maybe he's asleep, she thought.

Theo didn't want to be a pest, so she turned and walked back toward the car. Her joyous mood was fading with each step. She had anticipated a nice breakfast, good conversation, and a smooch or two. Now she'd have to settle for a drive-thru meal from the local fast-food joint.

Theo had totally misjudged Troy. Initially, she thought he was a heartless lady killer, but after spending some time with him, she realized that her assessment was wrong. He was a kind man. And the fact that he had saved her life had a lot to do with her shift in attitude. She didn't deny that he probably had a slew of women after him; after all he was charming, handsome, and single, not to mention a talented chef.

She opened the car door and got back inside. Theo felt

like a fool for popping by, expecting him to welcome her with open arms. She was acting like he was her man when they actually hardly knew one another. Theo put the car in reverse, turned her head, and began backing out.

"Hey! Wait a minute!"

She put on her brakes, turned around, and looked out the windshield. Standing in front of her car was Troy, frantically waving his hands. A slight smile crept up on Theo's face as she took in his muscular physique. He wore a pair of shorts, and a worn-out Jets T-shirt. His forearms were well-defined, as were his abs. He looked good enough to eat. She put the car in drive, pulled back into the driveway, and got out.

"Good morning," Troy said, smiling from ear to ear.

"Sorry to drop by so early; hope I didn't wake you," she said, feeling a little awkward.

"I wasn't asleep. I was out back picking some herbs from my garden."

"Oh, you have a garden?" Theo asked, sounding surprised. Troy didn't seem like the earthy type.

"Yep. Come around back and I'll show you," he said, leading the way.

When they reached the backyard, Theo couldn't believe her eyes. There was a large garden running the length of the yard. She couldn't decipher the various herbs from where she stood. The garden took up half the yard, while the other half was filled with rose bushes. There were white, yellow, red, and pink roses. His yard looked like something from *Better Homes and Gardens*. Theo was impressed.

"Wow! This is some yard. Do you maintain it yourself?"

"Yes, for the most part, except when I'm out of town, and then my aunt comes over and tends to it. Gardening relaxes me. And I like to use homegrown herbs in my dishes," Troy explained, and then asked, "You want some iced coffee?"

"Sure."

There was a slate patio near the sliding glass doors that led to the kitchen. Troy offered her a seat at the outdoor table and went inside to get the coffee. He came back shortly with a carafe of iced coffee and two tall glasses.

He sat in the chair next to her and poured them each a glass. Troy took a sip of the ice-cold brew and looked over the top of his glass at Theo. She was so pretty that he wanted to lean in and kiss her like he had done the other night, but he didn't want to make a move too soon. That night they had had wine to lower their inhibitions, but in the light of morning he wasn't sure that she would feel the same way.

They were silent for a few moments, and then Troy said, "So, what brings you by this morning?"

"Thought I'd put in an order for another delicious omelet," she joked.

"Oh, so you only want me for my food?" he joked back.

Food and another juicy kiss, she thought, but didn't dare voice her mind. "Who says that I want you?" Theo shot back.

"Touché. My bad," he said, holding up his hands in mock defense.

Theo was enjoying their jousting. She hadn't felt this comfortable with a man in a long time. After her divorce she had built a wall around her emotions, and now Troy seemed to be penetrating that barrier.

As they were talking, Theo thought that she heard a car door slam. Moments later, she heard the bell. "I think someone's at your front door."

"Really? I'm not expecting anybody." As he was talking, the bell rang again. This time he heard the chimes. "Excuse me, I'll be right back."

"Oh, okay." Theo didn't get a chance to tell him about apprehending Lars. *I'll tell him when he gets back*, she thought, and continued drinking her coffee.

Troy went inside the house, walked to the front, and opened the door. He stood there in shock. This was the last person he wanted to see.

"What the hell are you doing here?" he asked his unwanted guest.

[43]

"Would you stop ringing!" Remi yelled at the phone like it could heed her command.

The phone had been ringing nonstop since she had come home from the police station. The caller ID didn't register a familiar name or number. Since Lars hadn't returned home, Remi assumed that it was her husband calling from jail. She was still upset with Lars for trying to put her out of the room when the detective was questioning him. Out of spite, she refused to answer the phone.

The phone stopped ringing, only to start again.

She walked over to the nightstand, grabbed the cordless, and pressed talk. "Hello?"

"Where the hell have you been? I've been calling for hours," Lars said, sounding totally exasperated.

"I've been here. Where are you?" she asked calmly.

"In jail!"

"Why are you in jail?" she asked as nonchalantly as if he had said that he was at the golf course playing a round with his buddies.

"They think I had something to do with that Chyna

person's death!" He was talking fast, and was out of breath as though he had been running a marathon.

"Why would they think something like that? Do they have evidence to link you to the girl's murder?" she asked, with a coldness to her voice.

This news would have been alarming to anyone else, but it was lost on Remi. Lars's deception had her totally upset. First his affair, and then she learned in front of the detective that he knew the dead girl. At this point, Remi was feeling no love for her husband.

"Why would you ask me something like that? Remi, you know that I'm no murderer. Look, I need for you to call our attorney and have him get here as soon as possible to post bail. I can't spend another night in this awful place." Lars was sounding frantic, like a caged animal. He had never even been pulled over by the police for a traffic violation, let alone been arrested for a crime. He was totally out of his element, and wanted to get far away from the stench of jail.

"Sure. Let me go so I can call him," Remi said, ready to get off the phone.

"Thanks, honey. I love you," Lars said before hanging up.

"Yeah, right!" Remi said aloud once the line was disconnected.

Remi didn't call their lawyer. Instead, she went into the closet and began pulling clothes off the hangers. She gathered an armload of her things, carried them into the bedroom, and tossed them on the bed. She returned to the closet, and retrieved a pair of matching Louis Vuitton suitcases. Remi quickly folded her clothes and placed them into the luggage.

She went into the bathroom and gathered up her toiletries. Next, she went to the wall safe, cleared out her jewelry, took the six bundles of cash that were there for an emergency, and grabbed her passport, among other things.

Remi was getting out of town before the news of Lars's arrest spread like wildfire. She couldn't take the embarrassment of the townspeople talking behind her back, and worse yet, banishing her from the social roster. Remi had spent too many years building her reputation to watch it evaporate in an instant. She planned to go to Paris, where no one knew her, and start over. She had no remorse for leaving her husband. He had enough money to hire a team of attorneys to clear his name. Before the trial and media circus started, Remi would be ensconced in a new life. However, there was one more thing she had to do while still residing in her old life.

Remi finished packing, changed clothes, and headed out of the house. As she drove away, she glanced in the rearview mirror, taking one last look at her fabulous beach house. Although she would miss her home, she wasn't worried about starting over. She had more than enough cash to find a spacious apartment, and when the cash ran low, she'd sell off her jewelry, which was worth millions. Her exit strategy was perfect.

Instead of driving straight to the airport, Remi had

one stop to make. She drove down a familiar block. When she reached the house, she was surprised to see another car parked in the driveway. She started to leave, but another thought popped into her head. The timing couldn't have been better had she planned it!

Remi parked, got out, and walked up to the front door. She rang the bell and waited. There was no answer, so she rang it a second time.

Troy snatched open the door. "What the hell are you doing here?" he asked, sounding annoyed.

"I'm leaving town and wanted to say goodbye. Can I come in?"

"No. This isn't a good time." Troy didn't want Theo to see Remi. He was trying hard to win her over, and didn't want Theo thinking that he was seeing a married woman.

"Oh come on, Troy, don't be like that. I thought we could fuck one last time." She stepped close to him and rubbed her hand up and down his chest. "Remember how good it was the last time we were together?" she asked in a low, seductive voice.

Troy removed her hand from his chest. "Remi, how many times do I have to tell you, it's over?"

"What's the matter, your new girlfriend doesn't want to share?" Remi said, with venom in her voice.

"What are you talking about?"

Remi turned toward the driveway. "Isn't that the lady detective's unmarked car? I assume you're screwing her now."

"I think you'd better leave, before—"

"Before what? Before you call the cops? You won't have to call far, will you?" She laughed a sinister laugh.

"Goodbye, Remi," Troy said, and closed the door in her face.

He took a deep breath to compose himself, then returned to the patio.

"Is everything okay?" Theo asked, noticing the serious expression on his face.

"Yes, everything is fine. That was an acquaintance dropping by unexpectedly."

"This must be your morning for drive-by visits. I hope you didn't send them away on my account. I need to get going anyway." Theo stood up. "Can I use your restroom?"

"Sure. You know where it is."

Troy's bladder also started speaking to him. He followed right behind Theo and went to the guest bathroom.

While they were inside, Remi crept around the side of the house. She had been lurking around, listening to their conversation. She peeked around the corner, making sure that the coast was clear. She reached into her purse and took out a small envelope. She opened the lid, walked over to the table, and began pouring a healthy dose of OxyContin into Theo's glass. She assumed it was her glass, since Theo's tote bag was sitting in the chair. Her first attempt at poisoning Theo at Café Coco had failed, but this time she was going to make sure that Troy wouldn't come to her rescue. After seeing Troy and Theo driving through town the day following the attempted poisoning, Remi had assumed that Troy had somehow intervened and had saved Theo's life.

After she emptied the contents of the envelope, she reached into her purse and took out another one. She had gotten the drugs from the wall safe where Lars kept his stash. Remi poured a heaping amount into Troy's glass as well. The way he had treated her was unforgivable and she wanted to make him pay.

"Stop! Police!" Theo shouted, catching Remi red-handed.

At first Remi froze, like a deer caught in headlights. But then she took off running. Theo took off right behind her and caught up to Remi before she reached her car. Theo tackled Remi to the ground.

"It was you all along! You killed Chyna, and tried to kill me for getting too close to the truth! Remi Braxton, you're under arrest for murder!"

[44]

With Troy's help, Theo dragged Remi to the car and secured her in the backseat. Troy had heard the commotion and came running. He was surprised to see the two women on the ground, with Theo sitting atop Remi like she was roping a baby steer. Theo quickly told him that she had caught Remi spiking their coffee, and that she was taking Remi to the station to question her about Chyna's death. Before she drove off, Theo collected Remi's purse. She looked inside without disturbing any of the contents, and saw that it was filled with packets of Oxy, bundles of cash, and jewelry.

Theo radioed the station and told them that she was bringing in another murder suspect, and to have the interrogation room ready. She was eager to finally get to the bottom of who killed Chyna and why.

Theo drove to the station in record time, and within ten minutes, she had Remi sitting in a metal chair in the interrogation room, along with Rodgers, and was ready to extract the truth.

"Before we get started, I want you to know that I've

had the OxyContin found in your purse sent to the lab, as well as the coffee you tainted at Troy's, so don't even try to lie your way out of this. Once the lab reports come back and confirm that the drugs in your possession match up with what was found in Chyna's bloodstream, you're going down for murder," Theo said sternly, looking directly at Remi.

Remi was stuck. She should have driven straight to the airport instead of trying to get one last fuck with Troy. When she saw Theo's unmarked police car sitting in his driveway, she thought it would be the perfect opportunity to poison the nosey detective. Theo's investigation had led her too close to finding out the truth, and Remi wanted to shut her up for good.

"Are you going to talk, Mrs. Braxton, or are we going to sit here and wait until the toxicology report comes back? Either way, you're not going anywhere anytime soon," Theo told her.

Remi quickly weighed her options. She knew that the lab report would confirm what Theo had already suspected. Remi exhaled, and began speaking. "What type of deal will you give me if I cooperate?"

"I can't promise you anything. But I know that the judge will look more favorably upon you if you tell the truth instead of wasting the taxpayers' money by dragging this case through court," Theo said.

"First of all, I didn't mean to kill Chyna. It was that bitch Reece that I was after!" Remi blurted out.

Theo leaned in closer and asked. "And why was that?"

"At the party, I caught her in bed with my husband. When I walked in, they still had their clothes on, but I'm sure it would have been only a matter of time before they were butt naked and screwing like porn stars."

"Millions of people catch their spouses in the act, but that's no justification for murder. There must have been another reason for your actions," Theo said, trying to get to the truth.

"Of course you're right, I wasn't about to let that little tramp take away everything I've built over the years!" Remi spat.

"What do you mean?"

"During the party, I overheard Reece talking to Chyna, saying that she was going to call the cops on Lars for giving her drugs without a prescription if he didn't continue to feed her habit. I couldn't allow that to happen. If the police arrested Lars for dispensing drugs illegally, he would lose his license to practice medicine and be a disgrace to the community. Not to mention that it would be the end of our livelihood. I don't know about you, detective, but I grew up dirt poor. My mother was a single parent who struggled to pay the rent from her tips as a waitress. We were evicted so many times that I lost count. I survived the only way I knew how—with my looks and my brains. I ended up getting a scholarship to college, and that's where I met Lars. He automatically assumed, since I was high-yellow with light eyes, that I came with a pedigree, which was far from the truth. I was from New Orleans, all right, but not the ritzy French Quarter like most people assumed. I latched on to Lars because he had potential. He was a med student on his way to becoming a doctor, and with my help he not only became a doctor, but a world renowned plastic surgeon. And I wasn't going to let a little tramp ruin my life. I had finally become a respectable member of the community, with status and wealth. Reece threatened to destroy my world with a single phone call." Remi held her head down for a moment as if in remorse, and then asked, "Can I have some water? I'm thirsty."

"Sure. Rodgers, can you get Mrs. Braxton a bottle of water?"

"No problem."

When Rodgers returned, Theo continued her questioning.

"Okay, that explains your motive, but your act wasn't premeditated, so where did you get the Oxy on the night of the party?" Theo wanted to know.

"Lars had left it behind in the stateroom. After I caught them in bed and they both had left, I went into the bathroom, and when I came out I saw the envelope on the bed. I picked it up, looked inside, and then put the drugs in my purse. I had planned to throw them away, but the second I overheard Reece threatening to destroy my life, I decided right then and there that she had to go. I figured that since she was already taking

Oxy, people would think that she overdosed, and no suspicions would be aroused."

"How did Chyna end up with the lethal dose?"

"I went into the galley, slipped the drugs in a glass of champagne, and told the waiter to give it to Reece. He delivered the drink, but Reece set it down before taking a sip. Chyna then picked up the wrong glass and started drinking. At that moment, I knew I had done the wrong thing and an innocent person was being poisoned but it was too late. I had to follow through. I watched Chyna and Lars argue. From the way she was pointing her finger at Lars and talking fast, I could tell that the drug hadn't taken effect yet, so I waited. When Lars walked away, Chyna attempted to come back inside, but she stumbled. At that point I knew that the Oxy was taking hold of her, so I went out on the deck. She started slurring her words and stumbling, saying that someone had spiked her drink. No one was out there but the two of us, so when she turned around toward the railing, trying to throw up, I pushed her from behind. I assumed everyone would think she got drunk and fell overboard, and that would be the end of the story. But you came along and started in with your investigation. You were getting too close to the truth, so I tried to poison you, too," Remi admitted.

Theo nodded her head. She was satisfied with the story, except there was still one missing piece. "Remi, murderers who seem able to kill with as much ease as you did—going after more than one victim—often have a history of killing. Was this your first time poisoning someone?"

Remi looked at Theo with an evil look in her eyes.

Remi's mind quickly flashed back to Dena, Lars's college girlfriend. Lars had no intention of leaving Dena for Remi, so Remi had no choice but to slip the girl a lethal dose of antifreeze in her orange juice. Yes, she had committed a crime before, but that piece of information would forever remain a secret. She was in enough trouble, and didn't want to be charged with a double homicide.

She then said, "Wouldn't you like to know?"

"Rodgers, did we get her confession on tape?" Theo asked.

"Every last word, boss!"

[45]

"Good evening, everyone, and welcome to Chyna's Closet," Donovan said, standing at the podium and addressing the waiting crowd.

"As some of you know, Chyna Jones had a vision, and that vision was to open a boutique that highlighted the creations of some of Brooklyn's finest designers. Today her vision has become a reality. Although Chyna isn't here with us physically, I know she's looking down and smiling," Donovan said with tears in his eyes.

Seeing that her brother was getting choked up, Reece took the microphone from him. "Will everyone raise their glasses and let's give a shout-out to my girl Chyna." Reece raised her champagne glass, which was filled with sparkling cider. "To Chyna, may you rest in peace."

"To Chyna!" the room sang out in unison.

Chyna's mother, as well as Donovan and Reece's mother were there, both beaming with pride. Chyna's mom wanted to speak, but was overcome with joy and sadness at the same time—joy that her daughter's dream had come true, and sadness because Chyna wasn't there to see it for herself.

Now that Lars had been released and Remi was offi-
cially charged with Chyna's murder, Donovan and Reece,
as well as Chyna's family finally had closure and could
move on emotionally. Reece had the bright idea to
execute Chyna's business plan and make her boutique a
reality. Donovan was totally on board with the idea and
eagerly funded the venture. Reece had found the perfect
venue right in the heart of Brooklyn, a large, loft-like
storefront. She knew that Chyna would have wanted
her store to be close to their old neighborhood.

Reece also did research and found some talented local
designers. She even designed a few pieces of clothing
herself. The boutique was urban and edgy, exactly the
way Chyna would have wanted it.

Even death hadn't stopped Reece's best friend from
helping her. Chyna's new boutique had given Reece's
life new purpose, and as she strove to make Chyna proud
of her, Reece knew that she would never do drugs again.
With a portion of the profits from the boutique, Reece
planned on establishing an arts scholarship at their former high school in Chyna's name. To further occupy
Reece's time and keep her mind off of drugs and way-
ward men, she volunteered once a week at Worldof
Money.org, an organization started by noted author
Sabrina Lamb that teaches kids about finances, and how
to manage money. She had even picked up a few money-
managing tips of her own when she listened to the
experts making presentations to the kids. Reece had done

a complete one-eighty, and for the first time in her life, she didn't feel like a spoiled, selfish brat.

The opening was a major success with the press there, as well as a smattering of celebrities. Liza Lord lent a hand in organizing the event. She and Reece had started off on the wrong foot, but over the months, a friendship developed. Although Reece was still rough around the edges, she shared the same passion for fashion as Liza. Liza also enjoyed Reece's colorful vernacular. It was a refreshing change from the uppity "ladies who lunch" crowd that she socialized with in the Hamptons. And once Donovan got over his grief, he and Liza finally explored what they had started at the party. Liza couldn't have been happier.

Liza had been shocked to learn that Remi was the murderer and felt ashamed that the islanders had shunned Donovan and his family. The locals assumed that the rapper would bring a bad element to Coco Beach, when instead the bad element was already there, dressed in designer clothes, disguised as a respectable member of the community. The snobby residents were taught a valuable lesson—that having money didn't make you a better person; it only bought you better things. And in the end, material possessions meant nothing if the fiber of your character was corrupt.

Although Lars had been cleared of murder charges, he was convicted of dispensing drugs without a prescription and lost his license to practice medicine. He sold his penthouse, beach house, and yacht, and moved back to his hometown, leaving Remi to spend her days and nights on Rikers Island. Before he left town, he donated a significant amount of money to a drug rehabilitation facility—his self-imposed penance for breaking the law.

"This is a great turnout," Theo said to her date. She was glad that Chyna's dream had come true. Although she didn't know the young woman personally, she felt bad that Chyna's life had been cut short over something as trivial as status.

"Yes, it is," Troy replied, and hugged her close to him.

After the case was closed, Troy took Theo on a trip to the wine country to unwind. They spent seven glorious days romping through Napa and Sonoma Valleys, sampling some of the best wines the region had to offer. Their nights were spent sampling each other. Troy was a tender lover, and Theo relished every second with him.

"Don't you two look cozy?" Liza said, walking up to them. Initially, Liza held disdain for the detective, thinking that she was better than the working-class woman, but Theo proved her wrong. Theo had brought down one of the wealthiest women on Coco Beach, and now she was dating the island's most eligible bachelor. Liza had always based her bigotry largely on Theo's casual attire, but tonight Theo wore a couture black dress, a triple strand of pearls, and a pair of black Louboutins.

Troy kissed Theo on the cheek. "We are very cozy. Aren't we, babe?"

Theo smiled. "We sure are!"

Just then, Donovan walked up to the group, took Liza by the waist, and held her close. "Man, you really put your foot in this sea bass," he said, taking a bite of the delectable fish. Troy had catered the event, making his signature dish, among others.

"Thanks."

"You're going to have to give me the recipe, unless, of course, it's a secret," Donovan said.

"No, it's not a secret. Actually, it's easy to make. Fresh fish, some cream, a few sprinkles of garlic powder, salt and pepper, and a little this and a little that, and voilà... dinner!"

"Yeah, easy for you to say. You can cook that dish with your eyes closed and one hand tied behind your back," Theo chimed in.

The four of them cracked up laughing. A photographer then came up and snapped their picture. What a diverse group: the heir to the Lord billions, the rapper/mogul, the chef, and the lady detective, socializing like old friends without any social barriers, just as it should be.

ABOUT THE AUTHOR

Danita Carter, a Chicago native, is the author of *Peer Pleasure*, and the co-author of *Revenge is Best Served Cold*, *Talk of the Town*, and *Success is the Best Revenge*. A former Wall Street broker and fine jewelry designer, she splits her time between New York and Chicago. For more information, visit www.danitacarter.com.

DISCUSSION QUESTIONS FOR READERS

1. Can money buy class?

2. Why do those with "old" money consider those with "new" money tacky?

3. Do the wealthy have a false sense of entitlement?

4. Does having money take away a person's humility?

5. Should Donovan have tried to ingratiate himself into the community, or leave well enough alone?

6. Who did you suspect of murdering Chyna, and why?

7. Was Remi the least likely suspect? If so, why?

8. Would you stay in a loveless marriage like Remi had done, just for money and status?

9. Did Lars's actions (dispensing OxyContin to Reece), ultimately contribute to Chyna's death?

10. Was Kalvin justified in trying to kill Lars?

11. What did you like about Reece's character? What didn't you like?

12. If you could be one of the characters, who would it be and why?

13. What character transformed the most in the end? Reece, Troy, or Liza?

BY DANITA CARTER
AVAILABLE FROM STREBOR BOOKS

The video shoot wrapped up in two days, thanks to Lucas's professionalism, and his ability to follow directions. Now was the moment that he had dreaded for weeks—his first day at the new school. All the paperwork and payments had been taken care of by his mother weeks ago, so Lucas begged her not to come with him on his first day. He didn't want to look lame, being escorted by his mother, like it was his first day of kindergarten. Peggy didn't like the idea of him walking in by himself, but she understood, and agreed.

Lucas walked through the huge wrought iron gates of Walburton Academy, with his leather backpack swung over his left shoulder. He was nervous, but had that outward air of confidence. Lucas had never worn a uniform in his life, and felt awkward in the navy blazer with the gold crest on the left breast pocket, khaki pants, white shirt, and navy-and-gold-striped tie. He glanced around the courtyard, and saw himself mirrored in every boy on the grounds. They all looked like prep-school clones. The girls, on the other hand, were a different story. Although they also had on uniforms, they wore their skirts short, with socks pulled up over their knees. Instead of generic backpacks, they wore designer tote bags. And they all seemed to have on expensive looking shoes—designer no doubt.

"Hey! Watch where you're going!"

Lucas stopped in his tracks. "Sorry, man."

Ian and Lucas stared each other down.

Who is this nerd, with the crease running down his pants? That crease is so sharp I bet if I touched it, I'd cut my finger, Lucas thought.

This dude obviously doesn't have a Magdala at home to iron his pants, Ian thought, taking in Lucas's rumpled looking uniform. Even his blazer was wrinkled. "You must be new," Ian said, looking Lucas up and down.

"You could say that," he said, not wanting to admit that he, indeed, was the new kid on the block.

"New or not, you're walking towards the teachers' entrance."

Lucas felt stupid, but didn't let it show. "Yeah, man, I knew that."

"Ian, who's your friend?" Madison asked, walking up.

"I'm not his friend," Lucas quickly replied.

"No truer words have ever been spoken," Ian said, looking down his nose at Lucas.

Madison also gave Lucas the once over, and couldn't help but notice how rumpled his uniform was. "Did you enroll through the scholarship program?"

Lucas crinkled his face. "What?"

"Are you here on a scholarship?" she asked again, assuming by his appearance that he was from an underprivileged family.

"Naw, I ain't here on no damn scholarship! I'm paying my way, just like you," he spat out, obviously offended.

"Sorry. It's just that some of the urban kids are here on an academic scholarship, and I thought…"

Lucas cut her off. "Yeah, you thought that just 'cuz I'm black, I'm from an *urban*," he said, mocking her word, "area, and couldn't possibly afford to be here without a handout."

Madison's cheeks flushed candy-apple red. "No, it has nothing to do with race. As a matter of fact, my best friend is black, uh, African American," she stuttered, trying to redeem herself.

"Yeah, that's what they all say."

"Look, dude, she didn't mean anything by it," Ian said, coming to his girlfriend's defense.

"*Dude*, I really don't care what she meant," Lucas said, and strutted off, leaving them standing there looking stupid.

"What the hell is his problem?" Madison asked, once Lucas was on the other side of the courtyard.

"He's probably embarrassed to admit that he is, indeed, here on a scholarship. And when you called him out, he got mad."

Madison hunched her shoulders. "Yeah, I guess you're right."

"Right about what?" Reagan asked, as she joined them.

"See that dude over there in the wrinkled uniform?" Ian nodded his head in Lucas's direction.

Reagan glanced around the school yard until she spotted the new guy. "You mean the hobosexual looking dude? Looks like somebody shook him up in a bag, and then tossed him out?"

Madison giggled. "That's funny, where did you get *hobosexual* from?"

"Judging from the looks of him, he surely isn't meticulous about his looks like a metrosexual," she said, continuing to size him up.

"When we were talking to him, and I asked if he was here on a scholarship, he got all defensive, and basically accused me of being a racist."

"What? That's ridiculous! Did you tell him that I'm black?" Reagan asked.

"Yeah, that's when he said something smart and walked away," Ian said.

"He's probably mad because his parents couldn't afford to send him to Walburton without a scholarship. I mean, look at him." They all turned and stared in Lucas's direction. "He needs a haircut; those curls are all over the place. His uniform is too big, probably donated. If I had to bet, I'd say that he's one of those smart-ass kids from Harlem, Brooklyn, or the Bronx that scored high on his exams, and got offered a scholarship," Reagan said, making her own assessment.

"I'm sure you're right," Madison agreed.

"I mean he's cute and all, but unfortunately for him, I don't date broke dudes," Reagan stated, as she continued to stare at him.

Lucas had the feeling that he was being scrutinized underneath a microscope. Like all eyes were on him. He knew without a doubt that it was the red-headed chick, and Mr. Crease, so he turned in their direction. And sure enough, they were sizing him up like he was on display, but another girl had joined their little huddle. He squinted his eyes for a clearer view, and couldn't believe who was standing there with them. It was the girl he had bumped into at the shoot—Roshonda's friend. Except she looked different. Her hair wasn't wild like before, but straightened, and she didn't have on her old army jacket. *Damn, I thought that chick was cool, only to find out that she goes to this uppity school, with these rich brats. So much for trying to get with her,* Lucas thought and shook his head. Just then, the bell sounded, and he walked through the doors of Walburton Academy along with the rest of the "rich brats."